CW00738649

SACRIFICE

SAVAGE FALLS SINNERS MC #2

CAITLYN DARE

Copyright © 2021 by Caitlyn Dare

All rights reserved.

No part of this book may be reproduced in any form or by any electronic or mechanical means, including information storage and retrieval systems, without written permission from the author, except for the use of brief quotations in a book review.

Edited by Pinpoint Editing

Proofread by Proofreading by Sisters Get Lit(erary) Author Services

Photography by Michelle Lancaster

Model Anthony Patamisi

RHETT

"**S**hall we get out of here? Go somewhere a little more private?" Clarissa purrs in my ear.

But her words don't have the effect on me that she was hoping for, because the last thing I want to do is end up in a room alone with this chick.

My eyes scan the crowd for Sadie. She's the only reason I let Clarissa anywhere near me. She's the reason my head is fucked up. But I don't find her with Quinn like she was before. Instead, I find Quinn arguing with Dane.

The sight isn't unusual—everyone in the club knows that the two of them don't exactly see eye to eye. But the fact that Sadie is nowhere to be seen worries me.

"Maybe another time," I say, pushing Clarissa from my lap as I stand.

"Ow, Rhett," she whines, making me wince and confirming that I just did the right thing.

"Tell me where she is, Quinn," Dane demands as I get closer. "I know you're lying to me. If she's in dan—"

"What's going on?" I bark, looking between the two of them.

"Sadie's gone. And Quinn let her walk right out the fucking compound unaccompanied."

"You fucking what?" I roar, taking a step forward and getting right in her face.

Unlike most girls, though, she doesn't so much as blink at my aggression.

"Where the fuck did she go, Quinn?" I demand, my fingers twitching as I fight the urge to strangle the truth out of her.

If Sadie left alone and the Reapers... A shudder of fear races down my spine, the likes of which I've only ever felt once in my life before. Tuesday night, to be exact, when Dane called to tell me what had happened when someone ran them off the road.

Obviously sensing that I'm not messing around, Quinn swallows down her lies and looks me dead in the eye. "She went to meet Wes."

"Wes?" I bellow. "She went to meet Wesley fucking Noble? Why the fuck would she do that?"

Quinn shrugs, and I close the last bit of space between us.

"Cool it, bro," Dane breathes, sliding a hand between us.

"I don't know." Her brows pinch. "He texted her and she went to meet him."

"Fuck," I roar, my palm slamming down on the cabin wall behind Quinn's head. "Fuck. We need to find her."

"Let's go."

Dane and I take off toward the clubhouse with Quinn

hot on our tails. "Don't you already think you've done enough, Renshaw?" I spit.

"I didn't want her to go." Her voice trembles. "I told her it was a stupid idea. But you know what Sadie's like when she gets an idea in her head."

I scoff, knowing exactly what she's fucking like.

"Stay here."

"No, I'm—"

"Stay here in case she comes back," I growl, making her steps falter.

"Savage, Stray," Pacman shouts across the compound as we emerge around the corner. "Someone here to see you."

"Not now, Pac."

"It... er... looks pretty important."

"Fuck's sake." Upping my speed, I take off toward the gate, Dane right beside me. "This had better be life or fucking death."

"Oh shit," Dane breathes when we turn the corner and find who's waiting for us.

I barely register the blood running down his face or the fear in his eyes. All I see is fucking red as I fly toward Noble, pulling my gun from my pants as I go. "Where the fuck is she?" I demand, pinning him back against the clubhouse gates with my forearm pressed against his throat and the barrel of my gun digging into his temple.

"I-I—"

"Spit it the fuck out before I ensure you never say another fucking word again."

"Rhett, calm the fuck down, brother," Dane demands,

appearing at my side as Quinn finally rushes around the corner, clearly too fucking nosey for her own good.

"Oh my God," she cries. "Where's Sadie? Is she okay? What happ—"

"Renshaw," I growl, cutting off her incessant rambling. "Tell us where the fuck she is before I put a bullet through your brain."

"I don't know. T-they took her."

"Who's *they*?" Dane asks.

"Took her? Took her where?"

"I don't know," Wes cries. "I don't fucking know. They knocked me out and put her into a van. They were gone before I could do anything. I came straight here. I didn't know what else to do."

"Fuck," I boom, finally releasing him.

The clubhouse gates rattle as my fist collides with the metal. Once. Twice. Three times before I actually feel anything but pure fucking panic.

"It's okay. Let's get you fixed up and we'll figure this out. Rhett?" Dane calls, and when I turn back, I find he and Quinn are on either side of Wes, ready to help him inside.

"He's not fucking coming in here." Over my dead fucking body.

"Rhett, get over yourself," Quinn breathes, sounding totally exasperated. "Look at him."

"We'll clean him up," Dane adds. "Find out everything he knows, then go find her."

"If they've fucking got her, man..."

"We'll get her back." He meets my eyes and nods.

"Who? If *who's* got her?" Quinn demands.

"Shut the fuck up," I bark at her.

"It was Evan," Wes blurts out.

"*Evan?*" Dane echoes.

"I-I was with Evan. This is all him. I know it is."

"Stupid motherfucker."

"We'll go around the back. The less attention we attract the better," Dane says, pushing forward and forcing me to follow as we head around to the back of the clubhouse which will lead us to the secluded back door and into Dane's room.

Dane and Quinn lower Wes to the end of the bed, being entirely too gentle with him, seeing as he just got our girl fucking abducted by that sick cunt.

Grabbing Dane's chair, I drag it over and sit directly in front of him. "Tell us everything."

"There's a first aid kit in my bathroom," Dane says to Quinn, who rushes off while he stands behind me, waiting for information.

"We were walking through the park, heading to meet some of the guys. We were almost out when I saw her."

"Sadie?"

"Yeah. She called for me as if she was expecting me, but we were just going to meet the guys, so I don't know—"

"What happened next?"

He shakes his head as if he can't get his thoughts straight. "A white van pulled up and two guys jumped out. All in black. They... they hit her."

My knuckles crack with the tightness of my fists as I imagine someone hurting her.

"Then what?" Dane urges.

"I went to take off, running to help, but Evan hit me with something from behind and I blacked out. When I came to, they were all gone. I would have called her, but I don't have my cell. I don't know—"

I stand, the chair toppling over behind me as I begin to pace. "Where did they go, Noble?"

"I have no idea. I don't know what to do. I don't—"

"It's okay," Quinn soothes, reappearing with Dane's first aid box and laying it all out on the bed beside Wes. "We'll find her."

"Why was she even there?" he asks.

"You texted her, asking to meet," Quinn says.

"What the fuck?" He pales. "No, I didn't."

"I saw the messages."

I turn on him as Dane's body tenses in anger.

"I swear to fucking God, Rhett, I didn't text her. I didn't ask her to meet. I thought we were hanging out with the team. That's all."

"She got her cell?" I ask Quinn, who's doing her best to comfort Wes, which is pissing me the fuck off. He caused this; he doesn't deserve her fucking sympathy.

"Y-yeah I think so."

Dragging mine from my pocket, I open the tracking app I installed not so long ago.

"You put a tracker on her phone?" Dane asks, coming to look over my shoulder. "Jesus, bro."

"We had a job to do," I say, looking him in the eyes so he can hear my unspoken words.

"Right, so Riv and—" He tilts his head in Quinn's direction, "as well?"

"Yeah."

"Will you two stop talking in riddles?" she demands.

"Club business, Renshaw. None of your concern."

"My best friend is missing. It's damn well my concern."

"Just patch him up," I bark as the app continues searching. It already shows River and Quinn as being here, but Sadie's cell is taking longer to locate.

"There," I say, jabbing my finger onto the screen. "Let's go."

Dane opens the drawer beneath his bed and pulls out two extra guns, passing one over to me as a wide-eyed Wes looks between the two of us.

"Give me one," he demands, pushing Quinn aside and standing.

"Fuck off, Noble."

"I'm serious. I'm coming with you."

We both stare at him for a beat, and then I say, "You even know how to use one of these?"

"I know the basics." He holds his hand out, waiting for me to pass it over.

"Well?" Dane asks, getting impatient.

"You can come, but you're not having a fucking gun."

Tucking the extra piece into my cut, I take off for the back door once more. "Dane, get the keys to the truck and meet us out front. Don't raise the alarm. Not yet." Not until we know what we're dealing with.

"On it."

The three of us take off around the back as Dane heads through the main building to get the keys from the shop.

"Quinn, go back to the party," I say.

"But—"

"I said go back to the fucking party."

Her lips part to argue again, but I pin her with a look that cuts off whatever argument she might've had.

"Fine," she hisses, "but you call me the second you know she's safe."

I nod before looking at Wes. "Let's fucking go. And if you fuck this up, you'll be the one missing. You got that?"

"I want her safe as much as you do."

The image that's been on repeat in my head since the night Dane told me he caught Wes kissing her flickers through my mind and I turn toward him, stopping him from going anywhere other than straight into me.

"Let's get one thing clear here, Pretty Boy." His jaw pops in frustration, but he doesn't say anything. "Sadie is ours. We might be letting you tag along, but she has nothing to do with you, got that?"

He nods.

"Good. Remember that the next time you want to put your fucking mouth on her."

Without another word, I turn and storm away, assuming he'll follow but hoping like hell he takes off in the other direction and leaves us to it.

The location on the tracking app takes us to a warehouse on the outskirts of town. Seeing as it's a Friday night, it's completely deserted with only security lights illuminating the otherwise dark space.

Wes keeps his eyes on the app as Dane rides ahead of us.

"There," Wes pipes up, his arm shooting out as he points at the front corner of a van that's almost completely in the shadows.

"Not completely useless after all," I deadpan.

Parking at the other side of the warehouse, I kill the engine and we climb out as Dane pulls to a stop beside us. Pulling the gun from my pants, I release the safety and waste no time in locating the main door.

If it were anyone else other than Sadie inside, I would probably put a little more thought into my entrance plan. But seeing as it's her, and the only thing I can think of is getting her back safe, I rip the door open and race inside with my gun raised and ready to kill any motherfucker who might have touched what's mine.

What's *ours*.

2

SADIE

My eyes flutter open, a dull ache radiating through my skull.

What the—

Voices flit in and out of my head as I try to get my bearings, but I'm hit with too many thoughts at once and I flinch as pain ricochets inside my skull.

Wesley.

That traitorous asshole betrayed me.

But why?

"What the fuck, Justin?"

I can just make out a voice. It sounds vaguely familiar, but it isn't Wes.

"This isn't what we agreed. This isn't—"

"Quit being a little bitch, cous," someone replies. "You wanted to rough her up a little, here's your chance."

By the looks of it, I'm in some kind of abandoned warehouse. But before I can get a good look around, approaching footsteps send a bolt of fear through me and

I close my eyes again, slumping against the chair I'm tied to.

"Always wondered what Sinners pussy feels like," one of them says, his voice louder. The air shifts around me, panic rising inside me.

Think, Sadie. Think.

"Justin, man, this isn't—"

"For fuck's sake, Evan..."

Evan?

Evan fucking Henley is behind this?

I don't know what hurts more—that I let Evan get the jump on me, or that Wesley clearly betrayed me.

God, I'm an idiot.

All this time I thought me and Wesley...

I lock those thoughts down. There will be time to deal with his betrayal later. Right now, I need to focus on how the hell I'm going to get out of this.

Whatever *this* is.

Someone closes in on me. I don't open my eyes—I don't dare—but I feel them crouch before me, feel the warmth of their breath. And then I feel something else. The cool smoothness of... Fuck, a gun. Someone is gliding a gun along the curve of my thigh. Fear races down my spine.

Who the fuck are these guys?

I know Evan and Wes are here somewhere, but I've never heard of a Justin before.

"Shit, she's hot. Look at her tits, man. What I wouldn't pay to get a taste—"

"Seriously, J, I didn't want... this. I just wanted to

scare her a bit. Make her realize she was messing with the wrong guy."

"Relax, cous." The air shifts again and I sense Justin stand up. The urge to crack open an eye is strong, but I fight it. I don't want them to know I'm listening, not yet. Not until I figure out what's going on... or what they plan to do with me.

"Relax?" Evan balks. "You fucking knocked her out with a tire iron."

Well damn, that's obviously why my skull feels like there's a brass band in there.

"She's still breathing, and when she wakes up, we can have ourselves a little fun." He chuckles darkly. "That's what you wanted, isn't it? To see her on her knees for you?"

"Yeah, but..."

"You worry too much, cous. The guys will be back soon, and then we can get this party started."

I suppress a shudder. That doesn't sound good.

It doesn't sound good at all.

"You must have a death wish," I say, finally opening my eyes and glaring at Evan.

Justin left not long ago, after other guys arrived. I don't know where they are, but I can't hear them, so they must be outside or something.

"You're awake."

"Surprise." I scan the room again, my vision—and head—a little clearer. "Have you lost your fucking mind?"

Evan's brows knit as his eyes dart toward a door. When he glances back at me, I notice the unease there. "I didn't... It wasn't supposed to go down like this..."

I scan the room again, but there's no sign of Wes. "You need to let me go, now. Before Rhett and Dane realize I'm gone and rain down hell on you and your—"

"Well, well, the Sinners princess is awake." Justin appears, leaning against the doorjamb like he doesn't have a care in the world. He's worlds apart from Evan's all-American good looks. He's got shaggy brown hair and looks like he hasn't shaved in a few days. His jeans are scruffy, kissing well-worn black boots, and an array of ink peeks out from under the arms of his black t-shirt.

Throw in the gun tucked into the waistband of his jeans and the fact that he keeps calling me the Sinners princess, it's most likely he's in a gang. The MC might keep Savage Falls free from gangs moving in and trying to push hard drugs, but there are plenty of those criminal organizations in surrounding towns.

Who knew Evan's family had such connections?

I shift my arms, trying to reduce the amount of pressure on my wrists where the rope bindings are cutting into my skin. I have no idea how long I was out, but Dane and Rhett will know I'm missing by now. Maybe even my dad. The whole Chapter could be looking for me.

But a thought hits me.

What if they've taken me out of town? How will anyone track me?

Shit.

Shit.

Justin steps forward, a slow smirk spreading over his

face. "That's right, princess," he says as if he knows exactly where my thoughts just went. "They might be looking for you, but no one has any idea where we are."

"What do you want?" I ask, keeping an eye on everyone in the room. Justin and Evan are closest to me now, with two more guys standing sentry near the door. "Where's Wes?" I add when no one answers.

Evan flinches, his eyes flashing with something.

Dread trickles through me. "Oh my God, what did you do to him?"

Wes didn't betray me, not in the way I first thought. If he had, he'd be here, standing with them. But he's not. Which means something must have happened.

"Evan," I shriek, thrashing against my restraints. "What the fuck did you do?"

"Such a dirty mouth." Justin creeps closer. "I wonder if you suck as good as you cuss." He cups his junk.

"Go fuck yourself," I sneer.

He backhands me so quickly I don't even have time to brace myself for the fiery pain shooting along my jaw.

"Justin!" Evan steps forward but Justin whips his gun out of the waistband of his jeans and releases the safety, pointing it right at him.

"You never did have what it took to play with the big boys, cous." He tsks, waving the gun around. Evan looks ready to pee himself, the blood drained from his face as he holds his hands up in surrender.

"Get him the fuck out of here," Justin barks to the two goons by the door. They start advancing toward Evan and he inches back, trembling.

"Wait a minute, we had a deal... we had—"

"Deal just changed, Ev." Justin smirks, shoving the gun back into his jeans. "I think I'm going to enjoy a little one on one time with your girl here, and when I'm done, we can send her back to the Sinners in tiny little pieces."

"Justin, be smart," Evan tries to reason, but he's almost backed himself into the corner of the room.

He has nowhere to go, and the fear in his eyes tells everyone he knows it.

"No," he yells as one of the guys tries to grab him. Evan evades him but staggers right into the other guy's fist. A sickening crunch echoes through the room as his head snaps back, blood spurting from his nose.

"Don't go too hard on him." Justin chuckles darkly while Evan wails in agony. "The last thing I need is Mommy and Daddy landing a lawsuit on my doorstep. Although, if he knows what's good for him, he'll keep his mouth fucking shut. Isn't that right, cous?"

Between them, the two guys manage to wrestle Evan out of the room. Justin gives me his full attention then. "Now, where were we?"

"Fuck you," I snarl, lifting my chin in defiance.

"Brave... and stupid." He grabs a fistful of hair and yanks my head back, pressing the butt of his gun against my temple. "Scared yet?" His lip curves in mild amusement.

"When my club finds you, they'll make you wish you never laid eyes on me."

I've never believed in hurting innocents—and it happens sometimes in this life; innocent people get tangled up in club business and it doesn't always end well for them—but I would happily throw pieces of shit like Justin to the wolves. Guys who prey on the weak, who get off on exerting their power over women. Sickos who get off on pressing guns to the heads of their incapacitated captives.

Sick fuck.

"Evan told me what you did. Told me how you lured him in with your tight body and dirty words, and then made him look like a fool in front of your entire class."

"Your cousin is an asshole."

Justin guffaws at that. "Can't argue with you there." His fingers flex in my hair, making my eyes water. "But you see, darlin'," he leans in close, "what my fucking idiot of a cousin doesn't realize is that I don't give a rat's ass about helping him get revenge."

"What do you—"

"Hush now, it's time for some fun." He releases me, shoving me so hard I think the chair will topple, but it rights itself and I inhale a ragged breath.

Justin studies me for a second, his eyes running over every inch of me. His hungry gaze is like a thousand spiders under my skin, and my stomach churns. I have to swallow the bile rushing up my throat as he palms himself, obviously turned on by this whole interaction.

I need a plan, and quick. I need to get free of my restraints.

An idea hits me. It's risky, but it's better than sitting here like a lamb to the slaughter.

"What kind of fun?" I bat my lashes, moving my shoulders inwards a fraction so my boobs press together.

His eyes narrow. "What are you up to, little bitch?"

"Why don't you find out?"

"Or maybe, I just make you choke on my dick and fuck your mouth."

Oh God.

Fear threatens to consume me, but I inhale a steady breath, forcing myself to calm down. Panicking will get me nowhere.

"You could... but then, I can't touch you like this."

Heat blazes in his eyes as I purr out the words, but it quickly clears as he grabs my hair again and wrenches my head backward. "You think you can seduce me like you did my stupid fucking cousin?"

Fuck.

Fuck!

His spare hand drops to his jeans and snaps his belt, tearing the button open.

"No, please," I rush out, "don't do this. I'll do whatever you want. Untie me and I'll—"

"This'll do," he grunts, fisting his dick. "Open wide, princess. And don't even think about biting or you won't like what comes next."

He shoves my head down and thrusts his hips forward until I'm face to face with his dick. Bile rushes up my throat as I buck against his hold. "You don't want to do this," I plead, tears streaming down my cheeks.

I don't even realize he's released my hair until I hear the tell-tale click of the safety and the barrel of the gun presses against my temple. "Open. Your. Fucking—"

The rumble of an engine reverberates through the

warehouse and relief slams into me. I'd know that bike anywhere.

They're here.

My guys are here.

3

DANE

"**R**hett, no," I hiss, climbing off my bike and ripping my helmet off.

But it's too late. He's already dragged the door open and marched through it.

"Fucking hell."

Wes is out of the truck by the time I get to it. He stares at me with wide eyes, dried blood still caked on his face. But I can also sense that his need for vengeance is almost as strong as ours.

I have no idea what Wes's deal is, but I have no doubt he's on our side here. Convincing Rhett of that, however, could be a little more challenging.

"Stay behind me," I demand, pulling my gun from my waistband and following in the direction Rhett went only seconds ago.

I don't give him a chance to respond. Instead, I take off.

But even still.

We're too late.

The single gunshot echoes through the silent night air around us and turns my blood to ice.

I storm through the door with my gun raised and Wes hot on my tail, my heart thundering in my chest as I refuse to allow myself to even consider the possibility of that bullet hitting either my brother or our girl.

"Jesus fucking Christ," I mutter when we round the corner and find Rhett standing over a body, blood oozing from the guy's shoulder, and Rhett now pointing two guns at him.

"Wes," a soft, broken voice cries.

"Sadie," I breathe, following the voice and finding her tied to a chair, blood running down her chin but defiance fierce in her eyes.

Wes runs for her, dropping to his knees before her and going for her bindings.

"Here," I call, throwing my switchblade over to him.

"Stray," Rhett barks. "Two more went that way." He nods toward a door at the back of the space, and I take off.

The door crashes back against the wall as I fly through it, but the rumble of an engine in the distance tells me I'm too late. I race out into the parking lot as dust flies up behind a truck as they take off.

"We'll get you, motherfuckers," I mutter to myself. We'll never let anyone who hurts one of our own get away with it.

I'm about to rejoin the others when a pained groan sounds out from the darkness behind me. With my gun still raised, I edge closer.

"You stupid fucking cunt," I bark when a familiar, albeit bloody, face comes into view.

"I'm sorry... I'm sorry," Evan cries like a fucking pussy. "It wasn't meant to—"

"Shut the fuck up, asshole." Tucking my gun away, I reach down and grab Evan by his shirt, hauling him to his feet, not giving a fuck when he moans like a little bitch about the pain.

"Shut the fuck up or it's going to get a hell of a lot worse." I drag him back through to where the others are before unceremoniously throwing him at Rhett's feet. "They got away. But look who I *did* find."

"I'm sorr—"

Another gunshot silences Evan, but not before his eyes go wide in fear and he attempts to curl up into a ball.

"You really, really didn't think this through, did you?" Rhett mutters. "I'm going to enjoy fucking you both up."

Unrestrained anger oozes from every inch of Rhett's body. His eyes are so dark they're almost black and his body is trembling with his need to put a bullet through each of these assholes.

"Stray, line them up. I want to look them in the eyes when I end them."

He throws me some cable ties from his back pocket, but I don't move instantly. Instead, I look back at Sadie, my heart aching for her as I do.

She's curled up with Wes as he holds her, supports her.

Motherfucker.

That should be me.

"Stray," Rhett barks. His need for revenge and blood is too strong right now to focus on anything but ensuring that whoever these cunts are hear our message loud and clear.

"I'm on it."

Rolling Evan onto his front with my boot, I lean down and bind his wrists before hauling him against the wall in front of Rhett.

"Please, please don't do this. It wasn't meant—"

"Shut up," Rhett booms, his voice echoing off the bare walls around us.

I do the same to the other guy who is facedown on the concrete floor, blood still gushing from the bullet hole in his shoulder. He cries out in agony as I lift him and throw him against that same wall.

I take a step back from them, but not before I look into the guy's eyes. All the air rushes from my lungs as familiarity hits me. Although I have no fucking idea why, or who the cunt is.

He stares back at me, his face twisted in pain, but I swear to God I see the same recognition in his eyes.

"So you think it's okay to kidnap and tie up our girl, huh?" Rhett asks, his voice low and deadly, looking between the two of them. "Why?" he booms, startling both of them.

"I-I just wanted to—"

"Shut the fuck up, cous. You don't owe these cunts anything," the other guy barks.

"I want to get out of here alive," Evan whimpers as Rhett turns his gun on him. "Please. I'm sorry. I just wanted revenge from that night at the Arches. It wasn't meant to go this far."

"Stray," Rhett demands, and, without so much as

another word, I take a step forward and plant my foot into the asshole's stomach.

He grunts, doubling over as he tries to breathe through the pain.

"Still think it was a good idea?" Rhett barks.

"Rhett, Dane, please don't," a quiet voice pleads from behind us.

"Let us do our job, princess," Rhett says without looking back at her.

Ripping my eyes from my brother, I look at Sadie, at the exhaustion and concern on her face. Wes holds her tighter, whispering something in her ear.

Jealousy rips through me once more, and it's enough to cut through the anger and my own need for revenge to make me do the right thing.

Stepping up to Rhett, I place my hand on his shoulder. "We need to get her out of here. She's our priority."

His jaw tics with anger. He knows I'm right, but for some reason, he's refusing to accept it. Much like his feelings for her.

He doesn't say a word. He doesn't even look at me. Instead, he lowers to his haunches in front of the guy. "Who are you?" he hisses, and it makes me wonder if he's having the same feelings of familiarity as I am.

"Fuck you, Savage. I owe the Sinners nothing," he spits.

Rhett finally shoots a look in my direction, and I read his thoughts loud and clear.

He's a Reaper.

Rhett stands before pulling his arm to the side and

swinging the gun until it collides with the cunt's face with a painful crunch and he falls to the side, out cold.

"What the hell?" Evan wails.

"Put them in the truck. If we're right, we need to get out of here before they call in reinforcements."

"Get her out of here," I say to Wes. "Don't let her out of your fucking sight."

"You got it."

Rhett keeps his eyes on Evan and his cousin while I watch Wes and Sadie.

I wait until they've both left the warehouse before stepping up to Rhett. "She needs you, man. What the fuck are you doing?"

"They need to die. When I walked in, he—" Rhett swallows the words, shaking his head. "He was going to fucking rape her."

The fire in his eyes would terrify anyone else who'd be unlucky enough to look into them.

"But he didn't," I force out, trying not to lose myself to the same darkness he's drowning in right now. "We got her. She's safe."

"Yeah, and they're going to pay."

There's no talking to him when he's like this, so I nod. "Where are we taking them? Ray?"

"Not yet. I want to know what they're planning first."

"I don't think—"

"I don't give a fuck what you think right now, Stray."

My fists curl in frustration, but there's nothing I can do about it. He's made his decision, and there will be no changing his mind.

"Right, let's get them in the truck then."

We work silently like we have a million times before.

"Give me your keys," he demands once we're done.

"What?"

"Take Sadie and Wes to your place and meet me at our old storage containers on the edge of town."

"Nah, Rhett, you—"

"Give me your fucking keys, Stray."

With a shake of my head, I pull them from my pocket. "You're a fucking pussy, brother."

He doesn't acknowledge my words. Instead, he storms past me toward my bike.

"What's going on?" Wes asks the second I join him and Sadie in the truck.

"Can't tell you, man."

"Fuck that. You don't think I'm already in deep enough?"

"It's club business now, Noble. Let us deal with it."

"Are you going to kill them?"

I shrug, mainly because I don't actually know the answer to that. I've got a feeling Rhett has already made a decision, and whatever it is will be the result of this whole situation.

"Where are we going?" Sadie finally asks.

Looking over, I find her big green eyes staring back at me. Although exhausted, I can see the fear within them. But it's not for her, or for what she just went through, but for Rhett.

"My place. Wes can look after you while we deal with our new friends."

"Evan didn't mean for it to get this far," she whispers. "Whoever they are, they took it to the next level."

25

"Yeah, I got that," I admit, trying to tamp down my own anger.

"Are they—"

"We don't know," I answer before she gives Wes too much information. "But we'll find out."

"Don't let him do anything stupid, Dane."

I can't help but laugh, which I'm sure isn't the response she was after.

"If you think I—or anyone—can stop him from doing anything, then you don't know Rhett as well as I thought you did."

"I know, I just..." She trails off, blowing out a long breath instead. "I'm sorry." The regret in her voice hits me right in the chest.

"It's okay, Sadie, girl."

Reaching over, I find her hand and lace our fingers together while Wes holds her tight against his body.

Noble's stare burns into the side of my face as I'm sure he tries to figure out what exactly all this is, but he doesn't say a word. I'm not sure I'd have any real answers for him if he did ask.

I come to a stop in front of the building before pulling my key out. "Let yourselves in and use whatever you want. I've got clothes in the bedroom you can change into. There might be some food in the refrigerator or you can order in. Whatever."

"We've got it, Dane. Thank you." Her eyes hold mine, a million questions spinning within them. "Please, just try to make sure he doesn't do anything stupid."

"I'll do my best, Sadie, girl."

"I need both of you back in one piece."

"Y-yeah." I gulp, the emotion in her gaze overwhelming me.

Uncurling from Wes, she fully turns my way, wraps her hand around the back of my neck and pulls my lips to hers. I'm powerless but to respond to her, and my tongue sweeps into her mouth the second she parts her lips. But she pulls back almost as quickly, resting her brow against mine.

"Thank you for finding me."

"Always, babe."

"Come back to me. Both of you."

With one more chaste kiss to her lips, I release her and allow her to walk away with Wes.

"Noble," I call before they're too far away. He turns back instantly, his eyes locking onto mine. His jaw tics as I'm sure he waits for my warning about getting too close to Sadie.

"Look after her."

He releases the breath he was holding and nods once before I take off in the hope of doing what she's asked of me.

4

SADIE

"**W**es," I say, breaking the heavy silence.

He's been quiet ever since we left Dane at the truck ten, maybe fifteen minutes ago.

"I—fuck." His chest heaves. "I don't know what to say. Evan, he—"

"Come, sit." I pat the empty space beside me on the couch. "You're making me nervous."

Wes stops pacing and stares at me, his expression unreadable. "How can you be so calm about all this?"

"Calm?" Strangled laughter bubbles out of me. "I don't feel calm. I feel—God," the world spins around me as I touch a hand to my head, "that hurts."

"Sadie?" He rushes over to me and drops to his knees. "You're hurt. Shit..." His hands gently inspect my forehead, sweeping the bloody, matted hair from my face. "I didn't even... I think I'm still in shock."

"I'm okay." I'm not, but he looks like he's one second

from falling apart, so one of us needs to try to remain calm.

"Does Stray have a first aid kit lying around here?"

"Somewhere. Try the bathroom," I say, motioning to the hall.

His fingers linger on my brow, the air crackling around us. "What do you think they'll do to Evan?"

"They won't kill him,"—at least I hope they won't—"if that's what you're worried about." I offer him a wry smile, but he doesn't return it.

"I'm not." His eyes darken. "When I saw you... I wanted to kill him myself."

"Why?" My voice cracks, shocked by the intensity in his words.

"You know why." His thumb sweeps over my brow, sending shivers down my spine, and my eyes flutter.

"I'm theirs, Wes. I belong to them."

I'd seen the murderous rage in Rhett's eyes, the fierce possessiveness in Dane's. Rhett might not be ready to accept this thing brewing between the three of us, but tonight changes everything.

"Yeah," he sighs, pulling away. "I'll go find the first aid kit. Sit tight."

"I'm not going anywhere." I smile, inhaling a shuddering breath as the reality of everything crashes down around me. If they hadn't showed up when they did... I refuse to let my mind go there.

They did show up, and now Evan and Justin will answer to Dane and Rhett, and I'm safe here with Wes.

God, I was a fucking idiot to sneak out to go and meet Wes, especially with the Reapers sniffing around. But I was so angry at Rhett. I wanted to give him a taste of his own medicine.

"Okay," Wes returns with supplies, "I think I've got everything I need." He pulls over a small coffee table and lays out the first aid kit, a damp towel, and a small bowl. "Let me take a look at you."

"This is becoming a habit," I murmur, and he frowns. "Before, when you saw us leaving this place... there was an accident. The guys patched me up then, too."

"I bet they did." A knowing smirk tips his mouth, sending heat rushing through me.

"You can't say things like that to me."

"Just did." He winks, and I feel some of the tension ease out of my shoulders. If he's trying to make me relax, it's working.

Wes takes care cleaning me up, stopping every time I wince or flinch, giving me time to catch my breath.

"You're good at this," I say.

"I've had some practice."

My brows pinch at that, dread snaking through me. "What do you mean?"

"It doesn't matter." He continues attending to the gash in my head, but I snag his wrist, forcing him to look at me.

"It matters to me."

"Why?" He throws my question from earlier back at me.

"You know why." I don't think as I lean forward and press my lips to his. I just need the pain and the memories from tonight to vanish and selfishly, I know he's capable of making it happen.

"Sadie, fuck..." He inhales a ragged breath, touching his head gently to mine but not letting me deepen the kiss. "We shouldn't—"

"Yeah." Regret coats my voice. "I'm sorry."

"Don't be. Don't ever be sorry for the way you feel... but it's complicated, and I don't want to screw things up before..." He trails off.

"Before what?" I whisper, desperate to kiss him again. I don't know why I feel like this—why I want him the way I want Dane and Rhett. But I do.

"It's late. You should get some rest." He pulls back and grabs a dressing from the first aid kit, gently placing it on my forehead and securing it in place. "Come on, I'm sure Dane won't mind if you lie down."

"Wes, I don't need to—whoa." Everything spins again. "Maybe," I concede. "Just for a little while."

He offers me his hand, and I let Wes pull me up. He slides his arm around my waist and guides me down the hall to Dane's bedroom. Memories of what transpired the last time I was here flood my mind, but the steady pounding in my head makes everything a little hazy.

"I'll see if I can find you some Advil." Wes pulls back the covers and flicks his eyes to the bed. "I figure you might want to get out of your clothes, so I'll give you some privacy."

"Thanks." I perch on the edge of the bed, drawing in a deep breath, letting it calm my racing heart.

So not how I saw this night going.

I manage to peel out of my dress and find a clean t-shirt in one of the drawers. It smells of Dane, instantly settling the butterflies in my stomach. I wonder what they're doing... praying they're not risking too much for me. But Rhett's expression when his eyes found mine across the warehouse will haunt me for a long time.

Gingerly, I climb into bed and pull the sheets over me. Wes returns with a glass of water and some pain pills. "Here," he says, helping me sit up.

"Thank you."

"I'm going to be right outside, okay? You can rest. I'm not going anywhere." He takes a step backward, but my hand shoots out, snagging his wrist.

"Stay."

"Sadie, I—"

"Please, Wes. I'm not asking for anything, I just... I just don't want to be alone." Because I'm terrified that when I close my eyes, all I'll see is Justin's wicked smirk, his gun in front of my face, his hot breath—

"Hey." Wes pales as a violent shudder rolls through me. "You're safe now, Sadie Ray."

A surge of emotion crashes over me and I fight back the tears pooling behind my eyes.

"Sadie?"

"I'm... I'm fine." I blink them away, trying to be strong. I don't want him to see me like this. Weak and scared.

A dark shadow passes over Wes's face, his jaw clenched painfully tight. He kicks off his sneakers and walks around the other side of the bed, lying down beside me. I roll over and peer up at him, smiling when he slides his arm around me and draws me into his side.

"Thank you."

"Close your eyes, Sadie. I've got you," he says thickly. "I've got you."

I do as he says, sinking into his warmth.

And before long, the darkness envelops me.

I wake to an empty bed and the sound of raised voices.

"She asked me to stay with her," Wes says. "What was I supposed to do?"

"You could have kept your fucking hands to yourself, for starters," Rhett bellows. "You were all over her."

"I already told you, nothing happened. She was upset, I said I'd stay with her, and we fell asleep."

"You fell asleep... fucking asshole. I should just put you—"

"Rhett, ease up, brother," Dane says.

My head feels like it might explode, but I manage to summon the willpower to throw the sheets off my body and get out of bed. Slowly, I drag myself across the room, grabbing a hold of the door as I sway on my feet.

"What's going on?" I demand, stepping into the living room.

"Sadie, girl, shit..." Dane rushes over to my side, catching me as I stumble forward. He wraps his arm around me and scans my face. "You shouldn't be out of bed."

"I'm fine." His brow arches, and I add, "I heard arguing." My eyes slide to Rhett in question, and he glowers at me.

"Your boy Rhett got a little jealous is all. Isn't that right, Savage?" Dane teases.

"Wes only did what I asked of him." I hold Rhett's murderous gaze. "Besides, you left me here with him, remember?"

"Don't push him, Sadie, girl," Dane warns quietly, but I hear the lilt in his voice. He's enjoying this. Bastard.

My gaze flickers to Wes, and he gives me a weak smile.

"How are you feeling?"

"My head feels like it's been through a meat processor." Dane stiffens beside me, and I quickly add, "But I'm okay. What happened with Evan and Justin?" I ask Rhett.

"It doesn't matter."

"Doesn't matter?" I gawk. "Are you kidding me? They kidnapped me and... and that piece of shit almost—"

"Don't," Rhett grits out, his carotid throbbing. "Just don't."

"We can talk about this tomorrow, Sadie, girl. When you're feeling—"

"No." I wrench out of his hold and stare Rhett down. "I want to know what happened now. I have a right to—"

"Out," Rhett barks.

"W-what?" My brows knit.

"Pretty Boy, go with Stray and—"

"No way. No fucking way." Wes takes a step forward, and the temperature in the room drops.

"It wasn't a request," Rhett says coolly. "Go the fuck with Stray. Now!"

"Come on, Noble. I need to fill you in on some things

anyway. We can take the opportunity to... bond." He smirks.

"You're both fucking psycho if you think I'm going to just leave—"

"Wes," I say, fixing my eyes right on him. "It'll be okay."

"Fuck, Sadie. It doesn't feel right leaving you while he's—"

"Watch it," Rhett snaps.

"Okay, okay, enough of the macho pissing contest." I level each of them with a hard look before returning my focus back to Wes. "I'm okay, I promise. Thank you for staying with me. But I need to talk to Rhett. Go with Dane. I'll see you tomorrow, I promise."

He hesitates, his gaze flicking between me and Rhett and back again. "I don't—"

"She'll be safe with me," Rhett says, and I don't know who's more surprised—me, him, or Wes. Dane only looks amused by the turn of events.

"Fine." Wes releases a weary sigh.

"Thank you." I go to him, wrapping my arms around him and whispering, "For everything."

Wes holds me briefly before pulling away and moving to the door. With one last glance, he slips into the inky night.

"Give him hell, Sadie, girl." Dane winks at me and then follows Wes out.

The air is thick, suffocating, as Rhett stares at me. It's only when I look closer that I realize he's trembling, his fists clenched at his sides, as if he's seconds away from losing his thin rope of control.

"Rhett, I—"

"Don't," he whispers. "Just... give me a second."

So I do.

A beat passes.

And another.

Rhett doesn't take his eyes off me, searing me with his gaze.

I can hardly breathe under his intense regard. But then the air shifts again, the spell breaking, and he's storming toward me, pulling me into his arms and expelling a shaky breath.

"Fucking hell, princess," he rasps.

5

RHETT

I thought I'd lost you.

I swallow down the words that want to tumble from my lips as I breathe in her scent. But it's not the usual fresh cherry, because I can smell *them* on her.

My fists curl around Dane's shirt with my need to go back and end that cunt. It's what I should have done the second I stormed into that building. But knowing it would potentially stop us from getting any intel on why they felt the need to follow Evan's dumbass plan and take our girl meant I had to put the bullet in his shoulder instead.

"I'm okay," she whispers, but it does little to make me relax.

Every time I blink, all I can see is him with his hand in her hair, ready to—

"Rhett," she soothes, obviously able to feel me trembling as I attempt to do the right thing for once.

I know Dane should probably be the one to comfort her right now. I know he was desperate to get back to her, to know she was okay, but it needs to be me. I need to be here with her. I need to know she's okay, otherwise I'm going to lose my goddamn mind over all this.

Her tiny hand moves up my chest, making a shiver run down my spine as she pulls her head away from my shoulder and looks up into my eyes. I have no idea what she sees staring back at her, but it makes her gasp in shock.

"What happened tonight?" she asks, her brows knitting together.

I shake my head, not ready to talk about that, or anything, right now. "Not important."

"I think it—"

Pressing my fingers to Sadie's lips, I cut off her words. "Not now."

Her large green eyes bore into mine, and my heart rate picks up speed.

"Fuck, Sadie. *Fuck.*"

My lips are on hers before I know what I'm doing. Forcing her mouth open, I push my tongue in and search for hers as I pull her body flush against mine. A low moan rumbles up her throat and spurs me on.

Fuck, I need her right now.

But I can't. Not after what she's been through.

"Rhett," she moans when I drop my hands to the backs of her legs and lift her, her pussy pressing against my already hard cock.

"Shhh, princess. Let me look after you."

I walk through to Dane's bathroom and place her on the counter beside the sink. Just like the rest of this place, it's dated and mostly empty. I understand why Dane feels the need to have this place, though. He craves something of his own, but it's not necessary. He might not know his real family, but what he has at the club is all the family he needs. He's my brother in all the ways that matter, and I'd never let anything happen to him.

"What are you—" Sadie's words vanish when I take a step back from her, shrugging off my cut and dragging my hoodie over my head.

Her eyes immediately drop to my chest and her teeth sink into her bottom lip. It's a move I'm sure she's not aware she's making, but one I appreciate nonetheless. Sadie thinks she hides her feelings from me, keeps a lid on the things she doesn't want anyone to know, but I see it all.

Unsnapping my belt, I toe off my boots and drop my jeans, kicking them off as I move toward the shower. My cock tents my boxers and I have no doubt that she's already seen it and is getting ideas, but it's not happening. This is about her, not me.

"Arms up, princess." She hesitates, but when I lift the fabric of Dane's shirt, I leave her no choice but to follow orders. "Fuck," I groan when I drop the fabric to the floor and run my eyes down her body.

She fucking disarms me, and she has no idea.

"What hurts?" I ask.

"I-I'm okay."

Reaching out, I take her chin lightly in my grip. "No lies, Sadie Ray. What. Hurts?"

"My head."

My eyes lift to the bandage that I'm sure that prick Noble probably applied for her. I want to hate him, to beat the living shit out of him for being anywhere near her, but I also can't help but feel grateful that he looked after her for us while we dealt with business. And despite the fact that he was involved, I could see in his eyes the second I looked into them at the compound earlier that he wanted to protect her almost as much as we do.

Threading my fingers into the hair at the nape of her neck I move her forward a little and press a kiss to the skin beside the bandage. "Where else?"

She shakes her head, and I kiss down the side of her face.

"Sadie."

Holding her hands up, she shows me the red sores around her wrists from the rope she was bound with.

"Motherfuckers," I grunt, lifting one to my lips and gently brushing them over the sore skin. Holding her eyes, I watch her lids lower with each kiss.

"Rhett."

"Where else?"

"N-nowhere."

Dragging my eyes from hers, I run them over every inch of her body, looking for bruises or scratches, but I don't find anything.

Releasing her hand, I push my boxers down my legs and lift her from the counter, copying the move with her panties until we're both bare. I walk backward with her until the water hits me.

She watches my every move before she gets distracted by the rivulets of water running over my chest and down my body.

"Come here, but don't get your head wet."

She steps into my body, and I find her lips again,

kissing her as deeply as I can in the hope that she can feel everything I'm too scared to admit even to myself, let alone her. Her hot hands slide up my back, burning a trail everywhere they go as my cock bobs painfully between us.

"What are you doing, Rhett?" she asks when I finally release her.

"Washing tonight off of you," I admit, not wanting to tell her that she smells like that cunt and that dank warehouse. "Looking after you."

Reaching for the sponge, I pour a generous amount of Dane's shower gel onto it and set about washing every inch of her, once again looking for any signs she might be lying about not being hurt.

I cover her in fluffy white bubbles, memorizing every sexy curve and mark on her body as I go. "All done," I say regretfully, knowing she needs rest because her eyes are starting to flutter closed.

"But..." She reaches for me, and I capture her hand.

"Not about me, princess."

She nods, too exhausted to argue with me.

Turning off the shower, I wrap her in the only towel hanging on the rail and sweep her into my arms. I redress her in one of Dane's shirts before getting her into bed.

"Where are you going?" she asks in a rush when I take a step back, lifting the towel she'd used to wipe down my own body.

"I'll be right back, princess."

She nods, watching my every move as I back out of the room to grab my boxers. Dane will be back before long, and I'm sure the last thing he wants is me walking around his place naked.

To my amazement, she's still awake when I crawl into bed beside her. She instantly curls into my side and searches out my lips. Her leg curls around my waist, ensuring my cock grazes her pussy. Her burning heat calls to me, and I know that if I were to drop my hand to her right now I'd find her wet and ready for me, but I don't, as much as it pains me to do so.

"You need to rest, princess."

"I know... But when I close my eyes, I see him," she whispers, making my chest ache and my need for blood to return full force.

I think about the state of Evan when we kicked him out of the truck on the outskirts of Savage Falls and it helps to settle me. That stupid fuck isn't going to forget how badly he screwed up tonight for a very long time. And if he does, if he even so much as looks at Sadie ever again, I won't hesitate in following through with my threat of ending everything for him.

Justin, though, that fucking snake... thoughts of him really make my mouth water. He wasn't as lucky as his cousin, who got a chance of finding his way home. Justin isn't going to see the light of day again after we're finished with him.

Tomorrow we'll tell Ray what we've discovered, and I already know that he'll be as hungry for Reaper blood as I am.

Evan might be a stupid prick, but he's lead us right into the lions' den. Exactly where I wanted to be after last week's little warning when they ran Dane and Sadie off the road. We just need to make sure we act before they can strike again.

"Let me give you something else to think about, then." I kiss her once, twice, and on the third, she sucks my bottom lip into her mouth and sinks her teeth into it. "You're wicked, princess."

"I learned from the best." She smirks.

A growl rumbles up my throat as I deepen the kiss, distracting her from the events of the night. I kiss her until her body goes lax and she finally gives in to her exhaustion. Then, I pull her into me and hold her as she sleeps, reminding myself that she's okay.

I lose track of time as she lays sleeping in my arms, but it must be a couple of hours later when the front door opens and Dane's footsteps fill the silence.

It only takes him a few seconds to appear in the doorway, his eyes immediately landing on Sadie. "How's she doing?" he whispers.

"She's okay."

He walks into the room, dropping his cut to the floor and kicking off his boots. Gently lowering himself to the bed on the other side of Sadie, he carefully tucks a lock of her hair behind her ear as he checks her over, needing to see for himself that she's in one piece.

"You sorted your shit out?" he asks without looking at me, knowing that I'll never willingly open up face to face.

"Getting there," I admit.

"It's okay to need her... to want her, you know." His eyes bore into the top of my head as my heart begins to thunder in my chest.

"That how you feel?" I ask.

"You know I do."

"And what about him?" I look up this time, meeting his eyes as something passes between us. Apprehension, confusion, I'm not sure. But I think we can both admit that something big happened tonight, and it wasn't just about the three of us in this room. But I have no idea where it leaves us all.

"He cares about her," he says, "but he knows she's ours."

"That doesn't seem to be stopping him."

"He said nothing happened tonight."

"And you believe him?"

"I... uh..." He hesitates.

"Exactly. He wants what's ours, and we need to decide what we're going to do about it."

Because fuck... it's hard enough to think about Sadie with Dane, let alone that Pretty Boy motherfucker.

"Tomorrow, yeah?" Dane murmurs, pushing from the bed. "I'll sleep on the couch. Don't do anything I wouldn't do." He studies me for a beat, probably wondering if anything happened while he was gone.

"I only looked after her, bro," I say. "I did the right thing."

"Good." He gives me a stiff nod, his eyes flicking to Sadie once more. "She deserves it."

6

SADIE

I wake plastered to a wall of heat. My nose brushes a solid inked arm, and my lips curve as I blink and realize that Rhett is curled around me like a spider monkey. God, he feels so good, wrapped around me, protecting me.

I burrow closer, letting out a contented sigh when I hear something.

"*No, no,*" someone murmurs, and I stiffen. Muffled cries fill the apartment and I gently shake Rhett's arm.

"Rhett," I whisper-hiss. "Rhett, wake up."

He mumbles something, rolling away from me and turning over. So much for being my big, bad protector.

"*No, please...*"

Dane's panicked voice filters into the bedroom, and I realize that he's dreaming. He must be.

Gingerly climbing out of bed, I tiptoe across the carpet and slip out of the room. Moonlight bathes the apartment in a silvery hue, illuminating Dane's profile on the couch. He's asleep, curled up on his side like a child, but his brows are furrowed, his lips pressed into a thin line.

"*Don't,*" he jerks, his features freezing with fear, "*please don't.*"

Hurrying to his side, I crouch down and brush the hair out of his eyes. "Dane, it's just a dream. You're dreaming."

"*No, no!*"

My heart lurches into my throat as he thrashes on the couch, fighting some invisible monster. "Dane, wake up. It's just a dream... you're—"

He bolts upright, his eyes fixing right on mine. "S-Sadie?" His eyes blink furiously as he inhales a ragged breath.

"It's me." I smile. "You were having a dream."

"Nightmare," he breathes. "It was a nightmare." He runs a hand through his hair and drops back against the cushions, expelling a steady breath.

"Are you okay?"

"I will be," he replies tightly, shuffling back and patting the space beside him. I lay down next to him, our bodies flush and faces pressed together.

"Does that... happen often?"

"Sometimes."

He shrugs, and I ask, "Want to talk about it?"

"No point. I can barely remember anything."

My brows furrow. "What do you mean?"

"I think... I think they're memories..." His eyes slide to mine again, still alight with fear. "From before."

"Before you came to the club?"

He nods. "It's weird. I can sense things... a feeling or a smell, but I can't see things."

"Have you ever talked to anyone about it?"

"Grandma Irene used to try to talk to me about it, but I'd clam up and start shaking."

My stomach drops. "If you ever want to talk, I'm here, Dane."

"I know." He nudges his nose against mine, smiling. "I'm sorry I woke you."

"Don't be. I'm glad I was here."

"Yeah?"

"Yeah." I fight my own smile.

"How are you feeling, really?"

"I'm okay."

"You really scared us last night, Sadie, girl." Dane's eyes darken and my tummy clenches.

"I know, I'm sorry."

"I get it. Rhett is... well, he can be difficult, and it can't be easy being the club princess." A smirk tugs at his lips and I swat his chest.

"Asshole."

"Yeah, but you love it." His mouth hovers dangerously close to mine. "Gets you all hot and bothered." His hand slides over my hip, digging into my skin enough to make it hurt in the best possible way.

"Dane," I gasp, and he takes advantage, plunging his tongue deep into my mouth. Hooking my leg over his, his hand glides over my ass, toying with the edge of my panties.

"Need to feel you, Sadie, babe," he growls against my mouth, nipping my lips with his teeth.

"God," I smother a moan as his fingers shove into the damp material and find my pussy, slick and ready.

"This is ours," he grits out, spearing two fingers inside me.

Not his.

Not Rhett's.

Theirs.

"Dane, it's... ahhh..."

"Shh." He chuckles. "We wouldn't want to wake Rhett up. Something tells me he'd get pissed if he knew I had my fingers inside you while you're supposed to be resting."

He's right. I should be resting, but this is exactly the kind of distraction I need.

Dane presses deeper, hitting some magical spot inside me, and I bury my face into the crook of his shoulder, crying out.

"So fucking wet," he drawls, pumping into me faster.

My legs begin to quake, and I practically buck off the couch when his thumb joins the party, rolling lazy circles over my clit.

"You gonna come for me, Sadie, girl?" He winds his hand into the back of my hair and yanks my head up to look me in the eyes. "Come all over my fingers like a good girl."

"God, Dane," I choke out, his dirty words my undoing.

"Fuck my hand, babe. Show me how much you want it." He stills his fingers, making me work for it. My hips roll of their own volition, grinding against his hand. Dane watches me, his hungry gaze an aphrodisiac as I hurtle toward the edge.

"One day," he says huskily, "we're gonna have you pinned between us. Rhett fucking your sweet little pussy while I slide into your tight ass."

My eyes flare as I gush all over his hand. "You'd like that, wouldn't you, Sadie, girl?" Dane smirks. "Feeling both of us inside your body, worshipping you. Maybe we'll even let Pretty Boy into the mix. If you think you can handle the three of us."

I come hard, soaring into sweet oblivion.

"So fucking dirty," Dane kisses the corner of our mouth. "And all ours. We're lucky bastards, babe. You know that, right?" He brings his hand to his lips and licks his fingers clean. "Hmm, as sweet as cherries."

My cheeks burn as my heart settles. "That was..."

"Just the beginning." He pecks the end of my nose. "It's still early. We should try to get some sleep. Something tells me today will be a shit show." Something passes over his face, and I know he's referring to them telling my dad about what happened.

I get off the couch and hold my hand out. Dane frowns, and I chuckle. "Come to bed, Dane."

"I'm not sure—"

"I want you there. Rhett can suck it up."

I need both of them beside me, warding off the nightmares of what happened.

His brow arches but he complies, taking my hand and following me into the bedroom. I slide in first, burrowing myself into Rhett's side. He's still out cold, on his back with one arm thrown under his head, the other resting on his abdomen. Dane joins us, pressing up against me and curling one arm over my waist. His lips brush my shoulder, and a small sigh escapes me.

I could get used to this.

But I know things aren't that simple...

So I'm going to enjoy every second of it while I can.

The next time I wake, sunlight is pouring in through the curtains. I stretch my head from side to side, instantly aware of the two strong, hot bodies caging me in on either side.

"Morning, Sadie, girl," Dane murmurs from beside me.

"Hey." I glance over my shoulder and give him a smile. When I turn back, two icy blue eyes are staring at me. "You're awake."

Rhett's jaw tics as his eyes go over my shoulder. "Do I even want to know?" he asks, his voice thick with sleep... and something else.

"I... uh..."

"What can I say, brother?" Dane chimes. "I didn't want to miss all the fun."

Rhett lets out a steady breath, his eyes narrowing.

"Is this okay?" I ask, pressing my lips together.

"Doesn't look like I have much choice." His eyes run over my face. "You're okay?"

"I'm good, thanks to you. How did you know where to find me anyway?

Rhett's brows draw together as he watches me.

"Rhett?"

"Lucky for you, Pretty Boy has a good fucking memory. We ran the plates from the van."

"Oh."

"Don't think I've forgotten what you did." His eyes narrow. "I haven't." The dark edge to his voice makes my heart flutter.

"Bro, it's early. Save the lecture for after breakfast, yeah?" Dane chuckles, nuzzling my neck.

"I need to take a piss," Rhett growls, throwing back the covers.

"No, stay," Dane says. "We're cuddling."

"Yeah," I add, smothering the laughter in my chest. "Stay and cuddle. Please." I pout at him.

Rhett shakes his head, pinning me with a hard look. "Sorry to burst your bubble, princess, but I don't cuddle."

"Liar," I call after his retreating form. He'd held me last night. That's what I'd call cuddling in my book.

"He's such a morning person," Dane mumbles behind me. I turn in his arms and grin up at him, remembering what we did on the couch in the middle of the night. "Hi."

"Hi, yourself." He pecks the end of my nose. "This is nice..."

"It is."

"Maybe we should make it more of a permanent thing."

"Maybe we should. I don't think Rhett wants to be in our cuddle club, though."

"He might if we turn it into the cuddle fuck club." Without warning, Dane rolls me under him and pins me to the mattress. "Yeah," he says, grinding his hips into me. "I think Rhett would definitely get on board with that club."

"You're so bad." I roll my eyes, enjoying the feel of his weight on me.

"Damn right, I am." He kisses me. Once. Twice.

Rhett clears his throat and we both glance over at him leaning against the doorjamb, watching us. "Are you two done? I'm fucking starving."

"We could always have a pussy buffet?" Dane suggests, and I pinch his arm.

"Hey."

"What?" A lazy smile forms on his lips. "He said he's hungry."

"For food, asshole."

"Are you saying my pussy isn't good enough?" I tease, because it's Rhett, and he's too easy to rile up.

He just stares at us from the door with a scowl on his face. "You ran out on us, got lifted by the fucking Reapers, and almost..." His fist clenches so tightly the blood drains from his knuckles. "And you're both acting like... fuck this." He spins on his heels and leaves us.

Dane rolls off me, letting out a weary sigh.

"I guess we were being stupid," I say, suddenly feeling a little out of my depth.

"Nah, Sadie, girl." He shoots me a reassuring smile. "Rhett is just angry."

"At me." Guilt churns in my stomach.

"And himself. I'll go talk to him. Why don't you get cleaned up and find something to wear, then we'll feed the monster before he says or does something he'll regret."

"Yeah, okay." I climb off the bed, but Dane's hand shoots out, snagging me toward him. His mouth crashes down on mine, hard and unyielding. When he breaks away, I'm flushed, and my heart is racing in my chest.

"Everything's going to be okay," he says. "I promise."

He goes after Rhett, and all I can do is hope he's right.

7

WES

The sore spot on the back of my head thanks to Evan knocking me out continues to throb, acting as a constant reminder of what happened the night before.

Dane assured me that Evan was okay. Well, that he would be if he was smart enough to find his way home after they'd beaten him half to death and left him in the middle of nowhere.

It's no less than he deserves for pulling that stunt on Sadie, but even still, I can't help there being a little concern for the guy I've grown up with. His cousin, on the other hand... I feel nothing for him. The way he treated Sadie, the way he spoke to her, what he was going to do to her.

My fingers twist in the sheet beneath me as anger like I've never experienced before surges through me. If I thought the need to protect Mom from the monster that lives in this house was strong, then I have no idea what it was I felt when I followed Dane into that warehouse.

I never thought I'd wish death on anyone, but damn, I hope they kill that motherfucker for thinking he had any right to touch a woman like that, let alone Sadie.

He's clearly fucking stupid to go after the Sinners princess.

Just like you, a little voice pipes up, reminding me that I've somehow managed to find myself in the middle of something I really don't think I want to be involved in.

But Sadie.

Fuck.

There's something about her that calls to me. And as each day passes, I can only feel it getting stronger.

It's terrifying. It's exhilarating... It's probably a bad fucking idea.

She's theirs.

I shake the thoughts from my head, knowing that nothing good can come from them, before my heart jumps into my throat when the sound of tires on the driveway beneath my open window fills the room.

"Shit," I hiss, jumping up and rushing over.

Dad went out before I did last night, and, much to my relief, he still wasn't back when Dane dropped me off.

At least Mom was safe while I was busy worrying about Sadie. I'm not sure I have it in me to be concerned for both of them at the same time.

But when a car comes into view, it isn't Dad's but a black Honda pickup. I run for my bedroom door, but it seems I wasn't the only one who heard her arrival, because Mom's already greeting Sadie when I get to the top of the stairs.

"Of course, sweetie. Come on in," Mom says, as if

inviting anyone into this house is a good idea when Dad could come home at any moment.

"Jesus," I mutter, sweeping my hair back from my face but instantly regretting it when pain shoots down my neck.

"Hey," I say, forcing an easy smile on my face as I jog down the stairs, although I can't deny that the gesture comes easier the second my eyes lock on Sadie.

She looks better today, although it's impossible to miss the bandage still covering her head.

"You didn't tell me you had a girl coming around, Wesley." Mom beams.

"I'm sorry, Mrs. Noble. It's an impromptu visit," Sadie says politely.

"Well, you're more than welcome, Sadie Ray. And please, it's Victoria. Mrs. Noble makes me sound old."

I stare at Mom, wondering how the hell she knows Sadie's name. "We should go out," I suggest, taking a step toward Sadie in the hope that I can back her toward the door.

"Nonsense. Make yourself at home, Sadie." It's not until I edge closer to Mom, ready to ask her what the hell she's playing at, when I smell the alcohol on her breath.

Fucking hell, could this get any worse?

The three of us awkwardly look at each other before I relent, knowing it's safer if I'm home.

"Come on," I say to Sadie, running my hand down her spine and resting it on the small of her back. All the while, Mom watches on with excitement in her eyes.

I've never brought a girl home. Hell, I barely even bring friends back these days.

"Your mom is sweet," Sadie says once we're upstairs and out of earshot.

"Hmm..."

"She seemed a little—"

"What's going on, Sadie?" I interrupt before she brings up a subject I really have no intention of talking about right now.

"It's nice to see you too," she sasses, taking a leisurely trip around my room, her eyes running over everything.

She's wearing a black Sinners tank that shows off a decent amount of cleavage and a short denim skirt that showcases her curvy legs. Legs I'm busy staring at when she turns back to me.

"S-sorry," I stutter like an idiot. "I just wasn't expecting a visit. I assumed you'd be locked up in a tower to be kept safe."

She quirks a brow at me, clearly unamused by my attempt at a joke. "Them letting me out of their sight was the lesser of two evils."

"Oh?"

"They've gone to talk to my dad. To tell him about what happened last night so they can decide on what happens next." She runs her fingers over the football trophies I have on the top of my dresser, but I see the tightness around her eyes.

"Didn't they get their payback last night?"

"Yes and no." She glances at me. "I don't know how much Dane told you, but it's bigger than just Evan and Justin."

"Okay," I say, standing awkwardly in the middle of my room, unable to believe she's actually here.

"I'm not here to talk about them," she says, finally turning around to look at me.

"No? Then why are you here, Sadie Ray?"

Her eyes hold mine for a beat before they drop down my body. It's only then I remember that I'm only wearing a pair of sweats.

Lifting my hand, I rub the back of my neck as she takes her fill of me.

"I... um..." Sadie shakes her head and drags her eyes back up to mine. "I wanted to make sure you were okay. And say thank you, I guess."

"You have nothing to thank me for. The whole thing was my fault."

"None of that was on you. It was all Evan. You're okay, though, yeah?" she asks, closing the space between us.

"Yeah, Sadie Ray. I'm good. How's your head?" I ask, tracing my finger over the edge of the dressing I applied on her.

"I'll live."

The air between us crackles with tension and desire, and my fists curl at my sides as I fight the need to reach for her.

Memories of kissing her under the Arches come rushing back and my mouth waters.

She's theirs, I remind myself.

"Fuck, Sadie, I—"

My words are cut off when her breasts press against my chest and she reaches up to brush her lips against mine. Unable to stop myself, my hands lift, holding her cheeks and tilting her head to the side to allow me to deepen the kiss.

Her tongue meets mine and fights for dominance as her hands roam over my chest before sliding down my back and to my ass. My cock swells, pressing against her stomach as she kisses me as passionately as I do her.

Walking her backward, I lay her down the second her legs hit my bed and crawl over her, unable to stop now that I've started. "Fuck, Sadie," I moan, ripping my lips from hers and kissing across her jaw. "I laid here all night, thinking about you. About you with them."

"Jealous?"

"Hell yeah. You know I want you, Sadie Ray. Oh fuck," I bark in shock when she pushes her hand beneath the waistband of my sweats and wraps her fingers around my solid length.

She strokes up and down, her gentle grip fucking mind-blowing, and I have no choice but to drop my head to her shoulder as I lose myself to the feeling. My chest heaves as my body and head war about where this goes.

With regret, my head wins, and I push up from her body, looking deep into her eyes. "They'll kill me for this, Sadie."

"No, they won't."

"We can't. I can't... not after last—" The rumble of another engine forces me to sit up, and before I know what I'm doing, I've pulled Sadie's hand from my body and raced toward the window once more.

Dad's car door flies open, and he stumbles out. His suit is a mess, his hair is all over the place. He's clearly had a good night out.

"Fuck." Lifting my hand to my hair, I pull on the strands until it burns.

"What's wrong? Is that your—"

"Dad, yeah." I grimace. "You need to get out of here."

"It's okay, Wes. I can handle your dad."

"I have no doubt, but it's not happening. He'll freak out." Rushing to my chair, I drag a shirt on and shove my feet into my sneakers. "Come on," I say, throwing open the window.

"What the fuck are you doing?" she shrieks, standing in the middle of my room with her hands on her hips.

"Wesley?" Dad booms up the stairs, his deep voice causing goose bumps to cover my skin.

"Shit. Get out the window, Sadie," I demand, reaching for her and pulling her over.

"You can't be serious."

"Deadly. There's a ledge and then a trellis thing. Trust me, I do this all the time. You'll be safe. Safer than if he finds you in here."

She studies me for a beat before finally nodding and throwing her leg over the windowsill.

"I'm following you, but get in your truck and get ready to leave."

"Okay," she says, following my instruction and lowering to my makeshift escape route.

In seconds we're both in her pickup and she's got the engine running.

"Wait," she says, with the car already in drive. "What about your mom?"

I look to the house and then back at Sadie. "Just drive. You need to be as far from here as possible."

Mom's going to have to lie in the bed she's made for herself this time.

Neither of us does or says anything until Sadie turns into the next street. Reaching over, she uncurls my clenched fist and laces our fingers together. "Wes, what's going on?" she asks, pulling to a stop and looking over at me with her brows drawn together.

"My dad, he hates the MC."

"That's no secret, Wes. Tell me what that was really about."

"He's... he's a cunt, and if he finds you there, if he finds you with me, I don't know what he would do."

She thinks for a moment, and I fear what she might be in the middle of figuring out. "Last night when you said you'd had plenty of practice at patching people up. Y-you meant..." She swallows, her face hardening in anger. "Those bruises last week. They were him, weren't they?"

My teeth grind as I fight with myself to keep all this shit hidden, even though I already know it's too late. She knows.

"Yeah."

"We should go back for your mom."

Slumping down in the seat, I look up at the clouds as I suck in a deep breath. "She refuses to leave him. But I can't always protect her. And right now, I need to protect you." I turn to look at her so she can see how serious I am.

"N-no, you don't need to—"

Leaning over, I wrap my hand around the back of her neck and crash our lips together. The kiss is brutal, almost violent with my anger, but she gives me as good as she gets before I abruptly pull away.

"Take me away, Sadie, before I do something really fucking stupid."

8

SADIE

Wes sinks against my leather seat and closes his eyes, letting out a weary sigh. Anger ripples through me from his confession. I'd suspected that things with his dad were bad, but I didn't think... God. I can't even imagine.

"Hey," he says quietly, reaching over and sliding his hand along my knee. "I'm okay."

I glance at him, smiling weakly. "I'm taking you to the compound, okay?" He nods and I add, "I think we should tell someone... about your dad."

"Sadie, no." Panic flares in his eyes, but I try to focus on the road. "I can handle—"

"I won't stand around and do nothing, not when I..." I swallow the words, trapping them between pursed lips.

"When you what?"

"When I care about you." My eyes flick to Wes again, and this time, I find him smiling. "What?"

"Nothing." He grins. "Nothing at all."

We ride the rest of the distance to the compound in silence. It isn't awkward or uncomfortable, though. I can't explain it, but I feel safe with Wes. I feel like I can just be. It's weird, but I'm done questioning it.

Wes wasn't wrong earlier, when he said that Rhett and Dane won't like it. Rhett won't. I'm not so sure about Dane, especially after last night, the things he said. But it's too late to go back now. I want them.

I want them all.

And I'll do whatever I can to keep them. Even if it means Rhett throws a massive tantrum.

The second we reach the compound, Wes sits a little straighter. "Are you sure this is a good idea?" he asks. "The last time I was here..."

"If you hadn't come here to find them, I might not have—" I swallow the lump in my throat. "You saved me, Wes." My hand covers his, and the air crackles between us.

"Sadie, I—"

Steel crunches and cranks and the gate starts to roll open, and I give a little shake of my head. "Later," I say.

"Yeah." Wes runs a hand down his face, letting out a low whistle as I drive inside and park in my usual spot outside the shop. "Whoa, this is quite the... operation."

"Welcome to the inner sanctum of the Sinners MC." A smirk plays on my lips.

"Gotta say, I never thought I'd see inside those gates, and now I've seen it twice in less than twenty-four hours."

"Come on, let's go find my dad."

"Y-your dad?"

"Well yeah," my brows bunch, "the guys came to talk to him."

"Right." He pales, and I smother a chuckle.

"Relax, he won't bite. Much." I wink and shoulder the door, climbing out of the truck.

Wes joins me and we head for the clubhouse, ignoring the curious stares of the few bikers milling around. The second we enter, Pacman's head pokes up over the bar.

"Sadie, what is—I don't know you." He pins Wes with a hard look.

"Pacman, this is Wes. Wes, this is Pacman."

"What's up?" Wes gives him a small nod.

"And how exactly do the two of you—"

"Stand down, Pacman," I groan. "Wes is good people. He helped me out with... some stuff. Is my dad around?"

"In his office, but I wouldn't go down there if I were you."

I motion for Wes to follow me as I cut across the room toward the hall leading to the club's private rooms.

"Sadie," Pacman yells after me. "Come on, he said—"

"Thanks for the heads up," I say, waving him off.

Wes jogs up beside and whispers, "Perhaps we shouldn't go in there yet."

"We need to talk to them, now. Besides, you should probably hear whatever it is they have to say."

"I should?" His brows furrow, and it makes him look so fucking adorable I fight the urge to push him up against the wall and kiss him the way I wanted to earlier.

Raised voices cut off that line of thought, and I steel myself for whatever we're about to find on the other side of the door marked 'Prez's Office.' I knock once before grabbing the handle and walking inside.

"Not now—Sadie Ray." Dad gawks at me, running a hand over his beard. "Why am I not surprised?"

"Hi, Daddy." I flash him a meek smile.

One of his thick brows lifts. "Well, now you're here, you might as explain what the fuck you were doing sneaking out last night." Anger radiates from every pore as he glares at me. But it isn't just anger, it's fear.

My eyes scan the room, landing on Rhett and Dane. Dane shoots me an easy smirk, probably not surprised that I couldn't stay away. But Rhett... Rhett's expression is as thunderous as my father's.

Wes steps up behind me and Dane mutters, "Oh fuck," under his breath.

"Stray," Wes says coolly.

"You're playing a dangerous game, princess," Rhett seethes.

"We ran into a... complication," I say, stepping further into the room. Wes follows, closing the door behind him.

"Will someone tell me what the fuck Grant Noble's kid is doing standing in my office?"

"You didn't tell him yet?" I ask Rhett and Dane. Rhett's jaw clenches even harder.

"We hadn't gotten to that part, Sadie, girl," Dane soothes.

I'm hardly surprised my dad recognizes Wes. He makes it his business to know all the important players in Savage Falls. And Grant Noble has been a thorn in the club's side for as long as I can remember.

"Wes is... a friend," I explain.

"A friend? Since when did we start befriending the likes of—"

"Dad!" I hiss. "Before you jump to conclusions, if Wes hadn't told Rhett and Dane what happened last night, things might have ended differently."

"What the fuck are you talking about?" His murderous gaze slides to the two guys sitting on the couch pushed up against the wall.

Dane lets out a low whistle. "She's telling the truth, Prez. If it wasn't for Pretty Boy here, we might never have..."

"So what you're saying is I should be thanking him,"— his head whips in Wes's direction—"and not you two?"

"Does it matter?" I throw up my hands in frustration. "You're missing the point."

"The point?" His eyes narrow right at me. "The point, dear daughter, is that if you'd have stayed in the compound, none of this would have ever happened."

"Fine. I screwed up." I let out an exasperated breath. "I can admit that. But the Reapers obviously—"

"Hold up," Wes says. "The Reapers? As in, the Ridge View Reapers?"

"What do you know about the Reapers, Pretty Boy?" Dane asks.

"I know things got messy way back between the Sinners and the Reapers. It's why my old man wants Mayor Nixon to come down harder on the club. So nothing like that happens again."

"Take a seat, son." Dad motions to a chair and Wes

drops into it, and I stand there in the middle of the four men in my life.

God, when did shit get so complicated?

"Come on, Prez, you can't be serious," Rhett protests, levelling Wes with a cold look. "He's an outsider."

"Rhett," I hiss, silently pleading with him to not do this. Not here. Not when we both know his problem with Wes is much bigger than the fact that he was Evan's friend.

"Sadie made her choice when she brought him here." My dad sinks back in his chair, steepling his fingers. "Why exactly *did* you bring him here?"

"Like I said, we ran into a complication." My gaze lifts to Wes, but he shakes his head.

Not now.

Fine.

"But it can wait," I add.

Dane throws me a curious look that says *everything okay?*

I nod.

It isn't. I hate that we left Wes's mom there with his piece of shit dad, but he's right. Maybe now isn't the time.

"For fuck's sake, Sadie Ray, sit down. You're making me nervous." Dad's expression softens.

"I'm okay, Dad." I reassure him.

"Yeah?" He swallows hard, scrubbing his jaw, and I see the sheer relief there.

"What are you going to do with Justin?" I ask.

"I'm not sure you want to know the answer to that." His eyes darken, and I see a flash of Razor Dalton push to the surface. Dad looks to the ceiling and lets out a strained breath. "We need concrete proof this is Darren's doing. Once we have it, I can sit down with Nolan and Ritz."

"Then what?"

A chill goes through the room as my dad shifts in his chair. "That motherfucker kidnapped my daughter. He put his hands on you. Darren is mine."

"Nolan will never agree to that," Rhett protests. "He might be a loose cannon, but Darren is his nephew. He's family."

"Nolan won't want war, not now. Not while he's on his death bed. We get confirmation that Darren was working this alone, and then I go to Nolan and Ritz."

"And Evan?" Wes speaks up.

"Still loyal to that piece of shit, Pretty Boy?" Rhett practically growls the words.

"Relax, brother," Dane says, throwing his arm in front of Rhett to keep him on the couch. "Noble has proved himself. Cut him some slack."

"We'll see," Rhett snarls.

"Enough," Dad barks. "You can keep this pissing contest outside of club business. Evan Henley has been dealt with. He knows things will go south pretty quickly for him if he runs his mouth."

Wes nods, but I see a flash of anger in his eyes. Whatever tenuous friendship they had, it's over.

I don't doubt that, not one bit. If I did, I wouldn't have brought Wes here.

"Rhett, I want you with me when I pay our friend a visit. Stray, check in with Jax and the girls, and keep Sadie Ray out of trouble." His eyes finally settle on Wes. "And you... can we trust you?"

"I won't breathe a word of it to anyone, I swear."

"Why?"

"Because Sadie has been a friend, and that means something to me, sir."

"You look so much like her, you know."

Wes frowns, and I'm about to ask who he means when a knock on the door echoes through the room.

"Yeah?" Dad calls, and the door opens to reveal Pacman with a grim expression.

"We got company, Prez."

"Friendly?"

"It's Ritz."

Rhett shoots upright, and my dad stands.

"He's here alone," Pacman adds. "Says he came to talk."

"He knows," Rhett spits. "That motherfucker knows what happened."

Dread snakes through me, and I suppress a shudder.

"Get her out of here. Take her to your room," Dad barks at Dane, "and stay there. Don't move until one of us comes to get you."

"Seriously, Dad, I'm not—"

"What about him?" Rhett flicks his head to Wes, glowering.

"Two pairs of eyes are better than one. You good with watching my daughter while I deal with this?"

"Yes, sir."

"I am right here, you know," I mutter, but no one pays me any attention.

"It could be a trap," Rhett whispers, his stone mask already fixed in place.

Cold.

Cruel.

Untouchable.

"Let's go find out."

Neither of them look back as they storm out of the office to greet the VP of the Ridge View Reapers.

9

DANE

I follow Sadie and Wes out of Prez's office, noticing that the second the door closes behind the three of us, Sadie reaches out and threads her fingers through his.

Neither of them look at each other, but I can still feel the connection they share crackling between them. Most people would probably be jealous if they saw their girl with another guy, and I guess there is a part of me that is. But mostly, it just gets my cock hard thinking about watching her with him.

I squeeze my eyes closed for a beat as I remember her face last night as she came on my fingers. The way her cheeks heated and her lips parted as she sucked in heaving breaths. I probably shouldn't have done that while she was recovering from what happened, but my self-control is non-existent around Sadie. Besides, I needed to be close to her, to know she was okay. And I was pretty sure she felt the same.

Reaching down, I rearrange myself before overtaking

them, unlocking my door, and throwing it open for them to enter. "It's nothing like your mansion, I'm sure," I mutter as Wes looks around at the small space.

"Big houses aren't all they're cracked up to be," he mutters.

I keep my eyes on him as he takes in the posters on the walls and the crap that's strewn about everywhere, wondering what he's actually seeing, what he thinks about all of this.

"I'm going to use the bathroom. Can I trust you to play nice?" Sadie asks, her eyes narrowing on mine.

"Me?" I ask, mock offended. "I'm always nice. It's Savage you want to worry about. He was about two seconds from ripping Pretty Boy's head off when you barged in."

"Does that name have to stick?" Wes asks from behind me.

"Sure does, Pretty Boy." I shoot him a wink. "Nothing to worry about, Sadie, girl. We're good, right, Noble?"

"Sure, whatever you say."

He holds my eyes as Sadie slips into my bathroom and closes the door behind her.

"You kissed her." It's not a question, because I don't need to hear the answer. I already know.

"Uh..."

A smile curls up one side of my mouth, but it's anything but amused. "You're playing a very dangerous game here. You know that, right?"

He shakes his head. "I don't... Shit." Lifting his hand, he rubs the back of his neck.

"You want her. But what I can't work out is why. Your

family hates the MC, yet you're willingly... *actively*, making Sadie a part of your life. Why?"

He looks down at his feet for a beat before finding my eyes again. "Because she's the only thing that makes sense."

Fuck. I know exactly how he feels there. I've felt the same fucking way since I was about eight years old.

I study him, wondering what really makes him tick, what's really going on in his life to land him here in the middle of our club. "You made her come yet?"

"W-what?" he stutters, looking more shocked than I'm sure he would if I'd just hit him.

"Have you got her off yet? Made her come? Given her an orgasm?"

"This is the weirdest interrogation I've ever had, you know that, right?"

"Answer the goddamn question, Pretty Boy."

"No, okay? I haven't. Might have if we weren't interrupted earlier, though."

A knowing smile plays on my lips. I fucking knew they'd fooled around.

Wesley Noble is either really brave or really fucking stupid for touching our girl. Lucky for him, thoughts of him with his hands on her body only turn me on more than I already was. I've barely managed to get rid of my semi since finger fucking her on the couch last night.

If it were Rhett standing in my place right now, though, it would be a very different story.

"Interrupted by who?" I ask, not wanting him to think I'm not taking this seriously.

"My... um... fuck." He rubs nervously at his neck again, unable to hold my eyes.

"'Tell him." A soft voice comes from behind me.

Wes's eyes lift to Sadie, but I keep my gaze firmly on him.

"Sadie, I can't—"

"'Tell him, Wes. We can help. We can protect her." He swallows nervously as he holds her eyes. Sadie comes closer and stands at my side. "We don't have to be on a different team. Let us help you."

Lifting his hand to his hair, he pulls it back from his face, cursing, knowing that he's got no option but to confess whatever it is to me. "My dad. Okay. We were interrupted by my dad. I made Sadie leave the house via my bedroom window, so he didn't see her because he..."

"He..."

Wes looks at me before he turns his eyes on Sadie. Immediately the torment within them softens. "He hurts my mom."

"And you, Wes."

"Yeah, but I can handle that, it's her I—"

"Bullshit," Sadie snaps. "You shouldn't have to handle anything."

"It's my life. It's how it's always been." He shrugs and turns his back on us, his shoulders dropping in defeat.

"We can go and get her," I offer before my head has caught up with my mouth.

"We can't just walk in while he's there and take his wife, Dane," Sadie says.

"He was drunk. He'd been out all night. Fuck knows

what he's doing to her right now. But Sadie was a bigger priority."

"You're serious about this, aren't you?" I ask.

He stills, a humorless laugh rumbling from his throat. "I'm not going to lie about my cunt of a father hitting my mother."

"I didn't mean that, Pretty Boy. I meant Sadie. You're not playing here, are you?"

"Are you?" he asks, finally turning back to look at me.

Reaching out, I pull Sadie into my side. "Nah. She's fucking mine." With my hand in her hair, I drag her around in front of me and slam my lips down on hers.

My semi goes full mast in less than a second as her taste fills my mouth. Despite the fact that we've got an audience, she doesn't even try to fight me.

Maybe she's as big a freak as I am when it comes to being watched.

"Dane," she moans when I release her.

I reach for my belt and rip it open.

"What are you doing?" she whisper-hisses. I'm aware of the gravity of the situation happening only down the hallway, but right now, there's nothing to do but wait, so I figure we may as well have some fun while we're at it.

"Showing Pretty Boy here that if he's serious, then he's going to have to wait his turn." Shoving my pants down, I take my length in my hand. "Suck me, Sadie, girl. Show him exactly what he's missing out on."

Her eyes darken with desire, telling me what I already knew. She'd never deny me.

Shooting a look over her shoulder, her eyes collide with Wes's for a beat.

"Lock the door, then take a seat, Pretty Boy. Enjoy the show. If you're lucky, you might get a turn one of these days."

I lower down to the seat behind me, violently fisting my cock, which is already glistening with precum from just thinking of her sucking me into her hot mouth. "Knees, babe."

Dragging her eyes back to me, she looks down at where I'm holding myself, licking her lips as she does.

Before I get a chance to tell her again, she drops to her knees and takes over, licking at the tip and making my ass leave the seat as the sensation shoots through my body.

"Fuck, Sadie, girl."

Parting her lips, she sucks me deep until I hit the back of her throat. With my fingers twisted in her hair—the opposite side to her bandage—I guide her movements before looking up at Wes, who's watching us with a mix of shock and desire. Although the tent in his sweats clues me in as to which is stronger.

"Don't be shy, Pretty Boy. We're all about pleasure here."

He shifts, his hand going to his crotch, rubbing his cock through the fabric of his pants. It's easy to forget that not all guys are like those in the club, who'll happily fuck in public without a second thought.

"You want our girl to suck you off?" I ask, my eyes going back to Sadie.

She stills as if she's going to pull off me, but my grip on her tightens, stopping her from doing whatever is in her head.

"Fuck. Yeah."

"You should. She's fucking good." I force it a little deeper down her throat and she gags on me. "That's it, Sadie, girl." I encourage, watching her bob up and down as my balls start to draw up.

I never have been able to last long with her. I guess that's what happens when you've waited all the years I have.

"You know what's better, though? I ask, my release almost in touching distance.

"W-what?"

"Watching her come. She's so fucking beautiful."

My hips thrust up as my orgasm crests. Pulling her hair, I rip her from my length and sit forward, spilling my seed all over her chest so Wes has no choice but to see me mark her, claim her.

"So fucking beautiful. And all ours. Isn't that right, Sadie, girl?" Reaching out, I write my name in my jizz I've left on her skin.

She licks her lips, holding my eyes for a beat before hesitantly looking over her shoulder at Wes, who's staring at the two of us like he can't rip his eyes away.

"Pretty Boy?"

"Y-yeah." His eyes find mine, and confusion joins the desire that had previously flooded them.

"I want to see your skills," I tell him as I tuck myself away, not wanting him to get entirely the wrong idea about where this is going. I'll let him be in the room as much as he wants, but he ain't coming anywhere near me. "Get our girl off. I've already done half the work—she's wet as fuck."

Sadie gasps in shock, but she knows as well as I do that I'm telling the truth.

"Stand, Sadie, girl."

She does as she's told, rising to her feet at the same time as me.

After wiping her chest with a tissue, I place my hands on her hips and spin her around to face Wes. "You horny, baby?" I growl against her throat, lifting my hands to cup her breasts over her low-cut tank.

A whimper vibrates in her throat as I squeeze hard.

"You want Noble to get you off?"

"B-both of you."

My eyes find his over Sadie's shoulder. "That wasn't what I asked, Sadie, girl."

"You want to watch?"

"Yeah, babe. I wanna see if he's good enough for you."

"O-okay." Holding her hand out, she gestures for him to join us.

After a second, he stands, his cock trying to burst through his sweats. Fear flashes through his features until Sadie tugs on his arm and he steps up to her. Then it's replaced with determination before he lowers his lips to hers and sweeps her into his arms, taking her from me.

I hate the chill that covers my body when she leaves me, but it's soon replaced by something much more satisfying when his hands slide down her back until he grabs her ass harshly.

He stumbles back until his legs collide with the bed he was sitting on a few seconds ago and falls down, dragging her on top of him for a beat before he flips them over and pins her to the bed, lifting from her lips and staring into her eyes.

I have no idea what passes between them, but I do know it's crackling with chemistry and desire.

He whispers something to her and she drops her hands to the hem of his shirt, dragging it up his body and throwing it on the floor. He mimics the move with her before dropping his lips to the swell of her breasts.

I shove my pants down my hips once more as my cock swells, watching her enjoy herself.

"Wes," she moans when he bites down on her nipple through the lace of her bra.

"Take it off of her," I demand. "Make her really moan."

10

SADIE

My pussy clenches at Dane's order, heat coursing through me as Wes lifts his head and his eyes ask me a silent question.

Are you sure?

I nod, biting down on my bottom lip with anticipation.

"Fuck," he rasps, lust and longing swirling in his blue eyes.

"You'd better hurry before Rhett returns," Dane taunts, his own voice thick with desire, and I glance over, hardly surprised to see him jacking himself off.

Dane likes to watch. He likes to watch me at the mercy of Rhett... and Wes, apparently.

Fierce determination flashes over Wesley's face, and he smirks at me. Then he's unhooking my bra, leaving the straps over my shoulders as he sucks on each of my nipples. He trails hot, wet kisses down my stomach, swiping his tongue in my navel, making my tummy clench, hesitating when he reaches the waistband of my skirt.

Rocking back on his haunches, Wes pushes it up around my waist so he's got enough space to push my thighs apart and bury his face in my pussy. His fingers hook my panties to the side and his tongue swipes through my wet folds, spearing inside me so sharply I cry out, fisting Dane's bedsheets.

"Fuck, yeah," Dane hisses. "Tastes like cherries, am I right?"

Oh God. This is so freaking dirty. So wrong, given my dad and Rhett and the VP of the Reapers are right down the hall in my dad's office. But I can't stop myself. I need them to make me forget, to remind me that I'm safe and protected.

Wes lifts his head, making a show of licking his lips. "Tastes like trouble." He grins.

"Yeah, she does." Dane's deep chuckle fills the room, drowning out the slap of skin against skin as he pumps himself fast and hard.

"Less talking, more eating," he orders Wes, who seems all too happy to oblige as he dips his head again, devouring me like a man starved.

His tongue feels divine, sliding along the length of me, flicking my clit. He grazes his teeth against the sensitive bud before sucking it.

"Fuck," I pant, trying to smother the moans crawling up my throat.

"You need to stay quiet, Sadie, girl. Unless you want everyone to hear Pretty Boy getting you off."

"I... God, Wes. *God.*"

"Shut her up, man. Unless you want—"

Wes reaches up, forcing two fingers into my mouth, and I practically choke on them. But I don't care. His tongue feels too good, and then he's pushing two fingers inside me, stretching me. Owning me.

"Fuck, that's hot." Dane sounds breathless, his words choppy. "Make her come, make her beg..." he pants.

Wes chuckles against my pussy as I gush at Dane's words. "Dirty bitch." He practically breathes the words against my clit, making me squirm beneath him.

I'll be anything he wants, so long as he lets me come.

"Please," I rasp. "I'm so fucking close."

His fingers curl deeper as he works his tongue inside me, around me, licking and tasting.

"Yes," I cry around his fingers. "Oh God, yes."

Wes sucks the skin along my inner thigh, biting down right as he hits that place deep inside me, and I come apart.

"Yes, fuck yes," Dane grunts, finding his own release as my legs lock around Wes's head. Lazily, he laps at my pussy while I ride out the waves of pleasure crashing over me.

"I want to taste you," I say, huskily, gently tugging his hair.

His eyes connect with mine, the air snapping taut between us. He starts to crawl up my body and part of me wants him to fuck me, right here, right now.

Something tells me Dane would let him, so long as he could watch... maybe even join in...

Bracing himself over me, Wes kisses me, letting his tongue tangle with mine so I can taste myself.

"Alright, Pretty Boy, you've had your fun."

"What?" My head snaps over to Dane. He looks satisfied and a little bit pissed.

"This was about you, Sadie, girl. Not him." His eyes cut to Wes, who lets out a frustrated breath.

"A test," he deadpans.

"Something like that. Better fix yourselves before Rhett... in fact, better hurry, I think I hear footsteps."

Shit.

Shit!

I push Wes off me and quickly fix my tank and skirt before sitting up against the headboard and smoothing my hair down. Wes climbs off the bed and grabs his t-shirt, pulling it back on. Then he wipes his mouth with the back of his hand and perches on the side of the bed, putting plenty of distance between us.

I hear a door slam and heavy footsteps approaching, and soon enough the door handle moves, but it doesn't open.

"Open up," Rhett booms, "it's me."

Dane pads across the room to unlock the door and it swings open.

"Why is the door locked? Is everything—" Rhett pauses, his eyes running over the three of us, lingering on me. I shoot him a saccharine smile.

"What did Ritz want?" I ask innocently.

"What the fuck is going on?" he grits out.

"Nothing, we've been waiting for you," I say as calmly as I can, hoping he can't hear the slight hitch in my voice.

"Yup," Dane agrees. "Just grilling Pretty Boy and

getting to know him a bit better. He was feeling kinda hungry, but don't worry, I got him something to eat."

I smother a gasp, pressing a hand against my mouth and pretending to yawn. Rhett blinks, his eyes narrowed as if he isn't buying a single word of it.

"We're heading out," he says. "Take him home and get Sadie to Dee's house. The girls stay there until Ray says it's safe."

"Seriously, you're not going to tell us what happened with Ritz?" I balk.

"Later. We need to go."

"Fine, let's roll." Dane stands and moves toward Rhett, the two of them slipping into the hall while Wes helps me off the bed.

"You good after... you know." He rubs the back of his neck.

"Yeah, I'm good. Sorry things got a little bit... out of hand. Dane is—"

"I don't regret it." He runs his knuckles down my cheek. "I like you, Sadie. I like you a lot."

"I like you too."

"I won't pretend any of this makes sense to me. It doesn't. And I know I should probably walk away and never look back, but I can't. I won't. Even if Savage kicks my ass for it." Wes smiles weakly, and my stomach drops.

"I won't let him hurt you."

"I'm not scared of him."

"You should be," Rhett barks, his eyes fixed on the both of us. "Let's go."

We file out of Dane's room, but Rhett lingers, keeping me back while Wes and Dane disappear.

"What?" I ask when he doesn't speak.

"Are you... okay?"

"I'm okay. But I don't like all these secrets. And stop being a jerk to Wes. You owe him and you know it."

Rhett pushes his face into mine. "If it wasn't for him, you never would have left the compound."

"Seriously, you think that's why I left?"

His brows pinch. "What the fuck is that supposed to mean?"

"You know *exactly* what it means. We should go, they're waiting." Moving around him, I take a step ready to leave but he grabs my arm.

"This isn't a game, princess. If you don't want your Pretty Boy to end up hurt, you should—"

"Jealousy looks good on you," I sass, yanking my arm away and taking off down the hall.

This time, Rhett lets me go.

The atmosphere in the truck is tense as we head to Wes's house. I brush my hand up against his and he glances down, interlocking our fingers.

"Okay?" I ask, and he nods but his expression is vacant, as if he's worried about what he might find when we get there.

"We can still tell some—"

"No, I can handle it."

"She has a point, man," Dane adds. "If your old man is—"

"I said I can handle it."

I flinch at his tone.

"Shit, I'm sorry," Wes sighs. "I just... I'm not used to sharing the burden."

"You're not alone in this," I say. "Not anymore."

Dane's eyes burn holes into the side of my face as he drives across town, but I focus solely on Wes.

"Thanks." He offers me a smile, but it doesn't reach his eyes. "Maybe just let me out at the end of the street. I don't want to set him off again."

"Fuck that," Dane hisses. "We're not just going to abandon you."

My eyes snap to Dane and his lip quirks. "Thank you," I mouth, unsure if he knows what it means to me that he's being so cool about all of this.

Anything for you, his intense gaze seems to say.

"We'll make sure everything's okay and then we'll leave."

"Yeah," Wes concedes. "Okay."

The second we turn into his neighborhood, he lets out a steady breath, one I feel down to the pit of my stomach. I squeeze his hand, my heart crashing in my chest.

I immediately search for his dad's car, relieved when I see it missing.

"He's not here." Wes relaxes beside me. But the second the truck stops, he shoulders the door open and climbs out.

"I'm coming." I go after him. I have a bad feeling about this. I can't explain it, but dread unfurls inside me.

"Shit," Dane says as my feet hit the ground.

I don't wait for him, trailing after Wes as he enters his house.

"Mom?" His voice echoes through the high-ceilinged hallway.

Silence greets us.

Thick, sludgy silence.

Something isn't right.

"Mom?" He takes off, racing down the hall.

"Maybe she left with him?" I suggest, hurrying after Wes. He disappears through a door but draws to a sudden stop.

"Mom, fuck..."

I enter the kitchen and the sight before me steals the air from my lungs. "Oh my God."

Mrs. Noble is slumped on the floor against one of the counters, blood trickling from a nasty gash in her head.

"W-Wes?" She sobs. "Oh, Wes."

Guilt coils around my heart. We left her.

We left her here... and he hurt her.

Anger boils the blood in my veins.

"Sadie Ray? Oh, gosh. I didn't—"

"Shh, Mom. Let's get you cleaned up." Wes lifts her off the ground and I rush to the table to pull out a chair. Gently, he sets her down. "This is so embarrassing." She barely meets my eyes.

"I'm so sorry," I choke out.

"Oh. Sweetheart. It isn't... Grant's temper gets the better of him sometimes. It's worse than it looks. I was just..."

"Mom, stop. She knows." Wes's eyes shutter as he drags in a shaky breath.

But she isn't looking at me anymore. She's staring past me. "Hello, I don't think we've met."

Dane steps up beside me, a quiet storm. I reach back for his hand, and he laces our fingers together, letting me anchor him.

"This is Dane," I say, "my friend."

Wes's mom smiles weakly. "I'm sorry we're not meeting under better circumstances."

She's so calm and composed, my heart can hardly stand it. Or maybe it's simply shock.

Either way, we can't leave her here.

I won't.

"Did Mr. Noble—"

"He'll be out drowning his guilt, no doubt."

"Maybe we should call someone?" The words are out my mouth before I can stop them.

"Oh no, sweetheart, there's no need for that. It's just a little cut." Her smile is full of pain and anguish. "He doesn't usually..."

"Mom," Wes warns as he cleans up the cut and applies a small dressing.

"Maybe we should get out of here for tonight. Let him cool down," Wes suggests.

"But we have nowhere to go."

"We can go to a hotel. We can—"

"I know a place," I blurt out. "My aunt, I'm sure she'd let you stay and figure... things out." My eyes flick to Wes. "It's safe," I add.

"Sadie's right. I'm not sure I like the idea of leaving you here," Dane says, and I could kiss him for agreeing with me.

"What do you think, Mom? You know what'll happen

when he comes back... he'll be..." Wes swallows. "I'm not sure I trust myself around him right now."

"O-okay. Maybe, just for the night. But he can't know..." Her eyes settle on mine. There's no judgement there, but there is something. Regret, maybe? "We'll tell him we're staying at a hotel for the night to give him time to calm down."

"Okay," I say. "But we should probably go now."

Before he gets back.

11

RHETT

My bike rumbles beneath me as I follow Ray toward the warehouse where we left Justin tied up. My fingers tighten on the handlebars painfully as I recall the image I walked in on last night.

The need to end him rushes through me once more. I wanted to kill him last night, but Dane talked me down. He was right—we needed to tell Ray before we did anything. It was obvious that Justin was hiding things, and killing him wouldn't get us the information we need.

We know he's a Reaper. We know he's related to Evan and that's how he ended up doing that cunt's dirty work. But what we don't know is *how* it connects to the Reapers.

We turn left onto a dirt road and make our way to the hidden building. Thanks to Ritz's visit earlier, we know that Darren hasn't been seen for a few days, and although there's no evidence that he was involved in any of this, it's pretty fucking obvious that he's had a hand in hurting our princess.

"You ready for this?" Ray asks after we've climbed off our bikes.

I crack my knuckles, desperate to watch the life drain out of this prick's eyes for ever thinking he could lay a hand on someone that belongs to me.

"I was ready last night, Prez."

He eyes me curiously. "You did the right thing."

Maybe so, but it didn't feel like it as we walked away, knowing that he was still breathing.

The click of the lock on the huge metal door reverberates through me as Ray pushes it open and lets us both inside.

My heart pounds, my muscles tighten to finally put this motherfucker down. I wasn't expecting Ritz to hand him over. From the look on Ray's face, I wouldn't say he was expecting it either. But it seems that Ritz has enough to deal with without having to put this scumbag down.

It's nice to know that we still have some loyalties with the Reapers and they're not all after war for the shit that went down all those years ago.

Justin is silent as we walk into the small room he's contained in. The enclosed space smells of blood and piss, and I can't help but smile when we flick the light on and get a look at the sad fuck.

"Looks like you slept well," I boom, making him wince as the bright electric light burns into his eyes.

He looks like a mess. Both his eyes are almost swollen shut and his lips are split, dried blood down his chin and covering his shirt.

Ray circles him as I drop down to my haunches and pull my switchblade from my pocket, tucking it beneath the fabric I gagged him with last night. He flinches when I catch his cheek with the blade, but he makes no noise.

"You ready to talk now?" I ask, my voice sounding much calmer than I feel.

He stares at me, his jaw ticking in frustration.

"Wrong answer, asshole."

The sound of his nose shattering under my fist settles something inside me for a couple of seconds, but when he looks at me once more with the same defiance in his eyes, it only makes me crave more.

Cutting the rope around his wrist that attaches him to the loop on the floor, I lift him with his cut and force him to stand on unsteady legs. I hold him up with one hand, my other going to town on his face, splitting open the wounds I left him with last night.

"Who told you to take her?"

"Evan," he groans through the pain.

"Bullshit," I spit. "Evan asked you to scare her. Your cousin might be a dumb fuck, but he didn't want you to hurt her... to rape her."

I see Ray pale at my words out of the corner of my eye. But hearing and seeing it almost happening are two entirely different things, and I resume my assault.

"Okay, okay," he finally concedes, spitting blood from his mouth as he tries to breathe through the pain. "I told Darren what Evan asked of me. He... he told me to deliver a message to the Sinners via their princess."

"Fucking cunt." This time when I hit him, I let him drop to the floor.

My boot connects with his ribs with a satisfying crack. He cries out in pain, but I barely hear it as I continue to rain hell on him for thinking he could lay a finger on Sadie.

"Where is he?"

"I-I don't know."

"Liar." My deep voice echoes off the walls around us as Ray watches me with pride in his eyes.

"I don't know."

"You're fucking lying to me."

"No. *No.*"

Pulling my gun from my pants, I aim it at his head. I click the safety off and place my finger on the trigger. "One last chance, motherfucker."

"I don't know. He's got another place. No one knows—"

I look up at Ray, and he gives a single nod. My finger squeezes the trigger before my brain has registered.

The bang reverberates through the warehouse as Justin's body lies motionless on the concrete, a pool of blood growing around his head. My ears ring as we're plunged into silence and my chest heaves, my heart pounding as I stare at the cunt who touched our princess.

I feel better ending him. But not as good as I'll feel when we get our hands on Darren and do the same to him.

Ray takes a step forward and comes to stand beside me. "Who knew you cared about my girl so much?"

All the air rushes from my lungs at his words as my shoulders tense, and his eyes burn into the side of my face.

"No woman deserves what he was going to do to her."

"Hmm..." he mumbles. "I'll call the guys to come clean this up. We should get back to them."

———————

The last thing I expect when we get to Dee's is to find Noble still hanging around.

"I thought you'd got rid of him?" I snap at Dane the second I walk into the kitchen.

"You're a prick," Sadie hisses, jumping up from the stool she's sitting on between Pretty Boy and Dane.

"Never claimed to be anything else, princess."

"Ray, we need to talk," Micky says, emerging from the other room. The two of them disappear, leaving me looking between everyone else.

"What the fuck is going on?" I bark.

"There's an issue with Wes's mom," Sadie says while Wes looks like he wants to run and hide beside her. "She's... staying here tonight."

"Why the fuck is this our problem?"

Sadie takes a step toward me, her angry eyes holding mine. "Because, asshole, if it weren't for Wes then I'd probably be fucking dead right now." Reaching out, she lifts my blood-covered fists between us. "And I think it's clear to all of us how you feel about the guy who had me last night."

"Princess," I growl in warning.

"What happened?"

"Let's just say he won't be touching you or anyone else again."

"Good."

The air crackles between us as everyone else sits silently, watching our exchange. Dane, Quinn, River and Jax are used to us by now, but I can sense Wes's confused stare. I can understand why he's baffled by all of this. Hell, I'm fucking confused as to what's going on.

I'm not stupid. I knew something had happened between the three of them the second I walked into Dane's room earlier. If the guilty looks on their faces weren't enough, Sadie's pink cheeks that only burn that bright after an orgasm and the scent of sex in the air confirmed it.

What I don't want to acknowledge is the strength of the jealousy that crashed into me, knowing that they did whatever it was without me.

Heavy footsteps echo down the hall before Ray reappears. "We're going to clear out to give Victoria some space."

"No, I don't—" Wes starts, but when Sadie turns to him and whispers something he backs down. He nods and she slides her hand into his.

My fists curl at the sight before my eyes move to Dane, who unsurprisingly watches them together with desire building in his eyes.

Kinky fucker.

"Let's go. And it shouldn't need saying," Ray levels each of us with a hard look, "but none of you are leaving until we've figured out our next move."

I throw my leg over my bike as Dane, Sadie and Noble climb into the truck. River hovers, looking between Quinn and me.

"Go with him. I'm staying here," Quinn announces.

"Come with us, we can hang," Sadie calls from the truck.

"Nah, I think you've already got your hands full enough." Quinn's eyes narrow on Sadie, making me wonder just how much she knows.

"River, get on," I bark, more than ready to get the fuck out of here.

"O-okay." She races over and I hold out my helmet for her.

I still hate the idea of her on a bike, but at least if it's mine then I know I'm in control. The thought of her on the back of anyone else's bike terrifies me.

The journey back to Ray's is short, and the second we're all inside, he announces that he's going to his office and disappears, leaving us all standing awkwardly in the hallway.

"We should go and get drinks," Jax suggests, placing his hand in the small of my sister's back, making my teeth grind with my need to rip his arm from his body so he can't touch her again.

"Why don't you go out the back and start the firepit," Sadie suggests, and the two of them disappear, leaving the four of us with an unbearable tension crackling around us.

"Right, well as fun as this is," Sadie sasses, backing toward the stairs, "I'm gonna go take a shower. Try not to kill each other."

I watch her as she climbs the stairs, desperate to follow her and demand she tells me what happened between her, Dane and Noble earlier, but before I get a chance to move, Dane slaps me on my shoulder, pushing me toward the kitchen.

"You should probably clean up," he chuckles. "You look like a murderer."

"Funny you say that," I mutter, looking down at my blood-splattered arms and busted knuckles. "What I really need is a shower."

The memory of Sadie's wet body pressed against mine last night pops into my head and I almost spin around and follow her.

"Yeah, probably not the best idea with Prez down the hall. We don't want to be cleaning up any more bodies tonight."

Dane grabs a six-pack from the refrigerator as we pass through the kitchen. Knowing it's not going to be enough after the events of the past twenty-four hours, and the fact that I'm still having to look at Wesley fucking Noble and pretend he belongs here, I side step Stray and go straight for Ray's liquor cabinet, pulling out a bottle of whiskey and twisting the top.

I down nearly a quarter of the bottle with both Dane and Wesley staring at me like I've lost my mind before I finally walk to the sink to clean that motherfucker's blood from my skin.

By the time we get outside, Jax has the firepit roaring, and he and River are sitting around with a beer each in hand. With my eyes firmly on my sister, silently warning her to behave, I lower myself to one of the seats.

"We need to talk," Dane whispers, out of earshot of them.

"What?" I grunt, lifting the beer to my lips.

"You lied to Sadie... about how we found her."

"So?" I shrug.

"Rhett, brother, come on. When she finds out..."

"If I hadn't put that tracker on her cell, we might never have found her, and you're gonna rail me for it?"

He lets out a weary sigh. "You're playing a dangerous game, brother. She isn't some pet you can leash—"

Wes glances in our direction and anger explodes inside of me. "Why the fuck is he still here?" I bark, nodding at Noble, not even attempting to disguise my frustration.

"Because Sadie wants him here," Dane says with a shrug, knowing that it'll only piss me off further if his smirk tells me anything.

"And what the princess wants the princess gets, huh?"

"Don't remember you complaining before." He winks, and I'm relieved as fuck he's letting the tracker shit drop. So I put a tracker on her cell? I'd do it again if I had to. Sadie is a flight risk. She's wild and untamed, and I refuse to let her run riot on my watch.

"He doesn't belong here," I grumble again.

"*He* is sitting right here," Pretty Boy pipes up. "And don't worry, he doesn't really want to hang with you either."

My eyebrows shoot up in surprise. Well fuck me, maybe he does have some balls.

I'm still staring in shock when a shadow falls over us.

When I drag my eyes upward, I find Sadie standing with her hand on her hip and a fierce expression on her face. But it's not either of those that really steals my attention, because that's the damn near see-through tank she's wearing and the tiny shorts that I already know will show off half of her ass if she were to turn around.

"Looking good, Sadie, girl. Come sit with me." Dane holds his hand out for her, his other patting his lap. And like a good little girl, she goes.

A growl rips up my throat before I jump up, anger burning inside me. "Fuck this. Fuck all of this." I'm gone before I finish talking, making my way down toward the lake at the bottom of the Daltons' yard.

And I don't look back.

12

SADIE

Watching Rhett's retreating form, I lose my breath. "He's in a good mood."

Dane's arm curls around my waist, tugging me back against his front. His lips graze my neck, moving to my ear. "Leave him be. He needs to work through... stuff."

"Stuff?" My brow lifts as I twist slightly to look at him, and heat rises inside me as he tightens his hold on me.

His lips twitch into a knowing smirk, and I think he might kiss me, but the sound of Wes clearing his throat reminds me we're not alone.

"Sorry." I turn back and give Wes a small smile. River catches my eyes and smiles.

"I'm tired," she yawns. "I think I'm going to call it a night."

"Straight to bed," Dane warns, glancing between her and Jax. He pales, stuttering something about sleeping on the couch.

River blushes as she gets up and heads inside with Jax trailing after her like a puppy.

"Are they—"

"No," Dane barks. "Hell to the no. Rhett would cut off his balls if he ever thought he was going after his sister."

"Men," I mutter. It's obvious they like each other, and Jax seems different to the rest of them. Softer somehow. But I know all too well that it's the quiet ones that usually harbor the most darkness.

Silence settles over us and I ask Wes, "Do you think your dad—"

"I really don't want to talk about him right now." He stares at the flames flickering in the night sky, his expression tight. The pain in his eyes makes my heart cinch.

"Hey," I whisper to Dane. "Give me a second."

He nods, nudging me off his lap, and I go to Wes. He looks up at me through his lashes. "Room for me?" I ask.

He pulls me down onto his lap and buries his face into the crook of my neck, shuddering as he breathes me in. My arms slide over his shoulders.

"It's going to be okay," I soothe.

"I hate him." He lifts his head to look at me. "I fucking hate him, Sadie. I—"

"Shh." I cup his face, leaning in, brow to brow. "I'm here. I'm right here."

"I shouldn't have left..."

Guilt weighs heavily on me, so I can only imagine how he feels. "She's okay, Wes," I say. "She's going to be okay."

"Yeah." He lets out a long breath, lifting his bottle to his lips and taking a drink. "Savage isn't too happy about it."

"Rhett can go to hell. I want you here." I glance over at Dane and add, "*We* want you here."

He doesn't argue, but a strange expression passes over his face. My lips curve in a smirk. Dane is on board with this—whatever *this* is.

"Shouldn't we be a little careful in case your dad comes out here?" Wes says just as Dane's cell pings. He pulls it out and scans the message.

"Prez has gone back over to Dee and Micky's."

"He has?" I frown.

"Yeah, he's given me orders to keep you in the house. Looks like I'm on sitter duty." He winks and I roll my eyes at the amusement in his voice.

"You can stay here too," I say to Wes.

"I don't have to sleep on the couch with Jax though, right?"

Laughter bubbles inside me. "No, you don't have to sleep on the couch with Jax."

"Where will I sleep then?" His eyes darken, making my tummy clench.

"I think we can figure something out." I breathe the words against his lips. Dane is quiet, watching. I'm hardly surprised when I flick my gaze over to where he's sitting and find his eyes flared with lust.

Wes runs his hand over the curve of my knee and dips it between my thighs, stroking his thumb along the soft skin there. A shiver runs through me, and I let out a soft sigh. "You're so fucking hot, Sadie Ray," he whispers.

Memories of how good his mouth felt latched onto my pussy flash in my mind.

"What are you thinking?" he asks, not caring that Dane is still watching us.

"About how good your tongue felt on me. In me." I grin, ghosting my mouth over his.

"Fuck," he rasps, leaning in to kiss me, but I dart out of reach, smirking.

"Oh, it's like that, huh?" He gives me a lazy smile, draining the rest of his beer.

"Not out here," I say. Although my dad said he's gone over to Aunt Dee's, he could still come back at any moment, and I'm not sure how I'll explain the fact that I'm all over Wes. Not when he's already probably wondering if something is going on with me and Dane.

"Okay, lovebirds." Dane stands suddenly. "I'm going to check in with Pacman and then get another drink. You should probably get some rest." He lets the word linger.

"Are you sure?" I ask.

"Something tells me Pretty Boy needs you more than I do right now."

"Thank you," I mouth, snuggling closer to Wes, who remains silent.

"I'll see you both in the morning." He heads inside.

"Alone at last." Wes nuzzles my neck again, letting his mouth slide over my skin. I melt in his kiss, relishing how good it feels.

"We should go inside," I say.

"Or," he scrapes his teeth against my pulse point, "we could stay right here and you could let me thank you."

"For as much as I want to know what thanking me

looks like, I don't want my dad to find us out here. I kind of like having you around."

"Yeah?" He lifts his face to mine.

"Yeah. Come on." I get up, offering him my hand. Wes takes it, and I lead him back into the house. There's no sign of Dane or Jax, so I figure they're out front with Pacman.

"Drink?" I ask Wes, and he nods.

After grabbing two bottles of water, he follows me upstairs. "Aren't you worried River or one of the guys will see us?" he asks quietly.

"They won't say anything." Besides, I'm pretty sure Dane is handling that. There was something about the way he gave us his blessing earlier.

We slip into my room, guided only by the silvery hue of the moon bouncing off the walls. "Never thought I'd ever see the inside of Sadie Ray Dalton's bedroom." Wes pauses.

Glancing over my shoulder, I smile. "It's nothing special."

"Still," he shrugs, "it's your room. Your space." He surveys the walls, the collection of photos and old band posters. Then he goes over to my dresser, taking a closer look at the trinkets and keepsakes I've accumulated over the years.

"We don't have to do anything, we can just sleep." I don't know why I say the words, but he's hesitating, nervous energy rippling from him.

Wes's gaze snaps to mine. "You think I could possibly just sleep with you in bed next to me?" The words come out rough.

I gulp at the intensity in his eyes as he prowls toward me. He curves his hand around the back of my neck, burying his fingers in my curls. "So fucking beautiful." Wesley kisses me slow and deep, his tongue lapping at mine.

My stomach tightens, my skin vibrating with need. He kisses me like I'm air and he's drowning. His other hand skates down my spine, finding the hem of my tank, and he starts working it off my body. We break the kiss and I lift my arms, letting him pull it over my head.

"Fuck," he hisses, his hungry gaze fixed on my boobs. His hand slides up my stomach and over my ribs, until his thumb brushes my nipple.

"Wes," I moan, arching into his touch. His mouth crashes down on mine, hard and unyielding. He devours me, swallowing my moans as his hand pushes its way inside my shorts and finds me slick and ready.

"Ride my fingers," he demands, working me with skill and finesse. My legs begin to tremble, caught off guard by how quick he went from zero to sixty.

Dipping his head, he drags the flat of his tongue over my nipple, licking and grazing the sensitive bud with his teeth. "Tell me what you want, Sadie Ray." He whispers the words against my heated skin.

"I want... ahh, God," I moan, pressing my lips together to stop the desperate, needy sounds spilling out as he hooks his fingers deeper.

"I want to touch you," I manage to get out in between breathy moans, my hand finding the string of his sweats. After working it loose, I push my hand inside and grasp his cock.

"Fuck," he barks. "Yeah..."

My lips curve with satisfaction as I pump him hard and fast, matching the way his fingers move inside me. But it isn't enough. I want more... I want to feel him thick and hard inside me.

Pulling away, I grin up at him. "Get on the bed, Pretty Boy," I tease.

His eyes widen but he obeys, backing up, kicking off his sweats and boxers as he goes. I shimmy out of my shorts, baring myself to him.

"I think I died and went to heaven," he groans as I slowly move toward him, letting him drink in his fill of my curves.

Hooking my arm around his neck, I kneel over him, straddling his thighs. He grasps himself beneath me, letting the tip of his cock glide through my wet folds.

"Jesus, that feels good," he hisses. "And I'm not even inside you yet."

"You sure?" I ask. Because if we do this, if I have him, I won't be able to let him go. And things won't be simple, not with Rhett acting like a petulant child.

Wes hooks his other arm around my waist, dragging me closer until we're chest to chest. His lips brush mine. "This, me and you, you and them... we'll figure it out. But if I don't get inside you in the next five seconds, I might die a very slow and painful death of blue balls."

I throw my head back with laughter, but he has a point. Lowering my gaze to his again, I say, "I guess I'd better put you out of your misery then." Slowly, inch by inch, I sink down on him, savoring the way he stretches me.

"Fuck, Sadie, fuuuuck." He buries his face in my shoulder, his body shuddering. "You feel..."

"I know," I pant, letting my body adjust to him. It's so deep, so full. So good.

Wes exhales a slow steady breath, meeting my hooded eyes and staring at me.

"What?" I ask.

"Can I fuck you now?" He smirks, and I swat his chest.

"You'd better," I chuckle. "You have a lot to live up to."

13

WES

Holy fucking shit.

My fingertips dig into Sadie's hips, hard enough to leave marks on her skin, I'm sure. But I can't find it in myself to care if I leave bruises, because tomorrow when this is all over and she's with them, they won't be able to forget that I was here.

That for tonight, even if only for a few hours, she was mine.

"Wes," she moans, her head rolling back in pleasure at the same time she circles her hips over me.

Fuck, she feels like heaven.

Those two assholes could come storming in right now and end me for touching their princess and I probably wouldn't even be able to complain. Because being inside her after all the years I've imagined what it might be like is better than I ever expected.

Her tits bounce as she ups her pace, lifting up on her knees and dropping down hard until I'm balls deep inside her.

"Fuck, Sadie. You look... fuck."

A sexy smirk curls up at the corner of her mouth. Reaching out, she runs a fingertip from my sternum all the way down to my abs. She traces over the lines of my six-pack, sucking her bottom lip into her mouth as she focuses.

Her pace slows, and my need to take over, to fuck her like I've imagined time and time again, is almost too hard to ignore.

"Sadie?" I groan, my voice hard and strained as I try to keep control.

Her smile widens as her eyes find mine once more.

"You're wicked," I whisper, realizing that she's playing me.

"Tell me it's not exactly what you need."

"I can't, princess, because it's everything and then some."

She squeals as I flip her onto her back, lowering down until my nose brushes hers. "But I'm not good at losing control."

"Why doesn't that surprise me," she says, rolling her eyes.

"You love it," I growl, thrusting forward at the same time I suck her bottom lip into my mouth and sink my teeth into it.

A roar rips from her throat, her nails digging into my shoulders, the pain shooting straight for my cock and pushing me closer to a release I'm nowhere near ready for. I might have been waiting since the moment she walked into my bedroom earlier and showed me exactly what she'd come for, but even still. I want it to last.

"Shit, Wes... *Fuck*," she cries as I continue to pound into her.

"Sadie," I moan, watching her in disbelief as she takes everything I give her.

"Harder," she begs, her eyes holding a challenge.

Shaking my head at her, a smirk plays on my lips and I give her what she wants. Sweat covers our bodies as we move together, chasing our highs.

"Make me come, Wes. Fuck, I need—"

Pressing my thumb against her clit, I circle slowly for a couple of seconds until she cries out my name, her body locking up beneath mine as her pussy milks my cock, dragging my own orgasm from me.

"Oh fuck," I moan, dropping my weight onto her as my cock jerks inside her, filling her. "We didn't use—"

"It's okay," she whispers in my ear. "I'm on birth control."

"I'm clean, I swear."

"I know."

"I haven't been with anyone in..." I trail off, not even remembering the last time I let someone this close to me. All the girls at school want a piece and then dig their nails in as if it means something, as if I might actually want something more than just a hookup.

But how can I have more?

My life is a disaster. My family is imploding, and there's hardly anything I can do to stop it except continue trying to cover up the cracks.

"What's wrong?" Sadie asks softly, her hands rubbing up and down my back soothingly while I keep my face in the crook of her neck, breathing her in.

"Uh... n-nothing."

"Wes, don't do that. You don't need to pretend everything is okay with me."

She shoves my shoulder and I roll off her, knowing that I'm probably hurting her. Her eyes find mine, the hunger still there, but the thing that shines through the most is understanding and compassion. The sight of it brings a lump to my throat.

No one's ever got close enough to my life to see any of this before. I know that most of that is my fault because I've been terrified of allowing anyone to discover just how toxic my home life is.

"She's going to go back to him," I confess. "Tomorrow she'll wake up and think that a night away will have fixed everything, and she'll go back."

"I know," she soothes, brushing my hair back from my face and tucking it behind my ear. "It's going to take more to end the cycle."

"I don't even think she wants it to end. That's what scares me the most. She'll stay there until he finally takes things too far, and I won't be there to stop him."

"It won't come to that," she assures me.

"You can't know that. Every time, he gets a little bit worse, a little more violent."

"When did it start?"

I let out a sigh as I think back over my childhood. "Honestly, I don't even know. A part of me wonders if it's always been there. That I was just too young or naïve to see it. But the turning point was when my granddad died a few years ago."

She nods, keeping her eyes on mine as she absorbs every word I say to her.

It feels weird to talk about it. Even Mom and I have never properly discussed the things that happen in our own home. Like everything, she just brushes it under the rug in the hope it won't happen again.

"That's when he started drinking more, when his vendetta against the club ramped up."

"Did your grandfather have the same beliefs?"

"Yeah, I think so. Although, I was never close to him. He was cold, unfriendly. Exactly what my father is turning into. I don't think the same," I quickly add, needing her to know.

"I know, Wes. I wouldn't be here right now if I thought for one second you did. Neither would the guys."

"It's already a small miracle they haven't slaughtered me yet," I joke.

"They're not that bad."

I raise my brows at her. "Don't you remember what they did to me on the first day of school?"

"Can you blame them? They thought your alliances were with Evan and that you needed to be taught a lesson."

"I think I did. I never belonged with Evan and the team, but my skills on the field meant it was where I felt most at home. I was either with him or against him, and I chose the path of least resistance."

"Understandable." Sadie nods.

"I should have stood up to him sooner. Tried to stop him. I—"

"It's okay, Wes," she says, pressing her hand to my chest. "I get it."

"You shouldn't have to."

"And you shouldn't have to deal with the shit you do, but life sucks sometimes."

"Yeah," I say, leaning in closer and brushing my lips over hers, long past having the patience to talk about my cunt of a father while she's lying naked beside me. "But then other times, you end up in bed with a princess."

"Wes," she rolls her eyes. "I hate that nickname."

"Why am I not surprised? Don't tell me, you'd prefer to be our queen?"

Her eyes flash with something that I can't decipher. "You're really okay with this?"

"Do we even know what this is?"

"N-no, I—"

"Then let's not worry about it right now, yeah?"

I brush my lips over hers, not ready for our time to be over just yet. But just as I'm about to deepen the kiss, she slips out from beneath me and climbs to her feet. "Where are you going?" I ask, pushing to sit.

She pauses in her escape, her eyes dropping to my body and my more than ready cock. She bites down on her bottom lips as she stares at it.

"Sadie," I growl, my impatience getting the better of me.

After another couple of seconds, she holds her hand out for me. I have no idea where she's leading me, and quite frankly, I don't care. Right now, I'd follow her to the end of the Earth if it meant spending more time together.

Thankfully, she only takes me through to her

bathroom. She turns toward me and presses her hands to my chest, pushing me backward and looking up at me through her lashes. "I'm feeling all kinds of dirty right now."

A smirk curls at my lips as I drop my gaze down her body. "Oh yeah, you look filthy."

I let her push me into her shower stall, then, pressing herself against me, she reaches for the knob and we both get blasted with ice-cold water.

"Holy shit."

"Pussy," she jokes, reaching up on her tiptoes so she can whisper in my ear. "There's something I want to do. Something I can't stop thinking about."

"Oh yeah. Want to enlighten me?" I ask, hoping like hell the idea in my head is the same as the one in hers.

"How about I show you?"

Her fingers twist in my hair, angling my head so she can kiss me before planting soft kisses across my chest, getting lower each time.

"Sadie Ray," I groan when she starts kissing over my abs.

"What's up, Pretty Boy?" She smiles up at me and my heart tumbles over in my chest at the sight of her dropping to her knees before me.

Her hands run up my thighs as she studies my length that's bobbing impatiently in front of her.

"What are you thinking, princess?"

"Wondering if you'll taste as good as I'm imagining."

"There's only one way to find out."

"Hmm..." She hums, lifting her hand up and wrapping her fingers around my length. "I guess so."

Poking her tongue out, she licks the precum from my tip, making my hips thrust forward from the almost non-existent contact alone.

"Fuck, Sadie."

"That's nothing. Hold on."

"H-holy shit," I growl as she takes me in her mouth and sucks me all the way back. "Fuck. That feels good."

My fingers tangle in her hair, but I don't take over, instead just letting her do her thing and watching every second of her sucking me off.

Best fucking sight in the world.

In an embarrassing short few minutes, I already feel my balls drawing up. "S-Sadie, I'm gonna—" I try warning her, but all she does is take me that little bit deeper, forcing me down her throat, and my warning is obliterated as I explode.

The groan that rips from my throat and echoes around the bathroom doesn't even sound like my own as she swallows down every drop.

The second she's done, I pull her to her feet with my hands still in her hair and slam my lips down on hers. I press her back against the cold tiles and wrap her legs around my waist, knowing that I'm going to be ready to go again in a few minutes.

I always am when she's around.

I can't seem to get enough.

14

SADIE

I lie awake, cocooned in Wes's arms. He fell asleep almost the second we tumbled into bed, after making me come twice more in the shower.

God, he knew exactly how to touch me to drive me wild, willingly rising to the challenge of making an impression.

My lips curve, pure contentment washing over me. I probably shouldn't feel so smug at having three guys falling at my feet, but I can't help it. They're everything I never knew I wanted, and being with Wes like that... it was amazing.

He snores softly behind me, his warm breath tickling my neck. He's so different to the guy I thought he was, and I realize now, it's all a front. A mask. A shield. Wes plays a part at school; the person people expect him to be. When really, he's just trying to hold it all together.

A noise outside my bedroom catches my attention and I whip my head over to the door, listening. But there's nothing. Still, I can't sleep, so I gently ease myself out of

Wes's arms and tiptoe across the room, slipping into the hall.

"What the—"

Dane stares up at me from his position on the floor outside my door, a weak smile on his face.

"What the hell are you doing out here?" I whisper-hiss.

He reaches for me, twining our hands together. "I couldn't sleep..."

My stomach drops. "Another nightmare?"

Dane doesn't reply. He just nods, his mouth in a grim line.

"Come on," I tug his hand and he clambers to his feet.

When he realizes what I'm trying to do, he says, "I'm not sure this is a good idea, Sadie, girl."

"So you're sitting outside my bedroom, why exactly?" My brow lifts.

"Fine. But I'm not cuddling up to Noble."

I suppress a smile as I pull him into my bedroom. The air turns thick as Dane closes the door behind him. "You must have worn him out good," he says quietly.

"Jealous?"

"Jealous? No. Disappointed I didn't get to watch? Fuck yeah." His eyes flash with desire, sending a shiver racing down my spine.

"Thank you," I whisper. "For earlier."

"He needed you."

"And now you need me," I state.

"I just... I woke up and I reached for you—"

"Hey." I step toward him, laying my hand on his cheek. "It's okay. I'm here, Dane. I'm right here."

He turns into my touch, inhaling a shuddering breath. "Come on," he says. "It's late, and I need my beauty sleep."

He's deflecting, covering up his pain with a joke. I wonder if he realizes how similar he and Wesley are. Sure, their demons might be different, but they handle it the same—by letting the world see what they want them to see.

He taps my ass gently as I climb into bed, snuggling up to Wes's sleeping form to give Dane room to get in next to me. His hand curves over my waist as he lowers his head to mine until we're almost nose to nose.

"You make it quieter," he whispers, the sincerity in his voice shredding my insides.

"Sleep," I say, tracing my hand along his collarbone.

"Just a little taste first." He captures my mouth in a slow, passionate kiss. Our tongues tangle in lazy licks as we devour each other. Heat rises inside me, but I'm still exhausted from being with Wes earlier, and Dane is right. It's late—the middle of the night—and we should probably get some sleep.

He breaks away first. "Fuck, Sadie, girl. Kissing you will never get old." Heat simmers between us, but Dane doesn't act on it, pulling me closer instead.

I close my eyes, hyperaware of the two strong bodies on either side of me. Wes doesn't even stir, and within seconds, Dane relaxes into me, falling into a deep sleep.

And I lay there until darkness claims me.

Light trickles over my face, coaxing me from my dreams. Legs tangle with mine, a hot body pressed up behind me and arms possessively slung over my hips. Wes and Dane are still sleeping, but I sense someone watching me.

"You're lucky I'm not Ray," Rhett says coolly from his position by my door.

I push up on one elbow and meet his scowl. "What time is it?"

"A little after eight."

"Ugh," I groan, pushing the hair from my face. "You came back."

He nods curtly just as Dane stirs behind me.

"Are you going to stand there gawking, brother, or shut the fucking door and join us?" His hand drags me closer until his morning wood is pressed right up against my ass. "I reckon we could take her for a little morning ride," he teases, grinding into me with torturous precision.

"Dane," I hiss.

He chuckles, nuzzling my neck. "Mornin' Sadie, girl."

Rhett's eyes turn black with anger... and what I want to believe is jealousy. He keeps resisting this, resisting me, but I know he feels it.

"You're an asshole," Rhett snaps at Dane.

"And you're not fooling anyone with your 'I don't give a fuck' routine. The sooner you get on board with us, the smoother things will go. Then we can really have some fun." Dane's fingers slip under the oversized t-shirt I pulled on last night, brushing the underside of my boobs.

"You're a fucking dog."

"Never claimed to be anything else." Dane chuckles again.

"Can the two of you keep it the fuck down?" Wes grumbles, turning over to look at me. "Morning," he mouths, his blond hair tumbling over his eyes.

"Hey."

Silence descends over us, and I suddenly feel like everyone's waiting on me to break the tension.

"So... this is nice." I fight a smile, peeking over at a very silently fuming Rhett.

"It's not exactly what I had in mind," Wes adds, running his hand along the curve of my waist. "But I'm not complaining."

"You need to get up and get dressed before Ray gets home."

"He stayed at Aunt Dee's?" I ask, and Rhett nods. "Well, I don't know about anyone else, but I'm hungry."

"I've got something you can eat," Dane teases, but his laughter is cut off when something flies across the room and skims his head.

"Asshole," he murmurs, flipping Rhett off.

"I'll be downstairs. You might want to be discreet... Ray isn't here, but Jax and Pacman are. My sister too."

"Yeah, yeah, we got the memo," Dane says, pressing a kiss to my shoulder before he throws back the sheet and climbs out of bed.

"See you downstairs." He shoulders past Rhett and disappears into the hall.

His eyes linger on me where the sheet has fallen off my body, my nipples pebbled against my t-shirt.

"Something you need?" I quip, growing tired of his hot and cold bullshit.

His eyes snap to mine, but anger isn't the only thing I find burning there.

My brow arches as I await his reply. Dragging a hand down his face, he mutters something under his breath, then spins on his heel and storms from the room.

"Is he always so..."

"Grumpy?" I suggest. "Rhett isn't used to not being in control."

"Perhaps you shouldn't push him so much then," Wes counters, leaning in to brush his nose along my jaw.

"Where's the fun in that?"

"I like you, Sadie Ray. I like you a lot, and I think you're worth the risk. But I'd rather not end up on the receiving end of one of Savage's—"

"Stop. Worrying," I mutter. "I can handle Rhett, I promise."

Wes studies me for a second, his blue eyes so intense I feel a little breathless.

"What?" I ask.

"I could get used to this." He kisses me, soft and tender, his hand sliding deep into my hair as he takes what he wants from me.

My palms flatten against his chest as I hitch my leg around his waist and—

"Let's go," Rhett hammers his fist on the door, startling us.

"You were saying?"

Wes frowns, the moment between us is gone. "I'm going to clean up." He drops a kiss on my head, leaving me in bed alone.

I head downstairs last. I needed a minute to catch my breath and get ready to face everyone. Especially my dad. But to my relief, there's no sign of him yet as I enter the kitchen.

"Morning." I smile at River, who's picking apart a pastry.

"Jax got takeout from the coffee shop down the street," she says.

"Hmm, my hero." My eyes flick over to Rhett and Dane who are near the door, deep in hushed conversation. Wes catches my eye and gives his head a little shake.

Fine.

I won't pry, yet. I probably don't want to hear whatever Rhett is chewing Dane out for anyway.

I need coffee and something to eat before I get into it with him. Because we will have it out, one way or another. That conversation is brewing, like a storm circling on the horizon.

"How are you feeling?" River asks, and I don't miss the knowing smile on her face.

"I'm fine," I say, tilting my head slightly to her. "Why do you ask?"

"No reason." She gives me a half-shrug but barely keeps the grin off her face.

Once I grab coffee, I join Wes at the table. He's quiet but doesn't seem fazed by the awkward morning routine unfolding around him.

"Not hungry?" I point toward the array of breakfast items courtesy of Jax.

"I'm good," he says, his eyes dropping to my mouth. He looks starving but not for pastries, and I flush from head to toe.

Someone clears their throat and the simmering connection between us is broken. When I look up, I find Rhett glaring at us.

"Someone got up on the wrong side of bed," I sass, snagging a croissant and taking a bite.

"Sadie, girl," Dane warns as he joins us.

"He started it," I grumble.

"Seriously princess, you need to—"

Voices in the hall silence Rhett and he grinds his teeth, clearly not happy that he didn't get to reprimand me like a child again.

Asshole.

"Mornin'," Dad says as he stalks into the kitchen with Jax hot on his heels.

"Hey, Daddy." I smile.

"I'm glad you're all awake. We need to talk." He does a double take when he notices Wes in the seat beside me. "Your mom is fine. Dee is going to give you and her a ride back home when she's ready."

"Thanks, sir."

"Shit, son, don't call me that. Makes me feel all kinds of old. The name's Ray." He makes a beeline for the coffee machine. Once he's poured himself a mug, he turns around and leans against the counter.

"I wouldn't usually do this," he levels Wes with a stern look, "especially not with outsiders present, but since Sadie Ray dragged you into this mess, it seems only right you hear this too.

"The Reapers have a rogue member in their ranks. The prez's nephew, Darren Creed, has always been a loose cannon. He lost his old man in the war a way back, and he's always made it clear he wasn't happy with the truce.

"With Nolan Creed on his death bed, I got wind that Darren might try something stupid. I didn't think he'd come after my own, though."

Dad slides his eyes to me, anger simmering there. "He saw an opportunity with Evan and took it. Ritz confirmed that Darren is missing, which means Sadie Ray and River don't go anywhere without at least two guys on them at all times."

I scoff at that. "Seriously? And how is that going to work when we're at school?"

"You're out of school until we find him."

"What?" I balk. "You can't be serious? You're just going to lock us up like—"

"You were assaulted and held captive," Rhett snaps. "And you're acting like a spoiled brat."

"This is my life," I argue. "You can't just lock me away. What if Darren is gone? What if you can't find him? What if—"

"ENOUGH!" Dad slams his fist down on the counter. "I will not risk something happening to you again. Either of you." His gaze flicks to River, who has gone pale.

"You can't take us out of school," I say again. "It's senior year."

Rhett stares at me like I've lost my mind while Dane looks at me with nothing but pity. Of course, he gets it. He knows what it means to me to have my independence and freedom. Unlike Rhett, who's spent his whole life wrapping River in cotton to protect her.

"This is not up for discussion, Sadie Ray—"

"Dane and Wes are already there," I protest. "They can look out for us. Rhett too, if he ever bothers to show up for class. And Darren would have to be really stupid to show up at the school. You can tell Principal Winston, and he can have the security keep an eye out. I can't lose school, Dad. Please..."

He lets out a heavy sigh, dragging a hand down his face. "Straight to school and back home or to the compound. No deviations. No detours. No distractions. You ride with one of the guys at all times."

"Prez, come on—" Rhett starts, but I cut him off.

"Thank you, Daddy." I leap out of my chair and rush over to him. He opens his arms and pulls me into his big body.

"We'll get this fucker, Sadie Ray. And when we do..." A shudder rips through him.

"I know, Daddy." And I do.

Because while he might be overprotective and overbearing and suffocating at times, I know there isn't a single thing he wouldn't do for me.

15

RHETT

Unable to stand and watch as Sadie says goodbye to Wes before he climbs into Dee's car where his mom is waiting for him, I throw my leg over my bike and take off, leaving the clusterfuck that is the four of us behind.

I'm fucking pissed about what I walked in on this morning. But I'm not pissed she did it. If I'm being honest, I expected her to. What I'm angry about is the fact that I wasn't included.

It's your own fucking fault, asshole.

She looked so beautiful with her lips still swollen from their kisses, her hair a mess and red bite marks over her neck and chest. My grip on the handlebars tightens as I remember her rosy nipples poking through the thin fabric of her shirt.

I could have pushed everything aside and taken what I needed. I knew that, but fuck. Every time I think of her, I think of him and just how close he came to taking her away from me, making her do something she didn't want.

"Fuck," I roar as I turn down the street toward the clubhouse.

Space.

I need some fucking space from all of them to get my head together.

If I have to see one of them touch her, tease her again... If I have to watch her punish me by forcing herself on them, then one of us is going to get hurt.

"Savage, I just got—" One of the guys calls from the shop.

"Around the table, twenty minutes," I bark, cutting off whatever he was going to say and delivering the orders from our prez.

The second he's back here, he wants to talk. To all of us.

I swear to God, he'd better have some answers because now he's bent to Sadie's plea about going to school tomorrow, she's going to be wide open for that psycho to get to her again.

I know school should be safe. But we're not talking about some fucked-up kid here. Darren Creed is dangerous and clearly holds a serious grudge against our club. We need to keep her safe. River too. And letting them go to school is the wrong fucking move.

Ignoring everyone who so much as looks my way, I storm through the clubhouse and march behind the bar, swiping up a bottle of whiskey. I don't give a shit that it's not even lunchtime yet. I need something to take the edge off, and it's going to be this or some club whore I can lose myself in. And it can't be the latter.

I'm still swigging from the bottle when the others emerge.

"Prez is here," Micky says, heading toward the doors that lead to where we're all about to learn the latest and agree that we need to find and kill this cunt for even threatening to come after our princess.

With a nod, I follow him through and take a seat around the edge of the room.

Ray fills everyone in on the events of the weekend before moving on to explain his plan to work with Ritz to find Darren and take him out before he causes any more damage to either club.

"The Reapers are happy for us to take him out?" Pike asks with his brows pinched.

"Ritz's biggest concern is his father and the future of his club right now. He doesn't need a manhunt for someone who's going to threaten that. We're on the same team right now, and until that cunt is dead, he's a threat to all of us."

Working with the Reapers gets voted in before Ray turns to club business, specifically a gun shipment that's due soon. But before he dismisses us all, his cell rings.

He pulls it from his pocket and stares at the screen. Clearly, whoever is calling is worth interrupting Church for, because he lifts it to his ear.

He listens for a few seconds. "Motherfu— Yeah, yeah. Fine. Get him to put some fucking ice on them."

He hangs up, blowing out a breath, and then looks at each of his brothers around the table.

"Do what you need to do to get rid of this cunt. No one gets that close to my daughter and gets away with it."

"On it, Prez," Pike says before they push to stand.

"Rhett," Ray calls when I move to follow them. "A word."

I stand at the end of the table, waiting for the others to disappear, seeing as he doesn't want to say whatever it is he's got to tell me with them listening.

"There's a situation at the house."

My heart jumps into my throat.

Sadie.

"Pacman and Jax caught Sadie trying to escape."

"Stupid little—"

Ray raises a brow at me and I slam my lips shut.

"She was trying to get out to see you, apparently." His eyes hold mine, a million and one questions swirling within them.

"Me?"

"Something I should know about?"

I swallow down my apprehension. If he found out what's going on with all of us, he'd lose his goddamn mind.

Sex might be free and easy when it comes to the club, and relationships between numerous members isn't all that unusual, but having it involve the club princess sure makes it more complicated. Especially for our Prez.

"Probably something to do with the fact that I killed the man who was going to rape her." I force the word out, my fist curling as I think of what I walked in on Friday night.

"Yeah... maybe," he muses, clearly not believing a word of it. "I need my daughter safe, son. I need you, Stray, and anyone else to put her safety above theirs. But I need you to know that there's no one I trust with her more than you."

Guilt floods me. If only he knew the truth...

"Go to her. Find out what she wants. But if you do anything to hurt her, to make this situation worse, I won't hesitate on resolving it myself."

"I won't let anything happen to her, Prez. You have my word."

He nods once, dismissing me.

I swing by my room to change before knocking on Dane's door, but I don't get an answer. I'm assuming he left Ray's house after me, because if he were there, I have no doubt he'd have been able to keep Sadie in line.

I shake my head, thinking of Pacman and Jax trying to take charge. Sadie Ray barely listens to her father. There's no way she'd listen to a word that comes out of their mouths. But she also knows how serious this is. I saw it in her eyes on Friday night. The fear. So the fact that she's trying to break the rules tells me just how badly she wants to see me.

I'm still amused with the whole situation as I get back on my bike and repeat the journey I made not so long ago. The sun is beginning to set as I make my way across town, casting everything in an orange hue. I breathe in the early fall air and try to get myself under control before having to deal with that crazy bitch.

I know it's not working the second my cock twitches in my pants. She might be fucking insane, but hell if I don't need her. If her brand of crazy doesn't talk to mine.

There's no movement as I pull up at the house, and I

can't help but wonder what they finally did to keep her inside.

"Hello?" I call as I unlock the front door and step inside.

"Kitchen," a pained voice calls.

"What the fuck happened to you?" I ask when I find Jax laid up on the couch with a bag of fucking frozen peas on his dick.

"The princess happened," he grumbles. "She pulled a fucking knife on me, man."

I smother a laugh, because he looks less than amused by the whole situation. My eyes drop to the peas again and he continues.

"Pacman managed to disarm her, but she kicked me right in the nuts."

"Beaten up by a girl, Prospect. That's not going to look good when your patch decision comes up."

"She's fucking lethal."

"She's been trained by Ray, what did you expect? A soft fucking puppy?"

"You lot are fucking crazy, I hope you know that," he says, holding my stare.

"What are you—"

"Oh, shut the fuck up. I know you're all banging her. It's fucking obvious. What I can't work out is how Prez hasn't figured it out yet."

I take a menacing step toward him. "You need to keep your fucking mouth shut, Prospect."

"Wouldn't utter a word," he says, holding up his free hand in surrender. "Just... you know, try to keep her calm. This job is hard enough without injuries."

"Oh yeah, because you hate hanging around with River all the time." I lift a brow in accusation.

"We're friends." He blanches but tries to keep his expression neutral. "She's cool."

"Sure. Whatever you say. I'm gonna go and see what the princess wants."

"Be careful," he warns, making me laugh as I march toward the stairs, taking them three at a time.

"Wow, armed guard. It must be serious," I mutter when I find Pacman sitting outside her room with his piece resting on his knee.

"I'm not chancing anything. Prez will off me without a second thought if I let her out of my sight."

"I've got this, man. Go look after numbnuts downstairs."

"She got him good. Real fucking good. But fuck, my balls jumped into my body right along with his. He'll be lucky if he can have kids after that."

He disappears down the stairs and I suck in a calming breath. I'm going to need it for what awaits me on the other side of this door.

Pushing the handle down, I slip inside. I find Sadie on her bed, her knees bent up as she stares at the TV across the room.

"Causing trouble, princess?"

"What do you want?" she barks, not even bothering to look at me.

"That's rich. Weren't you the one trying to escape to see me?"

"Maybe I came to my senses."

"Yeah well, here I am. So have at it."

Lifting the remote control, she turns off whatever she was watching, slides off the bed, and finally, she looks over at me when she's at full height.

She's dressed much like she was last night in only a thin tank and a tiny pair of shorts. My cock swells as I take in her dusky pink nipples behind the white fabric.

"Tell me you weren't walking around in front of those two assholes looking like that."

"So what if I was?" she sasses, flipping her hair over her shoulder.

I take a menacing step forward, expecting her to take one back, but she doesn't. Instead, she just holds my stare, squaring her shoulders ready for the storm that's approaching.

"You're ours, princess. No one but us gets to see you like this."

"I'm yours?" She scoffs. "That's funny, because all I've seen of you recently is your back as you've run away. You're a fucking pussy, Rhett Savage. You say all the right things but you're too fucking weak to act on any of them.

"Dane, Wes... I know exactly how they feel, know precisely what they want. But you? You're nothing but a bag of mixed signals." She heaves a breath but isn't done yet. "You want me. You need me. You hate me. You can't bear to look at me. Yet, you what... you killed for me?"

I take another step toward her until we're standing so close the burning heat from her body seeps into mine. Her cherry scent fills my nose, and the only thing I can think about is kissing her and reminding myself just how she tastes.

My hand shoots out, holding her throat in a tight grip.

"You don't want to push me, Sadie. You know it's only going to get you hurt."

"Maybe I want the pain, Savage."

My jaw tics as I stare at her, willing her to do something other than wait me out, wait for me to say something, to open myself up to her like the other two have, like she wants me to.

"What do you want from me, princess?"

"Aside from your cock?" she asks with a smirk, ensuring that it goes full mast with the knowledge that she's thinking about it. "I want you to grow some balls and tell me what *you* want."

"You know what I want, princess."

"Sometimes I think I might." Her chin lifts with defiance. "But then you turn your back and run, leaving me with my head spinning and my body craving your touch."

16

SADIE

Rhett's fingers flex around my throat, his eyes flaring with a dangerous mix of anger and lust.

He hates it when I challenge him... but I know it turns him on too. I can feel it radiating from every inch of him.

"I don't share what's mine," he says, as if we didn't cross that line days ago.

"I don't see anyone else standing here, do you?" I step into him, pressing my body flush with his.

Rhett's fingers tremble around my throat as his thin rope of control frays. "What's happening with you and Noble?"

"You know what's happening."

"You let him fuck you?" His eyes darken.

"And if I did?"

Rhett lets out a low hiss, his jaw clenching tight.

"I want you, Rhett. I've made that pretty obvious. But I also want Dane... *and* Wes."

"Do you like being a dirty little whore, princess?" His

lips curl in a vicious smirk. "Letting three guys fuck you is—"

The crack of my palm against his face echoes through the room.

"You hit me." His words are cold. Lethal.

"You called me a whore." I spit the words as we stare each other down.

He's lashing out, trying to hurt me with cruel words and his rough touch. But I know Rhett, maybe better than himself. And this isn't about what I want—it's about what he wants. It's about the fact that he can't walk away from this.

"I'm not asking you to fuck them. I'm not even asking you to be with me when they're around... but you can't have me without accepting that I want them too."

"If you think your pussy is that good that I'm going to stick around while you let Stray and Noble fill you with their cum, you've got another thing—" My hand flies toward his face again, but Rhett catches my wrist midair. "I'm getting really fucking tired of you hitting me, princess."

"You're a bastard," I hiss, the words dying on my tongue as he squeezes my throat harder, shoving me backwards.

"I think I need to remind you of a few things." He snaps the belt on his jeans and pulls it free. "Turn around."

"Fuck you," I sneer, fighting a smirk. It's a game—this push and pull, the constant battle between us.

"If you're lucky." Rhett grins, and it's such a rare sight, my chest cinches. "Now turn the fuck around."

I comply, yelping when he grabs my wrists and forces them roughly behind my back. Using his belt, he binds my hands together and forces my body over the edge of the bed.

"Now if that ain't a pretty sight." He rubs his hand down my spine before shoving it deep into my shorts and spearing two fingers inside me.

"Oh God." The words get stuck in my throat as he fingers me with a vicious rhythm. I grind against his hand, desperate for more.

"So fucking greedy," he rasps, adding another finger, making my body tremble.

"More," I chant. "I need more..."

Rhett chuckles darkly, ripping his fingers away and leaving me aching. He drops to his knees behind me and yanks down my shorts, and then he's right there, eating my pussy like it's the best thing he's ever tasted. His tongue glides through my wet folds, dipping inside me. Greedy, big swipes. My knees buckle as I smother the needy moans spilling from my lips, but Rhett is there to steady me, his big hands clamped around my thighs.

"You taste like sin," he groans against my core.

"Rhett," I breathe as my orgasm starts to crest. "Fuck... *fuck*." My muscles twinge with pain as I strain against the restraint.

"You're going to come on my tongue, and then I'm going to fuck you so hard you never forget who owns this pussy."

"Yes, *yes!*"

He slaps my clit so hard I see stars, coming with an intense wave of pleasure that crashes into me.

Cool air licks the back of my legs as Rhett stands up, lazily pumping his fingers in and out of me, spreading my juices everywhere. "So fucking wet."

My lips fall open as he runs the tip of his cock through my slit, the steel ball making me shudder. One of his hands yanks on the belt, forcing me to arch my body as he slams inside me.

"Fuuuck, princess, yeah. Choke my dick." He pulls out slowly and thrusts once more. Pain laced with pleasure shoots off around my body.

His other hand curves around my throat and he leans over me, capturing my lips in a bruising kiss. Rhett isn't fucking me. He's branding me. Claiming me. I feel him everywhere. His cock buried deep inside me, his fingers on my skin, his tongue in my mouth. He's consuming me, but I'll happily drown in him.

He picks up the pace, jackhammering his hips in time with his tongue as he licks my mouth.

"Who do you belong to?" he demands, but I bite down on my bottom lip, refusing to give him the one thing he knows I can't.

Because I'm not only his.

"I swear to God, Sadie Ray." His fingers flex and I grow lightheaded as he pounds into me. "Who do you belong to?"

"Rhett, God... *God!*" I can barely talk, my body shattering apart in every direction.

He slows down, rolling his hips and changing the angle so that his piercing drags against my inner walls. "You really are a dirty whore, aren't you?" he snarls. "Are you imagining them here, now? Watching?"

I shake my head.

"No? Joining in then?" My pussy gushes around him and his brow lifts. "Yeah, you'd like that, wouldn't you? The three of us working you over at once. I'd get your pussy, Stray would want in your ass, and Pretty Boy... I guess he could have your mouth."

"God, yes," I cry as another orgasm tears through me.

I barely feel Rhett undoing his belt or flipping me over. Throwing my legs over his arms, he spreads me wide and impales himself deep inside me. He looks lethal, jaw set, eyes obsidian, his muscles rippling as he rides me.

"What would you give me if I let you have it, princess? If I agreed to share you?"

"Everything," I choke out. "Every-fucking-thing."

"Right answer." Rhett crashes his mouth to mine, drowning out my screams as another wave of pleasure rocks through me.

Growling against my lips, he tenses and then rips away from me to spray hot jets of cum all over my pussy. With a satisfied smirk, Rhett uses his fingers to spread it around, pushing some back inside me.

"You have no idea what you just agreed to," he says darkly, before tucking himself back into his jeans and disappearing into my bathroom.

I lie there, boneless and breathless, hardly able to keep the smile off my face. Rhett thinks he holds all the cards, but he just gave me exactly what I want—what I need.

A knock at the door has me bolting upright to grab the sheets. "Just a second," I yell, but the door opens and

Dane's head appears. His eyes instantly go to my legs and travel upward.

"Looks like I missed all the fun." He slips inside my room, closing the door behind him.

"Seriously?" I balk, trying to cover myself up.

"Don't," he demands, coming closer. His eyes flick to the bathroom door and then my body. "You two resolve your differences?"

"Something like that," I murmur, my body already stirring to life at the way he's watching me.

"He made a mess of you."

"She deserved it." Rhett appears.

Dane kneels before me, running his finger through Rhett's cum. "Fuck, that's hot," he says, bringing his finger to my lips. His eyes hold a challenge, and I quirk a brow.

"Do it," Rhett says tightly.

My eyes snag his and I see the curiosity there, the hunger.

With a dramatic eye roll, I take Dane's wrist and swirl my tongue over the tip of his finger before closing my lips around it and sucking.

"Fuck, yeah. Our dirty girl." Dane hums with approval.

Rhett moves closer, looming down over us. "I think she's hungry."

"She does look a little hungry, doesn't she?" Dane smirks, rising to his feet.

"On the middle of the bed, hands and knees, Sadie, girl." He palms his cock, rubbing it over his jeans.

My eyes flick to Rhett and he gives me an imperceptible nod.

141

Desire pulses through me as I shuffle back onto the bed and roll onto my stomach, pushing onto all fours. Dane stalks around the other side of the bed and crooks his finger toward me. "Come get it, baby." He fists his bare cock, pumping a couple of times.

"Put your lips on him, princess. Show him how hungry you are." The bed dips behind me as Rhett's knees hit the mattress.

"You gonna fuck her again?" Dane asks with a lazy grin as I close my fingers over his.

"I'm gonna clean her up." Rhett lowers his mouth to my pussy, and I gasp at how sensitive it feels. But then Dane's there, sliding his cock past my lips. He grabs my hair, forcing me further down on him until I have to hollow my cheeks and take him all the way.

"Holy shit, that feels good." He starts fucking my face as Rhett eats me, spearing his tongue inside me, making me moan onto Dane's cock.

Pleasure floods me as they give and take everything from me. I can barely stand it, my body splintering apart, but they don't let up. Rhett slides two fingers inside as he flattens his tongue against my clit while Dane pushes deeper, making tears pool in the corners of my eyes.

"Look at you." His thumb brushes my jaw. "I've imagined this, you on your knees for me while Rhett eats your pussy. How does she taste?" he asked his best friend.

"Like mine," he growls, latching onto my clit and sucking so hard my back bows.

"Possessive asshole," Dane chuckles through his teeth as I work him faster. "Shit, Sadie... yeah, like that."

His legs lock up, his fingers digging into my scalp as

his orgasm hits, and he spurts his cum down my throat. Rhett slaps my clit again, sending a bolt of pain through me before soothing it with his tongue and making me soar.

Dane drops to his knees, kissing me hard, swallowing my moans as pleasure crashes over me. I'm spent, wrecked and ruined by these two dirty-talking tatted bikers, and I wouldn't want it any other way.

Except maybe for Wes to be here. But baby steps.

Rhett slaps my ass as he clambers off the bed, and I sink onto the mattress. Dane chuckles, standing to tuck himself back into his jeans.

"We're doing that again, and soon," he says, levelling Rhett with a hard look. "But next time, you fuck her pussy and I'll fuck her ass."

My cheeks burn as I glance at Rhett for his reaction. He doesn't speak, but I see the answer in his eyes.

Next time is happening... and when it does, I'm not sure I'll survive it.

But I can't wait to find out.

17

DANE

Rhett and I watch as Sadie disappears into her bathroom.

"Well, that was fun," I comment, falling down onto her bed.

"How'd you know I was here?" Rhett asks.

"Prez. I went back to the clubhouse and walked right into him. He started quizzing me about the reason Sadie was so adamant about seeing you that she took out the prospect."

Rhett laughs. "You seen the state of him?"

"Sure have," I say, pride filling me for our girl. "She pulled a knife on him."

"I know. Crazy bitch," he mutters, rubbing his hand over his hair.

When his eyes come back to me, they hold a seriousness that wasn't there before. "You good?"

"Y-yeah, why?" I ask, not used to my best friend being quite so observant.

He rubs the back of his neck awkwardly. "I dunno.

After everything Friday night, you just seem a little... distracted."

"I'm good, man. It's just been a long couple of days."

"Ain't that the fucking truth."

"You're good with all this though, right?" I nod toward where Sadie is, wishing like hell I was in there with her. But I know she probably needs a little space after what just went down in here.

Rhett rubs the back of his neck, also looking at the bathroom door that hides our girl. "With you, yeah. Noble, though? I don't trust him."

I nod, knowing where he's coming from. At the beginning of all this, I'd have said the same... but after being in Wes's home, seeing the state of his mom, I've seen a different side to him.

The way he is with Sadie. He's serious and he wants her. I'm confident of that.

"Noble's solid, man," I say. "He's got a shitty home life. He's nothing like his father."

"Doesn't mean I want him anywhere near our girl," Rhett mutters.

A smile curls at my lips when he calls her our girl. Maybe he can share his toys after all. "Just give him some time. He wants what we want."

"That's the fucking problem," he mutters.

"Noble is the least of our problems right now. What did Prez say at Church?"

"Nothing you don't already know. Darren is a dead man walking. We just need to see who finds him first. If he's really un-fucking-lucky, it will be me. I want to gut that cunt alive."

The door opening cuts off his words, and we both watch as Sadie emerges with wet hair and wearing only a towel.

Fuck me, she looks hot.

"You're still here," she says, looking at Rhett.

"Yeah, why? Expect me to run, princess?"

"Yeah, actually I did."

"Glad you think so highly of me," he murmurs.

"I can only base it on past experiences, Savage."

"Sadie, girl," I warn. They've just managed to find some kind of common ground; the last thing any of us needs is for them to be at each other's throats again.

"You're right though," Rhett says. "I need to head out. I need to go and feed your dad some bullshit for why you tried escaping to get to me." He holds Sadie's stare for a beat.

"What? Someone needed to knock some sense into you."

"Maybe so, but I need to think up a way to stop him sniffing around, unless you want him to know what just went down here."

"No, no. I'm sure you can manage, big guy," she says, patting him on the shoulder as she passes. Both of us watch her move as she pulls open a drawer and fishes out a pair of panties. "Oh, I'm sorry, I didn't realize this required an audience," she sasses.

"You're naked, Sadie, girl. You can expect we'll always want to watch."

"Pigs," she mutters, turning her back on us and pulling her panties up her legs.

"You coming, Stray?" Rhett asks, dragging my attention back to him.

"Um..." I look back at Sadie, rubbing my jaw in uncertainty.

"You can stay. Rhett can take the pussy downstairs back with him, seeing as he's pretty useless here."

"Yeah, we're going to be having words about that," Rhett warns, narrowing his eyes at her.

"Oh shush. Like you can comment on a little excess violence."

"He's one of our own, princess."

"Yeah, and he wasn't listening to me."

"Because he was following Prez's orders."

"Aren't you leaving?" I ask, needing them to stop bickering.

"Yeah, alright. I'm going."

I expect him to reach for the door and disappear, so when he decides to storm across the room, my eyes almost pop out of my head. He threads his fingers through Sadie's wet hair and pulls her up on her tiptoes so he can smash his lips down on hers.

I stand there watching as he slips his tongue into her mouth, my cock swelling at the display. Just before I think it's going to get even more interesting, he pulls back and stares into her eyes.

"I'll see you tomorrow. Behave, for fuck's sake."

"I'm sure Stray will keep me in line."

With a nod at both of us, Rhett turns back toward the door and finally disappears.

"Well then... Just you and me now, babe."

She studies me for a beat. "You don't want to go back to the clubhouse to sleep, do you?"

"I... uh... I just thought Jax should probably head back to rest his balls."

"Rest his balls? What the hell was he doing downstairs that wasn't resting them?" she asks, her brows damn near hitting her hairline.

"Fine. Okay. I don't want to sleep there when you're here in a bed alone."

"Who says I'd have been alone? I may have another member of my harem that you haven't met yet coming to spend the night."

My face turns hard as I stare at her, totally unamused by her attempt at a joke. "If that was true, he'd be dead the second he came anywhere near you. I might be willing to share with Rhett and even Pretty Boy. But even I draw the fucking line there, Sadie, girl."

"Talk to me, Dane. Tell me what's really going on."

She drops the towel covering her body as she makes that request.

"You want me to talk while you've got the girls out? Jesus, Sadie, you really think that's possible?"

I take a step toward her; my hands are ready, poised to make a grab for her, but she quickly holds a top in front of her.

"Yes, Dane. I want to talk."

"Fine," I sulk, sticking my bottom lip out in a pout when she covers up.

"Order a pizza or something, I'm starving."

Pulling my cell from my pocket, I do as she says, jumping back on her bed. "Come lie with me, Sadie, girl."

She crawls up beside me and I wrap my arm around her waist, pulling her into my body, brushing my nose against hers.

"Talk, Dane."

"That guy on Friday night. The one who was going to—"

"Justin?" she interrupts, and I don't miss the shudder that goes through her.

"Yeah. There was something about him. Something familiar. I don't know. But since that night, my nightmares have been worse."

"You always get them?"

"Every now and then, but every single time I shut my eyes since that night, all these memories keep coming back."

"Memories of what?" she asks, her brow wrinkling in concern.

"That's just the thing... I don't know. I don't see events. I'm just... I'm scared. Fucking terrified. I remember being in the dark. I remember being in pain... the fear."

My body trembles talking about it even now in the daylight.

I wish I could remember. I wish I knew what happened to me before I was found at the clubhouse gates all those years ago. But no one knows, and it seems that my mind is content with playing tricks on me, only allowing me to see—*feel*—the basics. Nothing of importance, nothing that helps trigger any useful memories.

"You think he was involved?" Sadie asks, dragging me from my misery.

"I don't know. He just seemed familiar somehow."

"Have you ever spoken to anyone about this before?"

I shake my head. "Never."

She finds my hand, lacing our fingers together. "Thank you for telling me."

"I meant what I said last night, Sadie. You make it all quieter. When you're beside me, the nightmares don't come. I... I need you."

"I'm right here, Dane. Whatever you need."

"Thank you," I breathe, leaning closer to brush my lips against hers.

"You guys order pizza?" Pacman booms up the stairs.

"Fucking cockblock," I mutter against her lips.

"I think you've already had enough fun, don't you?" she asks, quirking a brow as she climbs off the bed.

"With you, Sadie, girl? Never."

I move to follow her but soon stop when she glances down at the impressive tenting in my pants. "Stay there." She smirks. "We don't want to give Pacman any more ideas than I'm sure he already has. I'll get pizza and beer. Want anything else?"

"You naked and beneath me."

"Jesus. What did I agree to?" she mutters as she slips from the room.

Falling back on her bed, I stare up at the ceiling, wondering for the millionth time since Friday night who Justin really is. Is he someone I should remember, or was it just a coincidence and it was the events of that night which triggered something inside my mind?

Sadie's cell rings on her nightstand, and, without thinking, I reach over for it. I almost answer it when I see Wes's name, but something tells me he'd be disappointed if he hears my voice on the other end, so I let it ring out.

Only a few minutes later, the door opens and the most incredible sight in the world appears before my eyes.

"My girl, pizza, and beer. Pretty sure I've died and gone to heaven."

"You're such a goof, Dane Stray."

"I've been called a lot of things over the years, Sadie Ray, but I'm not sure goof has ever passed anyone's lips in regard to me before."

"There's a first time for everything." She crawls back on the bed and flips the pizza box open.

My stomach growls loudly as the scent of tomato and melted cheese hits me.

"Here, Pretty Boy called," I say, passing her cell over as I scoop up my first slice.

"You mind?" she asks, holding up her cell.

"Of course not. I'm worried too."

She studies me, her head tilting to the side a little like a confused puppy dog. "Should I be concerned about how happy you are with the idea of Wesley joining... this."

"I don't want him, if that's what you're thinking. I've told you, Sadie, I only want your pussy. I just happen to like watching other cocks using it too."

Her cheeks heat at my words, images of the three of us filling her mind, I'm sure.

"That really shouldn't do the things it does to me, should it?" she asks, hitting her screen and lifting her cell to her ear.

"There are no rules, Sadie, girl. Just pleasure. Lots and lots of pleasure."

I watch as Sadie paces back and forth as she talks to Noble. My eyes track over every inch of her, memorizing every curve, mole and mark.

"And your mom?" she asks Wes.

"Okay. That's good, I guess. But you know that he'll... Yeah. Well, whatever you need. You know where we are... You too. I'll see you tomorrow though, right?"

She listens to whatever he's saying for a bit.

"Yeah, Dane's here," she says, looking up at me and smiling. She laughs. "I'm sure we will." Her eyes darken, making my body heat. "Call me if you need anything."

She nods as if he can see her. "Okay. See you tomorrow."

Dropping her cell onto the bed, she slips down beside me.

"Everything good?" I ask

"For now. His dad is being all nice and apologetic to his mom."

"Well, that won't last," I mutter. We might not know the ins and outs of their relationship, but abusive behavior as bad as Wes's dad's doesn't usually disappear overnight. Their bullshit however... that's usually pretty fucking solid.

We spend the night like... like a normal couple, I guess.

We hang out in Sadie's room watching TV. She even makes me do an assignment with her that we've both got due before she crawls under her covers with me, her naked skin pressed right up against mine, and allows me to hold her as we both succumb to sleep.

And for the first night this weekend, I don't wake up a few hours later trembling in fear and my body dripping with sweat.

18

SADIE

The incessant beep of my alarm rouses me from a deep sleep. "Ugh," I murmur, reaching over to hit snooze.

I wiggle backward, half expecting Dane to drag my body closer, but I only find cold sheets. "Dane?" I glance over my shoulder, frowning at the empty space.

My cell pings and I snatch it up.

Dane: Your dad came back last night after you fell asleep. I managed to sneak out just in time. But we owe Pacman big time for the heads up.

Thank God. I can only imagine how that would have gone down.

My cell pings again.

Dane: P.S. good morning princess.

I smile, my toes curling at his cute message.

Me: No nightmares?

Dane: I managed. There's coffee.

Me: I'll be right down xo

Throwing back the covers, I get out of bed and pad into my small bathroom. Once I'm done washing up, I grab some clean shorts and an old MC t-shirt and pull them on, tying the hem of the t-shirt around my midriff.

"Sadie?" River calls from the hall.

"Yeah?" I reply, trying to tame my curls out of my face.

The door swings open, and she pops her head inside. "I just wanted to see if you're okay."

"Why wouldn't I be?"

Her expression softens as she slips inside, closing the door behind her. "You know, with what happened and everything."

"I'm okay." At this point, I have no idea if it's a lie or not. I'm more than happy to bury the reality of what happened this weekend in favor of enjoying myself with my guys instead of thinking about just how serious the situation is.

"It's okay if you're not, too."

"Seriously, Riv, you don't have to worry about me. When you grow up in the club, you kind of get used to all the drama and violence." I shrug, ignoring the butterflies in my stomach.

Not the good kind.

"You were kidnapped, Sadie. That's not exactly usual club drama." Her brows knit. "If you need to talk—"

"I said I'm fine," I snap, harsher than I intended. But I don't want to talk about it, because if I do, I remember how it felt to be tied up in that warehouse with Justin leering at me. And remembering makes me feel weak, something I'm not well-versed in.

"Okay," she concedes, hurt lingering in her eyes, so, I add, "Thanks, I appreciate it."

She gives me a small smile.

"Come on," I say, "I heard there's coffee."

"Thank God, I need it."

"Didn't sleep well?"

We head downstairs together, and River shakes her head. "I'm a little on edge after everything."

"You know the guys won't let anything happen to you, right?"

"I know. I just... I didn't expect all this."

"It's not so bad." I meet her gaze. "The club and everyone in it, it's one big family. You'll never be alone here, River." She swallows, a flash of grief in her eyes. She rarely talks about her mom, but I know it's got to have been hard on her. "Listen, the same goes for you. If you ever need to talk—"

"I know, Sadie Ray. I know."

"Girls," Dad booms from the kitchen. "You gonna stand out there all day bitchin' or come eat something before Stray and Pacman clean up?"

SACRIFICE

Laughing, I start for the kitchen, but River grabs my arm. "Yeah?" I ask.

"I don't know exactly what's going on with you and... the guys, but I'm glad Rhett has you."

My brows knit together and I'm about to reply when she slips past me and disappears down the hall, leaving me standing there, wondering what the hell she means.

I find everyone in the kitchen. There's a huge spread of pastries again, courtesy of the bakery on the next block over.

"I'm quite capable of cooking, you know," I say, making a beeline for the coffee machine. Dane tracks my every move, his gaze like phantom fingers down my spine. I cast him a sultry look over my shoulder and he cracks a smile.

"Mornin'," he mouths.

"Morning." I grin, rolling my eyes when his drop to where my t-shirt rides up my stomach.

"We need to go over a few things," Dad says. "Get over here and sit."

"Not this again," I grumble, dropping into a chair. River joins us.

"One chance, Sadie Ray. You get one chance. You get a ride to school with Dane or Jax. You go to class, you don't wander off campus, and at the end of the day, you ride back with them to either here, the clubhouse, or Dee's. No sneaking off, no giving the guys the runaround. I mean it—"

157

"Jesus, Daddy, you make me sound like a spoiled brat."

Dane splutters his orange juice everywhere and even Pacman snickers. I shoot them both a death stare. My dad gives me a pointed look that has me suppressing a smile. We all know he's right—I am the club princess, after all.

"I know this is serious, but I need to stay in school."

"Follow the rules and we shouldn't have a problem."

"Fine," I mumble.

"Same goes for you, River. You stick with one of the guys at all times."

"I will." She ducks her head, blushing. But since Jax isn't here, I'm sure it'll go over Dad's head.

"Right," he drains his coffee and pushes out of his chair, "I need to head to the shop. Stray, Pacman, you get first shift. Rhett and Jax will meet you at the school." His eyes find mine again. "Behave."

Rolling my eyes, I wave him off. Dane snorts and I flip him off across the table.

"He has a point, Sadie, girl."

I poke my tongue out at him, flaking apart a croissant. "We should probably head out soon."

"Are you nervous?"

"No, why would I be?"

He lifts his shoulder in a small shrug. "Evan might have talked."

"I doubt he's stupid enough to come after me when I've got guard dogs."

"Guard dogs, huh?" Dane drags his bottom lip between his teeth. "I can be the dog, you can be the pussy."

Pacman chokes on his breakfast at that, and I ball up a napkin and throw it at Dane. "Asshole."

"Yeah, but you love me."

His words strike me like a physical blow. I don't love him. Or Rhett or Wes. We've barely established what we are or what this thing is between us. But now the words are there, in the ether, taunting me.

If we keep down this road, it's likely my feelings for them will grow. I already care about them—each of them. And I know they care for me, in their own ways. But can it truly work, the four of us together?

I guess only time will tell.

The rumble of the bike as Dane drives to school drowns out my thoughts. Which is fine by me, because I don't want to think about what happened.

I want to forget.

Dad and the guys will handle it. They'll find Darren Creed, and when they do, they'll make him wish he'd never looked twice at me.

But by the time we pull up outside school, my nerves get the better of me.

"You good?" Dane asks over his shoulder as he cuts the engine.

"Yeah." I smile, but it's tight.

He nudges me off the bike, following me. Gently taking the helmet and hanging it off the handlebars, Dane stares down at me. "We can always go back to the compound or your house, just say the word."

I shake my head. "I need to do this." My eyes dart away, but Dane slides his finger under my chin and forces me to look at him.

"You don't have to prove anything, Sadie, girl."

"I know."

"And you know we won't let anything happen to you."

"But you'd still rather I was locked up at home."

"It isn't like that, and you know it. We just want you safe. And I don't want to have to get in between Rhett and Henley's guys if they start causing shit."

As if on cue, the familiar rumble of Rhett's bike draws our attention, and we watch as he drives toward us. The second he stands, he swings his leg over the chassis and approaches. "Everything good?"

Dane nods. "I was just telling Sadie we can turn around and go home, but she's pretty insistent we stay."

"Because she's a pain in my ass."

"*She* is standing right here." I jab Rhett in the ribs. His eyes darken, dropping to my mouth. Dane clears his throat with a chuckle.

"You two might want to tone down the bedroom eyes."

"Asshole," Rhett grumbles.

I like this. It's nice—normal.

Well, as normal as it can get for a girl tangled up with not one, but three guys. A girl who a rival MC wants to use as leverage.

I suppress a shudder but I'm not quick enough, and they both notice.

"Sadie, girl?" Dane tilts his head, studying me.

"I'm fine." I brush him off, heading for the club's truck. River and Quinn pile out and Jax joins us.

"Pitbull," Rhett says. "You know the score?"

"On it, Rhett." He lingers like he's about to say something to River, but he thinks better of it and goes around to climb back in the truck. Backing into a parking spot on the edge of the lot, he cuts the engine.

"Seriously, he isn't going to sit there all day, is he?"

"Sure is."

"Rhett, that's just—"

"Necessary." His eyes flare again.

Just then, Wes arrives. I go to greet him, but Dane snags my wrist.

"Let him come to you," he whispers.

"Stop being so weird. We're at school. Nothing is going to happen here." They have security. CCTV. It's a school campus, for God's sake.

"Bad things happen all the time at high schools," River says, and I widen my eyes at her.

Ducking her head, she mutters, "Sorry."

"Hey." Wes strolls up to us and I immediately notice the dark circles under his eyes.

"What's wrong?" I reach for his hand, surprised when no one—mainly Rhett and Dane—stops me.

"I'm okay." His eyes hold mine, saying everything he can't. Or won't. "We should probably get to class," he adds. "We're drawing a crowd."

He's right.

Kids linger, watching us. Watching Wes with us.

A line has been drawn today.

But something settles deep inside me knowing I have the three of them on my side.

19

WES

My skin tingles with what feels like the attention of the entire school as I make my way toward the entrance alongside Sadie, Dane, Rhett, River, and Quinn.

It's surreal. All of it.

Everything that's happened since going to meet Evan Friday night has been like a dream.

I want to say a nightmare, but I can't call it that, because amongst all the pain and violence there has been Sadie making everything that little bit better, allowing me to feel something other than the desperation and helplessness I usually do.

Swallowing down my unease, I keep my head held high, my grip on Sadie's hand tightening. I know I should let go, that by allowing others to see our connection I'm only going to bring more attention to myself, to her. But I can't bring myself to do it.

Her touch alone makes breathing that little bit easier.

School has always been my safe haven. A place I've

been able to live my life without constantly looking over my shoulder, waiting for whatever blow Dad is going to land on us next.

Okay, so I might have had to deal with Evan and his unique brand of assholeness, but I always thought he was a puppy compared to my father. Turns out I probably should have been a little more concerned about his intentions when it came to Sadie. I always thought he was all talk. Clearly, I didn't know him as well as I thought I did.

More eyes turn to us as we step into the hallway, but it's nothing compared to when the team looks our way.

Sadie squeezes my hand and tucks herself into my side. "It's going to be okay," she whispers. "You've got us, remember?"

"I know. We need to get to class."

Stopping at each of our lockers in turn, we then split up, Quinn and I heading for the science department, while Sadie, River and their bodyguards head for English.

I walk away with a heavy heart, wanting nothing more than to pull her into my body and kiss her. But I guess that's a step too far when the entire school is watching our every move.

"If you need me, call me," she whispers before reluctantly releasing my hand and letting me go.

"You too."

With my head lowered, not wanting to invite anyone to join me, I make my way outside, once more a few steps behind Quinn, who took off while I was talking to Sadie.

"Yo, Noble, wait up," a familiar voice calls, and when I glance to my side, I find Jamie stepping up next to me.

"What the fuck is going on, man? First Evan gets jumped on Friday night, and then you turn up and walk straight into the club whore's arms."

I've moved before my brain has caught up with my body and I pin him to the wall with my forearm pressing against his throat. His eyes widen as he stares back at me.

"You wanna say that again?"

His lips part, and I almost expect him to repeat his words. He never was the fucking smartest. But when he does speak, different words come out.

"I-I'm sorry. It was just a joke."

I press against Jamie harder, making his eyes widen in panic. "If I ever hear you call her that again, you'll be lucky if you don't end up in a worse state than Henley is in now," I growl.

"T-that was you?"

"No, it wasn't fucking me. We were jumped on the way to meet you guys Friday night. Stupid fucker mouthed off at them and when I came to, he was gone." The well-rehearsed lie rolls off my tongue.

"Well, you were lucky. They've done a real number on him."

I want to say good, the asshole deserved it. But I fear that I may have already said too much, connected myself and the club to his cuts and bruises. Even if he did bring it on himself.

Releasing him, he sucks in a heaving breath. "You've lost your mind, you know that, right?"

"Just keep your opinions to yourself, Beckworth, and we'll be good."

He looks over at me, confusion written all over his face.

I know that I never really stopped Evan being a dick to Sadie, but I never fucking agreed with it either. I probably should have stood up for her a little—hell, a lot—more. But between my dad and Evan, I knew it was a battle I'd never win. So I just decided to keep my mouth shut and watch her from a distance, knowing that I'd never get a shot with her anyway.

Well, everything has changed now, and I don't give a shit what anyone else thinks about Sadie and the club. I'll be standing right beside them. My dad can go fuck himself if he thinks I'm going to bend to his wishes. I'm going to do the complete opposite. I'm going to find a way to make Mom leave him, and we're going to get the hell away from his vicious insults and brutal punches before he kills one of us. If he's really unlucky, I'll set the club on him for beating a woman, and he'll wish the only thing he lost was his family.

I've only seen a glimpse of what Rhett and Dane are capable of. And there are plenty more where they come from. If I tell them to make it hurt, I have no doubt they will.

Jamie doesn't say anything else as we head for our chemistry class, but I know that's not because he's lacking questions. I'm sure every single person walking these hallways wants to know why one of its star football players is now slumming it with the Sinners.

Well, they can all go fuck themselves, because for once, I really don't give a shit about what they think.

The day drags. Each class seems to take longer than the last, and each teacher piles on the homework until I swear I'm going to drown in it.

The only good thing about the day is that I blow off the team at lunch and spend it sitting at another table in the sun with Sadie and the guys. I keep my back to the rest of the school, not wanting to witness them all gawking at me. I don't need to turn around to know they're doing it; I sense it every time Rhett or Dane growl at someone.

"Who knew you two could be so protective," Sadie murmurs with a smile playing on her lips, clearly aware of what they're both doing.

"We're looking after you, princess. Don't read too much into it. We couldn't give a fuck about Pretty Boy here."

"Sure," she says, reaching over and placing her hand high on my thigh. Her heat burns through the fabric of my jeans, making my cock harden.

I glance over at her and she smiles at me, knowing what her touch does. I drop my hand to hers and pull it higher letting her feel my length. Her fingers squeeze me through my jeans and I damn near come in my boxers from her touch alone.

Leaning over, I brush her hair away from her ear. "Wanna blow off last period and go have some fun?"

Her breath catches at my suggestion before she shoots me a wicked smirk. "I know something I want to blow."

She winks and I groan in pain, desperate to feel her lips wrapped around me again.

"You should make use of the girls' bathroom by math. They've got these mirrors..." Dane bites down on his fist, lost in thought. "There's nothing fucking better than watching what she does to you."

"Dane," Sadie hisses.

"What, babe? I know you loved it just as much as I did. Being able to watch my co—"

"Enough," she barks, throwing one leg over the bench and turning her attention to me. "As much as I'd love to, I've got to go to class. I've got a test."

She's right; if I miss any classes, no doubt it'll somehow get back to my dad and he'll delight in teaching me a different kind of lesson the next time he has the opportunity to get his hands on me.

He was on his best behavior when he got back to the house not long after Mom and I were dropped off by Dee yesterday. It was cringeworthy listening to Dad apologize to Mom, telling her that she's the single most important thing in his world.

All of it was bullshit, but she sat there and soaked up every word like he wasn't saying the same things he has to her over and over.

Reaching up, I run my fingers through my hair, pushing it out of my face. "Let me walk you to class?" I ask, although I'm already aware that the other two won't be very far behind. They've made it more than obvious that they don't trust me to protect her if shit were to go down.

I, however, know that I'm more than capable of

protecting what's mine. I just haven't had a chance to prove it yet.

"Sounds good."

Dumping our trash in the nearest can, the four of us head inside. "I've got practice after school," I tell Sadie.

She looks over at me, something brewing behind her eyes.

"What are you thinking about, trouble?"

"Can I come watch?"

"Practice?"

"Yeah." Desire darkens her eyes.

Turning toward her, I force her up against the wall, aware that our shadows come to a stop somewhere behind us. Her breasts brush against my chest and she gasps at the sensation.

"I'll let you do anything that puts that look in your eyes, princess. We'll be out on the field. I suggest you and your bodyguards come and find a spot on the grass to... Work on your assignments." I wink.

"Will you take your shirt off for me?"

"You're wicked, Sadie Ray Dalton." I lean in, brushing my nose against her.

"You love it."

"Damn right."

"Come on, kids. Class calls," Dane announces, the joy in his voice telling me that he's enjoying cockblocking me a little too much.

"Weren't you the one suggesting we make use of the bathroom not so long ago?" I ask him when he joins us.

"Yeah, and she turned your ass down in favor of a test, so let's go."

"Asshole."

"You love me." Dane blows me a kiss and Sadie bursts out laughing.

"I think he's got a thing for you," she says through her laughter.

My face must show all my thoughts because Dane quickly jumps in. "You might be pretty, Noble, but it's gonna take more than a pretty face to turn me. Sorry."

"Fucking hell, let's go." An impatient bark comes from behind us and when I turn, I find Rhett standing there with a murderous expression on his face.

He hates school, that much is obvious at the best of times, but right now he looks about three seconds away from putting someone out of their misery.

"Come on, Sadie Ray. Let's get you to class."

I take her hand and pull her away from the wall, resuming our journey.

"We'll see you after," she says, looking up at me with her huge green eyes when we come to a stop outside her class.

"You've got to convince them that they want to spend two hours watching a bunch of guys run around the field."

"I've got a way of making them see things the way I want," she sasses.

"You sure do. That's a powerful skill right there, Sadie Ray."

"I'll make sure I use it wisely then."

"Good luck on your test."

"Is it bad that I'm regretting my decision?" She bites down on her bottom lip.

"You can make it up to me another time."

"Deal."

I drop a quick kiss to her nose and allow her to duck into her class before she's late.

"Come on, Pretty Boy. Let's get you and our boners to class."

Flipping Dane off, I march ahead of them, assuming that they don't actually want the three of us to hang out like we're all friends or some shit.

20

SADIE

The week drags on much the same. River, Quinn and I are chaperoned to and from school, at least one of the guys with us at all times. By the time Friday rolls around, I feel like I can't breathe.

Don't get me wrong, I like having the constant attention of three hot guys, but I hate being imprisoned at my house, or Quinn's, or at the compound. I'm not used to being confined; I never have been.

I get it. Darren Creed is still on the loose, and every day that ticks by is another day my dad and the guys grow even more pissed—and worried—than they already are... but I need my space.

I need to breathe.

"Sadie, girl, let's go," Dane yells from downstairs.

"Yeah, yeah. Two minutes."

God, he's insufferable. They all are. If Dane isn't hanging around the house, bossing me around, it's Rhett. They come over to hang, study, and sometimes to remind me who I belong to. But with everyone so on edge, there hasn't been a lot of time to kick back and relax.

Even Wes has been over. He and Dane have developed a strange comradery, playing basketball in the yard or sitting around the firepit drinking beer and shooting the shit. I can tell Wes is just grateful to have somewhere to escape to.

"Sadie, let's—"

I storm over to the door and almost rip it off its hinges. "I said I'll be two fucking minutes," I yell, slamming the thing shut so hard it reverberates through me.

Seconds later, heavy boots thud on the stairs and I'm hardly surprised when Dane throws the door open and appears in the doorway. "What's up?" He narrows his eyes right at me.

"Nothing." I wave him off, finishing up my hair.

"Bullshit. You've been pissy all week." He comes up behind me and loops his arms around my waist, meeting my eyes in the mirror. "Talk to me."

"I'm just sick of it, being on house arrest. It's... it's driving me insane."

His brows pinch as he nuzzles my neck, keeping his eyes on me. "You're restless." I nod, inhaling a deep breath. "Maybe we need to figure out a way to destress you." His eyes dance with amusement, and other dark and dirty things. "We've been neglecting you."

"We haven't exactly had much time alone. The house is always full of people. And my dad—"

"Don't worry about Ray." He kisses my neck, drawing a soft moan from my lips. "Right now, all he cares about is finding Darren and making sure you're safe."

"You really think he'll come after... the club again?" I ask because the words I really want to say were stuck in my throat.

Dane hugs me tighter as if he knows exactly what I'm thinking. "We won't let that piece of shit hurt you again." His eyes sear into mine. A silent promise lingers between us.

"And what about you?" I whisper, turning in his arms and sliding my hands up his chest. "Who'll protect you?"

A smirk tugs at his mouth. "You don't need to worry about me, Sadie, girl. I ain't going nowhere." He leans down, ghosting his lips over mine. My hands curve over his shoulders as I press my body against his. I need more, so much more. But as our tongues meet, a voice pierces the air.

"Stray," Jax yells. "We need to head out."

"Motherfucker," Dane mumbles under his breath, pulling away. He brushes his thumb over my lips and sighs, "Later."

"Yeah." I pull away, but he snags my waist.

"We'll find him, Sadie, and when we do, we'll end him."

With a small nod, I slip out of his hold, grab my bag and head downstairs. At least it's almost the weekend; maybe I'll be able to talk Rhett or Dane into taking me out somewhere.

A girl can only hope.

Wes is in his usual spot, waiting for us to pull into the parking lot. The second he sees the truck, he strolls over. Quinn shoots me a look, but I ignore her. She's taking things even worse than I am, but I'm hardly surprised since she's always had one foot in the club and the other firmly out.

"Hey," he says, offering me his hand as I climb out.

"Hey." I smile. "Any sign of Evan?"

"No. I heard he'll be back in school next week."

"Something to look forward to."

It's been surprisingly quiet on that front. Without their fearless leader, the football team and cheer squad pay me little attention. Although I can't help but wonder if Wes has something to do with that.

"God, I want to kiss you," he breathes, crowding me against the side of the truck. My heart flutters as he reaches for me, but then Dane is there, slinging his arm around Wes's shoulder and dragging him away.

"You're with me, Pretty Boy. Rhett wants a word with the princess."

I scowl. All three of them have taken to calling me that.

"Where is—"

Dane points over my shoulder, and I turn to find Rhett leaning against his bike, his inky-blue gaze fixed right on me.

"Guess I'll see you in class," I say to Wes, shooting Dane an irritated look.

"See you later, princess," he chuckles, leading Wes away.

"You don't always have to listen to them, you know," Quinn says, coming up beside me. "They're not your keepers."

"Quinn," I sigh. Because I don't want to do this, not here. Not now. River joins us, lacing her arm through my cousin's.

"Come on," she says. "We should probably get to class."

Quinn holds my gaze, daring me to say to hell with it and ignore Dane's message that Rhett wants to talk. What she doesn't know, though, is that I want to talk to Rhett too. Although he's been around this week—more than he ever has—he's kept me at arm's length. And I know it's because he's still coming to terms with everything. Not to mention the fact that he's barely containing his rage over Darren still being on the loose.

"Go," I say. "I'll catch up with you."

Quinn snorts, pulling River away, who shoots me an apologetic smile, but she has nothing to be sorry for. If anything, River is the one who seems to understand my predicament. And she's the one who hasn't judged me for it.

Rhett tracks my every step, sitting up straighter as I reach him. "Hey," I say.

"Hey."

Okay then.

"You wanted to talk?"

"Stray said you're restless."

"Stray has a big mouth." My lip quirks.

"Listen, I know this isn't easy, but your old man already let you stay in school—"

"Because I'm safe here," I snap. "No one is going to come into school in the middle of the day and hurt me."

Rhett grinds his teeth, letting out a steady breath. "Is it really so bad having the three of us trailing around after you like puppy dogs?"

I gawk at him. "Did you just... make a wisecrack?"

"It was a simple question."

"It sounded a lot like a wisecrack question to me." My lips curve. I can't help it. Things have been strained between us, so to hear the softer tone to his voice... well, it cracks something inside of me.

"Are there no leads on Darren at all?"

"Nothing." His stone mask slides back into place. "Wherever he's holed up, he doesn't want to be found."

"God, I hate this."

"Want me to whisk you away for the day? I'm sure I could find some less-than-innocent ways to distract you." His brow quirks, and heat floods me at the huskiness in his words.

"Another wisecrack. Who are you and what have you done with Rhett?"

"Don't push me, princess. You might not like it when I snap."

I lean into him, unable to fight the connection simmering between us. "You forget something, Savage. I really like it when you snap."

"Fuck, Sadie..." He inhales sharply. "You should probably get to class before I do something I'll regret."

"Later, then?" I ask, hopeful.

"I don't know. Prez wants us to—"

"And what about me, huh? What about what *I* want?"

His nostrils flare, carnal need rolling off him. I'm two seconds from asking him to make good on his word and take me away from here. But something catches Rhett's eye over my shoulder, dousing me in ice water.

"You should go in. I need to speak to Jax for a second."

I glance back and see the source of Rhett's sudden interest. "Fine." I don't bother to disguise the hurt in my voice. "I'll see you later."

The two of them watch me all the way, until I'm entering the school building.

"Everything good?" Dane is waiting at my locker for me.

"Yeah, fine." I yank it open and grab my books, except something's wrong. "What is—"

"Sadie?" Concern coats Dane's words as I stagger back, icy-cold dread flooding me. "The fuck?" He plucks the photograph from my locker and cusses under his breath.

"What is it?" Quinn rushes over to my side. "What's wrong?"

"A photo..." I croak. "There was a photo in my locker."

"A photo?" She glances from me to Dane and back again. "Let me see that." She snatches it off Dane, and we both stare at the grainy image.

Dane has his arm slung casually over my shoulder as I smile up at him. It's innocent enough, only someone has scratched out his eyes with a knife, leaving jagged black holes, and added a thick scrawled red pen mark across my throat.

"Holy shit, that's..."

"We need to go," Dane says, his cell to his ear.

"G-go?" I stare wide-eyed at him.

"Yeah, clearly this place has been compromised."

"Compromised, right." I inhale a shuddering breath.

"You think it's Darren?" Quinn whispers, scooting closer to me.

"Or someone doing his dirty work." Dane's eye dart up and down the hall. "Either way, we need to get out of here until we know for sure."

"But it's class, we can't just—"

"We've got a problem," Dane says to someone, and I sense Rhett come up behind me. He takes the photograph from Dane and mutters something under his breath.

"We're leaving."

"Yeah," Dane agrees. "You take Sadie, I'll bring Quinn and River."

"What about Wes..." I blurt out, panic riding inside me. "He's a part of this."

"Like fuck he is," Rhett hisses, and I pin him with a pleading stare.

"Please."

He regards me for a second, a storm brewing in his gaze. "Fine. Dane can get him. But we leave. Now."

"He's right, Sadie. You two should go." Quinn touches my arm. "We'll make sure Wes comes with us. Go."

Rhett presses his hand on the small of my back, nudging me away from them. But I'm still paralyzed to the spot, the chilling image stuck in my head.

"Princess," Rhett growls, and I look up at him. "If you

don't want me to throw you over my shoulder and carry you out of here, I suggest you move."

21

RHETT

Sadie looks over her shoulder at Quinn and Dane, who both silently beg her to do as she's told for fucking once and get the hell away from here.

My fingers flex against her back, my need to do as I just threatened almost getting the better of me.

"Do not leave here without him," she warns, looking directly at Dane.

Fucking Noble.

I have no idea what either of them see in him. He's a douchebag football player, as far as I'm concerned. And as much as he might tell us that he doesn't agree with his father about the MC, I still don't trust him.

Grant Noble has made it his life's mission to take us down, to convince Mayor Nixon and Police Chief Statham to stop working with us, turning a blind eye when our indiscretions inadvertently help the town. I find it hard to believe that someone who's grown up listening to that poison doesn't feel the same, let alone suddenly want to be one of us.

He's either after something or... Sadie's pussy is just that damn good.

Thoughts of how true that statement is hits me, and despite the current situation, my cock swells at the memory of sliding balls deep inside her the other day. Of just how good she tasted as she soaked my face while she sucked Stray off at the same time.

"Let's go," I bark, dragging her into my side, my impatience getting the better of me—mostly to get her out of any danger, but also to get her alone.

It feels like it's been forever since it was just the two of us—or even the three of us. There's always been another bodyguard around to put a stop to our fun.

I'm on full alert as we push through the main doors, my eyes scanning the tree line, looking for any kind of movement, any sign that someone could be waiting for us to bail on school the second we found that photo.

Is this a trap?

Have we played right into their hands?

"W-what's wrong?" Sadie asks when I pause.

Seeing nothing of concern, I push forward. "Nothing. We need to leave."

"You're overreacting."

"I don't need your opinion right now, princess. I just need you to follow orders."

Her chin drops to argue, probably to cuss me out, but I cut her off before she gets the chance. "We all need you in one piece." I release a strained breath. "Me, Stray, even fucking Noble. Now shut the fuck up and follow my lead."

She rolls her eyes at me but wisely keeps quiet.

Jax slips from the truck as we approach. "Everything okay?" he asks, glancing between us and the school building waiting for the others to appear with us.

"No, it's not. The others are coming. Take them all straight back to the compound."

"Okay."

"And be on fucking alert. No one is dying today."

His eyes widen at my words, but he immediately nods in agreement—unlike Sadie— and hops back into the truck, starting the engine so he's ready to go the second they all pile inside.

I climb on my bike and Sadie quickly joins me as I turn the engine over. She wraps her arms around me, but it's not tight enough.

Fear coils around me like I'm bound in barbed wire. I need to know she's there. I need to know she's with me. Curling my hands around her wrists, I pull her arms tighter, squashing her breasts against my back, her warmth seeping through my cut and settling a tiny bit of my unease.

"Don't let go," I growl over my shoulder.

"Oh yeah," she calls back. "I was planning on jumping right off."

My teeth grind at her ability to write all this off as if it's nothing when the reality is that her life is on the fucking line.

Not wanting to think about it anymore, I gun the engine and fly out of the parking lot, leaving a cloud of dust in our wake. Her hold on me doesn't let up the whole way back as my anger, my fear has my fingers gripping my handlebars until my hands start to cramp.

I fucking knew letting them go back to school was a bad idea, but she was adamant and pulled those puppy dog eyes at Prez and got her way.

I push the speed limit the whole way, taking more risks than I usually would, but thoughts of being followed, of being watched, don't leave my mind, and I know I need to get her within the safety of the compound gates.

A growl of frustration rips from my throat as we make the last turn toward the compound. I have no doubt she felt the vibration of it with how tight she's holding me, but I don't give a fuck. I need to do something to expel this pent-up energy that's zipping around inside me. Not that I really think anything other than killing that cunt or fucking her into next week will actually help.

The second I pull the bike to a stop, she climbs off and begins marching toward the clubhouse.

"Where the fuck are you going?" I shout after her.

"Going to lock myself away like a fucking princess. Isn't that what you all want?" she screams, turning to face me. Throwing her arms out in frustration, she presses her lips into a thin line.

Marching up to her, I wrap my hand around her throat and push her behind a stack of tires, out of sight from the guys working in the shop. "No, princess," I growl, my lips so close to hers they almost brush. "That isn't what I fucking want."

"So the two of you don't want me to be the kind of girl who's seen and not heard, the kind of girl who just sits around letting her guys use and abuse her at any given opportunity?"

She's angry, I get that, but fuck, having a hissy fit isn't the fucking answer right now.

"Watch it, princess, or that is exactly where you're going to find yourself. At my fucking mercy."

Her eyes dilate at my words, proving to me that she doesn't find the idea of being at our beck and call that terrible.

"At least we would know you weren't off doing something fucking stupid and putting yourself in danger."

"One thing," she seethes. "I did one fucking thing."

"One thing that almost got you... raped and killed." The words punch the air, making her breath hitch. But a stone mask slides back over her face as she narrows her eyes on me.

"And what about Dane, huh?"

"What do you mean?" I demand, my brows pinching.

"The day of the accident," she says, "they went after both of us. Today, that photograph... It was of me *and* Dane. Not me and you, not me and Wes. Or me on my own. He's going after both of us."

My chin drops as I think about what she's saying.

"Fuuuck," I hiss, looking toward the compound gates as if his bike is about to appear any second. I know he's not; I can't hear the rumble of his engine. "Fuck," I bark, the weight of what she's figured out pressing on my shoulders.

"Why the fuck didn't you say something sooner?"

"I don't know, I..." The color drains from her face. "I froze, okay? Besides, you practically dragged me out of there. But it makes sense, Rhett. When you add up all the—"

Sadie squeals as my fist connects with the brick wall beside her head. "Now you understand why I didn't want to leave without them?" she sasses.

"You need to quit the fucking spoiled brat act, or your ass is gonna be so fucking red you're not going to be able to sit for a week."

"Fuck you, Savage. Fuck. You."

She storms off, and this time I let her go as I shake my sore hand out.

I catch up with her less than a minute later in the clubhouse.

"Sorry, sweetheart. Your dad and Micky are out meeting Chief Statham, hoping he can spare a couple of his men to help the search for Creed. They should be back in a few hours. Anything I can help you with?" Pike says.

"No, I'm good. If you see him before me, tell him I need him. I'll be in Stray's room." She turns on her heels, her entire body locking up when her eyes collide with mine.

"Stray is at school."

"He won't be for long," she mutters, walking toward me.

"Princess," I growl, refusing to move.

"Savage." She holds my eyes, defiance shining bright in hers.

There are plenty of men who wouldn't have the balls to go up against me, but it seems our princess has plenty.

"You're not going to Stray's room." My warning is low enough so that only she can hear me.

"I'm done listening to you." She barges past me and takes off down the hall.

But she doesn't make it farther than my door before I reach for her arm and drag her inside, pushing her up against it the second it's closed. "You're really trying my fucking patience, princess."

"Good, because you've fucking ruined mine. If something happens to them, I'll never—"

"Nothing is going to happen."

"You didn't think that when you dragged me away like the place was on fucking fire."

"That's because you're—" I slam my lips shut, trying to get a rein on my emotions.

This girl drives me in-fucking-sane.

"Because I'm what, Rhett?" she taunts.

"You're my responsibility."

She laughs right in my face. My fists curl and my shoulders tense.

"Rhett Savage, loyal to the core. Follows his prez's orders without question like a good little club member," she mocks.

Anger burns through me, my blood boiling just beneath my skin. "I have to protect you."

"Because he told you to."

I hold her eyes. She's playing me.

"Come on, Rhett. It's time to stop hiding." She leans in closer, taunting me. "Tell me how you really feel." My teeth grind, but she adds, "I dare you."

She gasps when my hand finds its home on her throat, squeezing hard enough to make her eyes widen. "You are my responsibility, Sadie. My job is to keep you safe. To protect you."

"Why?" she urges, not willing to let this go.

My heart thunders in my chest. I know what she wants, but I also know that I can't give it to her. Dane might be willing to bare himself to her, tell her how he really feels, but I'm not that kind of fucking person.

"Because—"

"Savage, open the fucking door," Dane booms before his fist rains down on the wood.

"Saved by the bell," Sadie mutters as I drag her away from the door and pull it wide open, allowing Dane, Jax, Wes, River, and Quinn to spill into my space—the last fucking place I want everyone.

"You get here okay?" I stupidly ask.

"What does it look like?" Dane asks with a smirk as he walks over to Sadie and pulls her into his side, dropping a kiss to her temple.

The smile she gives him makes my chest ache. That's what she wanted from me. And I gave her the complete opposite. I gave her the only thing I'm capable of: rough touch and barbed words, because I'm too terrified to let myself do anything else.

"Prez isn't here."

"Then we wait." Dane drops onto my chair, pulling Sadie down onto his lap while the others hover awkwardly.

"Jax, take the girls to the clubhouse and get them a drink." Noble's name is on the tip of my tongue. But after not being able to give Sadie what she needs right now, I figure that I can at least give her this.

"But I—"

"Now, Jax," I boom, ripping my door open and pointing through it.

Quinn levels me with a look that I think is meant to scare me. "Do not make this any fucking worse, Savage."

"Wouldn't dream of it, Renshaw. Look after my little sister, yeah?"

"Fuck you."

River meets my eyes, silently asking me if I'm okay. I nod, and a smile twitches at her lips.

I fucking hate that I dragged her into this life, but I know that what Dane has said to me time and time again is true. There's nowhere else she'd be safe. No one else I'd trust her with more other than my brothers.

The second the door closes behind her, the atmosphere in the room ramps up to almost unbearable levels.

"Sadie," I say. "Tell Stray what you told me."

She gives me a double take, momentarily forgetting her suspicions before it hits her and she nods, turning to Dane to break the news.

22

SADIE

"I don't think this is just about me." I stand up, needing to pace as my words perforate the air.

Dane blinks at me. "What?"

"Think about it. They tried to run us off the road, and I wasn't the only one in that photo, Dane." My stomach knots.

"Maybe they think you're together," Wes suggests. "Maybe it's a two-for-one kind of deal. Take out the club's princess and her guy as retribution."

"Hey, asshole," Rhett growls. "Watch it."

Wes snorts. "You know I didn't mean—"

"Stop," I snap. "This isn't helping. I'm just saying that photograph, what they did to it, it felt... personal." My eyes linger on Dane, but he isn't looking at me. He's staring at the wall, his eyes cloudy.

"Dane?"

"I recognized him."

"Who?" Rhett spits.

"That motherfucker who hurt Sadie... Justin."

"But that's not possible. He's one of Darren's guys. Our paths barely crossed the Reapers until recently."

"Yeah," Dane says, but I see the doubt in his eyes.

We're missing something. I don't know how I know, but I do. And it has something to do with Dane, I'm almost certain.

"What do you remember about when you arrived here?" I sit on the edge of the bed.

"Shit, Sadie, girl, it was a long time ago."

"I know. But it could be important."

"What are you thinking?" Rhett asks, clearly confused.

"I don't know." I shrug. "But something doesn't add up."

Dane stares at the wall again, that forlorn look on his face. I open my mouth to say his name, but Rhett snags my gaze and shakes his head.

Releasing a shaky breath, I hug myself tight. "What happens now?" I ask, a lick of fear racing down my spine.

"We wait for Prez and Micky to get back and go from there."

"But we're on lockdown?" I meet Rhett's dark gaze, and he nods.

"Until we know more, yes."

"Fine. I'm going to find Quinn and River."

"Hey," Rhett snags my wrist as I reach him, "you good?"

"No, not really. But it isn't like I have a choice, is it?"

He stands up, towering over me. "Sadie—"

"Let's not. It's going to be a long weekend. I need a drink." Or three. "Wes, want a tour?" I ask him.

"Sure." He follows me to the door after I yank out of Rhett's grip.

"You two need to watch it," Rhett hisses. "The last thing we need is Prez thinking that—"

"Seriously, that's what you're choosing to focus on right now?" I arch a brow, cutting him with a deadly look.

His lips press into a tight line, but he holds my gaze. God, when he looks at me like that, I want to believe he's in this with me.

With us.

Rhett steps aside, and I slip out of his room with Wes hot on my heels. I'm too restless to sit still. And being in the same room as all three of them... it's the sweetest kind of torture. But now isn't the time to play, not when a psychopath is gunning for blood.

My blood.

A shiver runs through me, and Wes touches the small of my back. "Sadie, I—"

"Don't." I shoot him a weak smile. "I'm fine. I just needed some air."

"They're just worried," he adds. "We all are."

"Yeah, I know. But I don't know how I'm supposed to feel right now. The bike accident was one thing... but the photograph in my locker... it feels different somehow. More personal."

"No one—"

"Sadie Ray?" Dad's voice echoes through the clubhouse, and I hurry into the main room, rushing into his arms.

"Shh, sweetheart, I've got you." He hugs me tight, and

until this moment, I didn't realize how badly I needed to see him.

"I need to meet with the guys, okay?" Easing me back, he holds me at arm's length. "You and the girls sit tight with Pitbull and Pacman. The women will be here soon." He drops a kiss on my head. "I won't let anything happen to you, Sadie Ray. Not you or anyone else in this family." His eyes hold mine, full of fire and promise.

"I know, Daddy," I whisper.

The clubhouse doors open, and Aunt Dee, Rosita, and the other old ladies pour inside.

"Dee," Dad goes to her. "You know the drill. We're on lockdown until I give the word."

She nods softly, something passing between them. I can't remember the last time we had to go on lockdown, not like this. Sure, there have been threats over the years, but never such an open declaration of war.

"Sadie, sweetheart," Rosita approaches me, "how are you holding up?"

"I'm okay, thanks."

"You're built of strong stuff, sweetie." She leans in, smiling. "And something tells me you have plenty of guys looking out for you."

I glance over my shoulder to find Wes watching me. Dane and Rhett have also appeared, standing over by the bar, their eyes fixed in my direction.

"I..." I trail off, not really sure how to answer her.

She lets out a small chuckle. "The heart wants what it wants, Sadie Ray, don't you forget that." Cupping my face, she leans in and presses a kiss to my forehead before walking over to join the other old ladies and girlfriends.

"Come on." I beckon to Wes, and he follows me over to where Quinn and River are sitting.

"Everything okay?" my cousin asks, and I nod.

To my relief, she doesn't say anything else as she and River dish up a pack of cards and start a game of rummy.

One by one, my dad's top guys disappear down the hall to head to Church.

"They're meeting?" Wes asks.

"Yeah. Probably to vote on how to handle the latest threat. But like Rhett said, it's likely we'll be stuck here all weekend at least."

"You made Dane and Quinn come for me. Why?"

I release a small breath, my eyes darting from his face to my hands and back again. "You know why."

"Yeah." He swallows, raking a hand through his dirty blond hair. "Does that mean I get one of those?" He flicks his head to Jax's cut, and I can't help the laughter that spills out of me.

"Do you want one of those?" I tease.

"I dunno, I reckon I could pull it off."

"Have you ever ridden a motorcycle?"

He shrugs. "I'm a fast learner."

"Somehow, I don't see it."

Wes leans in closer, close enough that I can feel the warmth of his breath. "Maybe one day, I'll surprise you."

I wet my lips, desperate to kiss him. To let him take me away from all... this.

"Will your mom be okay? Won't she wonder where you are?"

"She's fine." His jaw ticks. "Dad is in his guilt phase.

It'll last a few days at least. And don't worry about me, I'll cover my tracks."

"I don't want to cause you anymore troub—"

"Hey." Wes brushes his hand over mine, the table obscuring them from sight. "I already told you, you're worth it."

"Senior year wasn't supposed to go down like this." I sigh, turning my hand with my palm up so we can lace our fingers together. No one is watching us, the women too busy organizing to notice. Quinn, River, and Jax are used to us by now, so they barely glance in our direction. And Pacman is distracted by something on his cell phone.

"I know things have been hard for you, but I don't know... I'm kind of glad with how things turned out." The corner of his mouth tips in an adorable smile.

"I totally see why they call you Pretty Boy."

Wes chuckles, his smile morphing in a smug smirk. "Oh. Is that right?"

"Discreet, Sadie Ray, real discreet." Jax snorts across the table, and I flip him off.

Everyone laughs then, and the six of us all play cards for the next hour, pretending it's just another day.

By the time the men reappear, the atmosphere in the clubhouse is more relaxed. Aunt Dee and Rosita came prepared to make enough food to feed everyone, and most of the guys make a beeline for the buffet table at the far end of the room.

"Pigs," Quinn murmurs.

"What was that, Renshaw?" Dane smirks as he grabs a stool and drags it over to where we're sitting. Rhett is still hovering with my dad, the two of them in hushed conversation.

"So, what happened?" I ask casually.

"Nice try, Sadie, girl. But you know the rules. What happens in Church—"

I grab my bottle cap and flick it at his face. Dane ducks just in time for it to sail past him. "That wasn't very nice," he grumbles.

"I'm not feeling in a very nice mood."

The air around us thickens as everyone watches our interaction.

"Don't be a brat, Sadie Ray." His voice is a low warning. "It never ends well for you." The faintest of smiles tugs at the corner of his mouth, and heat splashes inside me.

How does he manage to make everything sound so sexual?

Wes chuckles quietly beside me as if he knows exactly where my thoughts are at. But then Dad appears, looming over us.

"Son," he says to Wes. "How is your mom doing?"

My brows knit at the softness in his voice.

"She's okay, thank you."

Dad's eyes slide to mine in question. "I guess we have you to thank for him being here."

"He's in this, Daddy, whether you like it or not." I lift my chin in defiance, aware that nearly everyone is watching us now.

"Tread carefully, Sadie Ray. He might be your friend,

but he's still Grant Noble's kid, and that man has been a thorn in the club's side for longer than I care to remember." His words sound menacing, but I catch the glimmer of humor in his eyes.

"If it's any consolation, sir, I hate my father probably more than the club does."

Dad gives Wes a curt nod, fighting a smile as he tries to maintain his tough guy attitude. "You should all eat something. It's going to be a long couple of days." He stomps off toward Micky and my aunt. Rhett doesn't join us, grabbing a beer and perching on one of the stools instead.

It's weird, being here with all of them. It doesn't help that the three of them can't take their eyes off me.

So much for warning me to tread carefully.

"I'm going to play pool," I announce to no one in particular.

They don't follow, and I'm grateful. I need to catch my breath, to try to calm my racing pulse.

"Rack 'em up," I challenge Pyro, one of the club's older members. He's a bit of a loose cannon. No old lady. No morals. And a heap of wicked-looking flame tats curling up his neck and around his head. Hence his nickname.

"Ah, hell, Sadie Ray. You know I don't like to beat your ass at pool."

"Big words, Pyro. But I'm feeling lucky."

Rhett's eyes drill into me as Pyro racks the balls. "Ladies first," he drawls.

There's nothing sexual about the way he looks at me. Pyro isn't like that. He's more interested in blood and violence—so much so that my dad keeps a tight leash on him. Most of the time.

We play for a few minutes, and it's pretty even. He sinks a ball, I sink two. He sinks two on his next shot, while I miss. But then the tide changes and I'm winning.

"Wily little thing, aren't ya?" he hisses.

"Don't be such a sore loser." I wink across the table as I sink another ball.

"Motherfucker," he grumbles, cracking his cue down on the edge of the table.

"Pyro, rein it the fuck in," Uncle Micky barks.

I snort, and his eyes flare.

I have the game in the bag, lining up my shot onto the black ball. It glides in the corner pocket, and I whoop with victory.

"Sorry, Pyro, better luck next time." I chuckle, just as someone snickers, "Got your ass handed to you by a girl."

I walk away, but the sound of smashing glass makes me whip around. Pyro has overturned a table of drinks, spraying glass and liquid everywhere. Someone screams as he grabs a bottle and launches it across the room, right in my direction. It misses me by a mile, but Dad and Micky are already storming toward him.

"Fucking hell," someone grunts as we all watch them manhandle him toward the door.

"Go cool off, now."

"Sorry, Sadie Ray," Pyro mutters, skulking out of the clubhouse.

Dad's eyes fix on mine, flaring with confusion. "Something I should know?"

It's only then I feel them behind me. Rhett, Dane, and

Wes flank me like sentinels, and I glance up at Rhett, frowning.

"He wasn't going to hurt me," I say incredulously.

"We didn't know that." His jaw clenches.

"Seriously, I'm fine." I glance at each of them, unsure whether to be flattered or offended that they jumped up to defend me.

Regret glitters in Wes's eyes, as if he knows they just crossed a line. Dane looks as relaxed as ever, an amused glint in his eye. But Rhett... he's visibly shaking as he stares at the mess Pyro left behind.

"I'm fine," I say, reaching for him.

He flinches, snatching his hand away. My stomach sinks, the walls closing in around me as I realize we have an audience that contains most of the club.

"My office," Dad barks, raking his hand through his shaggy hair. "Now."

23

WES

Sadie looks back at the three of us with fear in her usually bright green eyes as a similar feeling races through me.

We shouldn't have done that, but the second the guy with the menacing tattoos looked like he was threatening her, my ass was off the seat, and I was making my way over.

I guess I should have predicted that I wouldn't be the only one who'd want to protect her from the crazy, pissed-off biker.

"I'm sorry," I mouth, feeling guilty that I've made all of this worse for her.

Maybe it wouldn't have been so bad if just Rhett and Dane stood up for her—that is their job, after all. But me... That screams suspicious, and I can totally understand why Ray is calling us out on it.

The intrigued stares of everyone in the room burn into my back as I follow Sadie and Ray down to his office.

After sharing a concerned glance, Rhett and Dane follow as well.

Our footsteps on the concrete floor echo around us, my heart thundering in my chest as I try to predict what could happen next. I have no idea what I'm going to say if Ray turns those cold, critical eyes on me.

My hands are already beginning to tremble at the thought. Not that I'm going to allow any of them to see it. Sadie asked me earlier if I wanted to be a part of this. Wanted my very own cut. This might just be the time to make that decision as I prepare to go head-to-head with her father, the Prez of this MC.

Sadie, Dane, and I take a seat in Ray's office, but Rhett remains by the door. Not wanting to be near us all or wanting to run, I have no idea. Although, I wouldn't have thought it would be the latter; I can't imagine Rhett Savage running away from much.

"I'm waiting," Ray booms, and I have to fight the flinch that wants to rip through me at his demand.

"We're just looking after our princess, Prez," Rhett says, his voice cold, his face unreadable.

Ray regards him for a moment before running his eyes over the three of us. "Stray?"

He looks a little more nervous as he glances between Rhett, Sadie and Ray. "J-Just doing our job," he confirms, much to Ray's irritation if the pulsating vein in his neck is anything to go by.

I can't imagine this will go well for them when he discovers—if he doesn't already know—that they're lying to him.

"You know," Ray starts. "I've been watching the four of you. At first, I thought it was Dane who was stupid enough to put his cock on the line." He lifts his hand from beneath his solid mahogany desk and places a wicked-looking knife on top.

Fucking hell.

"Daddy," Sadie pleads, but he's having none of it.

"Then Pretty Boy showed up, and I thought maybe you were straying outside of the club. But then the way Rhett took Justin down last weekend in your honor... Well, let's just say that threw a cat amongst the pigeons." Ray scrubs his jaw, keeping one hand on the knife.

"Daddy, please let me explain..." Sadie sits forward between the two of us, trying to placate her father.

"Yes, Sadie Ray. Please, enlighten me, because I'd really like to not have to kill two of our brightest young members and prove to Grant Noble that he's right, that we are a bunch of brutal savages, after I deliver his son back to him in tiny little pieces."

I swallow nervously. He's joking.

Right?

Of course, he's joking.

I glance at the others to see zero reaction on their faces. Is this shit just normal club life, or are they better game players than I expected?

"Don't be ridiculous. You're not going to touch any of them," Sadie says calmly, her voice strong and determined as she stands, staring right at her father, whose fingers are still flexing around the handle of his knife.

Ray's eyes narrow at his daughter. "Sadie Ray," he growls, the vein in his temple joining the one in his neck.

"I care about them, Daddy. All of them." She narrows her eyes, and I'm struck by how similar they look in this moment. "You will not threaten them, you will not go after them. They're protecting me. Each of them is making this shitty situation that little bit better."

Ray's lips part to respond, but in a move I never thought I'd see, he closes them again, totally lost for words.

"I'm sorry, Daddy, but there's nothing you can do to stop me from seeing any of them."

His chest heaves as he looks between us, a deadly warning in the depths of his scary eyes. "Pretty Boy?" he suddenly barks, making my spine straighten.

I hate the Pretty Boy nickname they've given me, but I figure that it's their way of showing they've accepted me, so I just have to suck it up.

"Yes, sir."

"Your father know about this?"

"No, sir. He'd probably kill me." The words were meant to be a joke, but even as I say them, I know they could well be true.

Sadie drops back down beside me and laces her fingers through mine, a move that Ray doesn't miss but it doesn't seem that she cares.

"Is he going to be a problem? We've got enough shit on our plate right now; we don't need your over-opinionated cunt of a father distracting us."

"I'll make sure he's not."

Ray stares at me, probably wondering how the hell I'm going to keep that promise. And in all honesty, I have no idea myself. But I know I need to keep it, because without it, he has every right to kick me out of the compound and keep me away from Sadie.

He holds my eyes for a beat longer before turning back to his daughter. "You... Fucking hell, you're playing with fire, Sadie Ray."

"I can handle it, Daddy." She smirks.

His teeth grind at her response. "Whatever... *this* is, you will not flaunt it around my club. I appreciate that they're all looking out for you... But as for the rest of it... Well..." He drags a hand down his face.

"You don't need to worry about me, Daddy. I'm a big girl, I can make my own decisions."

"I know that, sweetheart, but your independence and constant need to push the boundaries at every turn terrify me."

"Nothing will happen to her," Rhett growls, speaking for the first time in what feels like forever.

"Like being driven off the road and abducted?" Ray deadpans, cutting off anything else Rhett might have wanted to say.

"Sadie Ray, Pretty Boy, get the hell out of my office."

She stands, pulling me with her.

"And stay out of trouble," he adds. "We're in enough shit as it is right now."

"Yes, Daddy," she agrees, leading me around his desk so she can drop a kiss to his cheek. "Be nice to them, please? They're kind of important to me," she whispers, making him scoff.

Clearly by not being a member, I'm getting off lightly here. Either that or he's lulling me into a false sense of security by letting me walk out unscathed.

"I can't make any promises, sweetheart."

Knowing that's as good as she's going to get, Sadie pulls me to the door, looking between Rhett and Dane as she does.

A second later, we're slipping out of the room and into the empty hallway.

"Do you think they're going to make it out alive?" I ask.

She turns back to me, her dark eyes meeting mine, making my stomach flip in excitement. Sadie slams her palms against my chest and I stumble back, hitting the wall. She presses the length of her body against me as she reaches up on her tiptoes and presses her lips to mine.

"I'm sorry," she murmurs into our kiss.

"You're worth it and more, princess."

A low growl rumbles in her chest as her tongue pushes between my lips. The urge to lift her and switch our position burns through me, but I lock it down, knowing that anyone could walk down here and see us.

Almost as quickly as it started, she pulls back, putting an end to our kiss, leaving my chest heaving and my cock hard.

Clearly being able to feel it against her stomach, she palms me through my jeans.

"Princess," I growl as she squeezes.

"I'll make it worth your while," she promises. "I've got a plan. Come on."

She takes off down the hallway, leaving me to quickly rearrange myself before following.

All eyes turn to us as we enter and I swallow down

my nerves as several scary bikers stand, clearly also on board with protecting their princess.

"Stand down, boys," Sadie announces with amusement. "There's nothing to see here."

She marches straight over to Quinn, who's standing with the wives, and whispers something in her ear. Quinn scowls, clearly not happy with whatever Sadie's plan is, but after a couple of seconds, she finally concedes and nods.

The two of them hug before Sadie marches behind the bar and collects up a few things. "Come on, Pretty Boy," she says. "We've got a private party to attend."

She passes me a couple of bottles and I take off after her, more than ready to lose the attention of everyone in the room.

There are a few guys out by the shop, but none of them pay us any attention as we pass. The heat of the afternoon sun warms my skin as I watch Sadie's ass sway in front of me. I have no idea where she's leading me, and quite frankly, I don't care.

"What is this place?" I ask as we walk down a path that appears to be outside of the compound, although I'm not stupid enough to think it is.

"Just wait and see."

"Is it safe?"

"Do you have a gun?" she asks, turning back to look at me.

"Um... N-no," I stutter, my pulse ratcheting. "I wasn't aware that—"

"It's okay. I have." She smirks. "I borrowed Dane's spare when he wasn't looking."

I choke on my own spit as the image of Sadie wielding a gun pops into my head.

"You okay there, Pretty Boy?"

"Y-yeah, I'm good."

"Good, because I need you ready for what I've got planned." She winks and turns around again.

I can't help but glance at our surroundings. But I can't see anything other than trees. It doesn't seem safe, not given the circumstances, but Sadie doesn't seem too bothered.

"This whole place is protected, Wes. We're as safe down here as we are up there. Trust me?" she asks, shooting a sultry look over her shoulder.

"Of course."

"Good. What do you think?" The path opens up before her and she steps aside, showing me the view.

"Oh wow," I breathe, taking in the gushing waterfall beyond, the clear blue water twinkling in the afternoon sun.

"It's my favorite place in the world. Well, maybe not the whole world—I've never really been outside of Savage Falls, so..." She trails off, probably realizing that she's rambling.

She leads me over to a lush patch of grass and we lay the bottles in the shade before sitting down. The second her ass hits the ground, I reach over and pull her to me, desperate to continue what we started back in that hallway.

"Hey," she breathes, looking up into my eyes.

"Hey yourself." She smiles seductively, making my

cock swell once more. "Are you okay? All of this it's... crazy." A resigned sigh slips from her lips.

I tuck her closer, rolling her beneath me, needing to feel her body pressed against mine. She shrugs, her large eyes holding mine and allowing me to see everything she's feeling. "It's my life. Crazy is normal."

"I think this is beyond normal, Sadie. Someone is after you."

"They won't get to me," she says, sounding much more confident than I feel.

"You can't know that."

"I've got one of the best clubs in the country looking after me. I've got my three guys protecting me. What more could I need?"

My mind flickers back to the office we left only minutes ago. "You think they're going to be okay?"

A smile curls up at her mouth. "My dad might look scary, but when it comes to me, he's a huge teddy bear. He's just laying down some new ground rules."

"New?"

"They broke all the old ones when they touched me."

"I touched you too, so why am I not in there right now?"

"You never had the original rules. You're in a totally different situation. But rest assured, he will catch up with you."

"Great," I mutter, already dreading that conversation.

Sadie chuckles, amusement glittering in her eyes. "Just tell him how awesome you think I am and I'm sure you'll get along fine."

"I think you're awesome?" My brow lifts.

A smile twitches at her lips as her hand slides down my back until she squeezes my ass. "You sure do, Pretty Boy." Her eyes darken with lust. "Wanna show me just how awesome?"

24

SADIE

We make out until we're both breathless.

"Fuck, you get me so hot," Wes breathes, sliding his hand between our bodies to cup my breast. He yanks on the neckline and trails his tongue down my skin, licking and nipping. I smother a moan.

"Seems like they started the party without us." Dane's gruff voice pierces the air and I glance over to see them heading in our direction. Wes stills above me, but I grab his hair, guiding him back to my chest. Dane chuckles. "Greedy little bitch." His words make my pulse flutter.

Rhett's eyes narrow, anger and jealousy simmering there, whereas Dane looks eager to join in as he looms over us.

"Bite her tit," he says thickly. "She fucking loves that."

Wes complies, pulling my boob from my bra and grazing his teeth along the sensitive bud.

"Ah," I cry, arching into him as he bites harder. It hurts in the best possible way.

"Fuck yeah." Dane palms himself through his jeans.

My eyes flick to Rhett and I realize he's stayed back, dropping down onto an overturned tree trunk. He sips his beer while watching us.

Watching me.

"You both look okay." I check them for any bruises, my voice thick with lust.

"It's cute you care," Rhett drawls.

"What's that supposed to mean?" I nudge Wes off me and push up onto my elbows.

"He knows."

"And? Maybe it's time for the truth to come out."

"It's not that simple." Rhett's eyes flare with irritation.

"Seems pretty simple to me," I quip back, sitting upright and pushing the curls from my face. "I meant what I said in there, Rhett. I care... about all of you. If you can't handle that, that's on you."

"Sadie, girl," Dane hisses, dropping down beside me and Wes. "Don't poke the beast."

"Fuck the beast," I snap. "I'm not ashamed of how I feel or what we're doing. I don't know why he,"—I flick my head toward Rhett—"has such a problem with it."

I clamber to my feet and stare Rhett down. He glares back, sipping his beer and refusing to engage.

Asshole.

"I'm hot," I blurt out. "I'm going for a swim." Before I can second guess myself, I start stripping out of my clothes.

Kissing Wes got me all hot and bothered, but being alone with the three of them twists me up inside. It's like

I'm burning from the inside out, and I need to cool off before I combust.

"Fuck," Wes hisses, his eyes drinking in the sight of me.

"I'm in." Dane jumps up, almost falling over his feet as he starts stripping out of his clothes. "Pretty Boy?" He glances at Wes, who shrugs.

"Yeah, why not."

My lips curve deviously. I hadn't intended on anyone joining me, but maybe I can use this to my advantage. Turning my back to them, I unhook my bra and slide it off my arms, casting them a glance over my shoulder. "Last one in is a little bitch."

Pushing my panties off my hips, I kick them off and take off toward the water's edge, not hesitating as I leap into the river. I go under, relishing the way the cool water bites against my hot skin. It feels divine, and I swim further out before breaking the surface.

When I look back at the embankment, Wes and Dane are almost naked. The way the sunlight peeks through the trees and hits their strong, powerful bodies makes my tummy clench. The silvery scars that mar Dane's chest seem to be highlighted by the sun; concern pushes some of my desire aside.

I remember them from when we were kids, and seeing them now makes me realize how he hardly ever removes his shirt.

My stomach twists once more. It's no longer just with desire but with worry, too.

I know I'm right. There's more to this Darren thing than him just wanting me. I'm sure of it.

Rhett doesn't move; he just sits there, glowering. But if my plan works, he won't be like that for long.

"You'd better swim, Sadie, girl," Dane teases, dragging my attention back to him as he dives effortlessly into the water. He soars toward me, snagging one arm around my waist and pulling me under with him. We surface together, my back to his front as he treads water for both of us.

"Gotcha," he rasps against my neck, kissing me there.

Wes swims toward us, his gaze full of heat and promise. "You need to swim faster next time, Pretty Boy. I got to her first, which means I get to fuck her first."

"Pig." I elbow him again, harder this time, and Dane falls away from me with a grunt of pain.

Laughing, I swim toward Wes, wrapping myself around him. "Hi." I kiss him lightly.

"Hi." Humor dances in his eyes, but it changes to sheer lust when I wiggle closer, feeling his cock press up against me.

"Looks like Pretty Boy gets me first." I cast a dark look back to Dane.

"Oh, it's like that, huh? It's on, Sadie, baby. It's so—"

I push away from Wes and take off, swimming as hard as I can toward the waterfall. My body cuts through the water like a rocket. I don't swim out here much anymore, but when I was a kid, it was one of my favorite things to do in the summer.

Inhaling deeply, I duck underneath the surface, gliding toward the waterfall. There's a hidden cave inside, perfect for what I have in mind. The force of the fall hits the water above me, but I barely feel it as I swim underneath. When I break the surface again, I'm in the cave.

With a smug smile, I swim to the far side where the water becomes shallow and laze in the pool. It's warmer in here, the air balmy from a small hole in the cave ceiling, sunlight bouncing off the walls, making everything look ethereal.

Dane appears first, Wes hot on his heels. My lips curve as they swim toward me. "Took you long enough," I sass. "Rhett still sulking?"

"Something like that," Dane mumbles. Snagging my ankle, he yanks me through the water. "Hold her," he barks at Wes, who comes up behind me. The water barely reaches their waists; I can't take my eyes off Dane's cock resting thick against his thigh.

"See something you like?" he drawls, and I lick my lips. "Later. First it's my turn to play." His hands slide up my thighs and he cups my pussy.

"Dane," I cry out.

"I'll never tire of hearing my name on your lips." He spreads me open, running a finger down my slit and dipping it inside of me. "Do you think Prez knows we're out here, ruining his princess?"

"Big words when you're barely touching me."

His brow lifts, as he shoves two fingers into me roughly, stealing my breath. "You were saying?"

"Asshole," I breathe, pleasure shooting through me as he curls them deep inside me.

"That can be arranged, princess. Just say the word and I'll sink deep into your ass while you suck Pretty Boy off."

"God, Dane," I gasp, wildfire burning me up inside at his dirty words.

Wes is hard behind me, but I can't move to touch him, not while I'm spread out between them. One of his hands slides around my waist and over my stomach, coming up to cup my boob. "So fucking soft," he murmurs, squeezing gently.

Dane drops to his knees, the water sloshing around his chest. Sliding my legs onto his shoulders, he leans forward, licking the length of me.

"Fuck," I moan. "That's—" The words get stuck in my throat as his fingers sink back inside and his tongue finds my clit, licking with perfect precision. I reach for Dane's head, burying my fingers into his hair as he eats me like a man starved.

"Should I make her come?" he asks Wes.

"I want to fuck her mouth while you fuck her." Wes's throaty confession does things to me.

"I like your style." Dane nods. "Move closer to the edge, where it's shallow."

They work together to make sure I stay above the water. My stomach is coiled tight with need, every nerve ending heightened and desperate for more.

"What do you think, princess?" Dane spears two fingers inside me. "Do you think we should let you come?"

"You'd better, asshole," I snap, and he chuckles.

"Fuck, I love your dirty mouth." He bands his arm around my stomach and flips me, but to my surprise I don't sink under the water; my knees hit the ground, steadying me. Wes is leaning back against the rocky edge, fisting his cock.

"Now put your lips around him and suck."

Wes groans as I let him feed his cock into my mouth. "Fuck, she's good."

"Yeah," Dane shifts behind me, palming my ass as he drags his cock through my wetness, nudging my clit. I moan around Wes, and he grunts, thrusting up into my mouth.

"Hold on," Dane says, softer, and I brace my other hand on Wes's thigh as Dane slams into me. "Fuck, Sadie, girl, you feel—" He pulls back and thrusts again, shoving me forward. I have to grip the base of Wes's cock to avoid choking on it, but I love the way they own my body, taking what they need and giving me what I desire.

Our moans bounce off the cave walls, drowned out by the ferocity of the waterfall beyond. No one—not even Rhett—will know what we're doing in here. Although I hope he knows exactly what he's missing.

"Who owns this pussy?" Dane rasps, fucking me with fast shallow thrusts.

"You do," I pant, licking Wes's shaft, up and down, around and around like a popsicle. His jaw is clenched tight as he tries to hold on while I tease him to the point of no return.

Dane's thumb traces my ass, pressing gently on the puckered hole. "You gonna let me in here soon, Sadie, girl?"

"Yes... *yes*," I breathe, barely able to think straight. It feels too good, being between them like this. He could ask me anything and I'd say yes, so long as he keeps fucking me.

Dane pushes a little harder—not enough to fill me there, just enough to let me feel it, to let it fuel the sensations coursing through me. Wes is close, his grip in my hair harder, his thrusts more eager.

"Come in my mouth." Our eyes connect, and he mumbles something as his legs lock up and he shouts my name, spurting hot jets of cum down my throat.

"Fuck, that's hot," Dane grits out, slamming into me harder, so hard I'm sure I'll have his fingerprints on my hips. "Pinch her clit," he orders Wes, who slips a hand into the water and finds his target, pinching hard.

I shatter apart, crying both their names. Dane isn't done, though. He grabs the back of my neck and yanks me upright so he can kiss and suck my skin. "Savage doesn't know what he's missing out on," he chuckles darkly, fucking me so hard I see stars.

A second orgasm hits me right as Dane comes hard, biting down on my neck. We stay like that for a while, riding the intense waves rushing through us. When I can finally breathe properly again, I twist my face to look at him.

"Hmm, that was fun," I say with a sated smile.

"Damn right it was." He kisses the end of my nose. "But looks like your fun is only just getting started."

"What—"

Gripping my chin, Dane moves my head and I find Rhett in the shadows near the entry of the cave. He stares at me, his nostrils flared and jaw set.

"Come to play?" I purr, my body already stirring to life again under his intense regard.

"Fuck," Dane guffaws behind me.

Rhett's eyes narrow, and I can see the turmoil in his eyes. He wants me—wants this.

The question, though, is if he's man enough to do anything about it.

25

RHETT

The water rains down on my back as I stand and watch Dane pull back from Sadie, his shoulders relaxed and a sappy smile playing on his lips.

The second they followed her like little fucking puppy dogs, I knew I wouldn't be able to sit there letting my imagination run wild about what they were doing in my absence.

Dane's arms band around Sadie's waist as if he needs to protect her from me.

He might.

Sadie's chest heaves as she stares at me, her eyes blown with desire and her cheeks, neck and chest all flushed from the orgasms Dane just dragged out of her.

"You just going to stand there, brother, or are you going to come and join the party?" Dane asks with a smirk.

Smug fuck. He knows exactly what he's doing to me.

He knows how I feel about Sadie without me ever

having to utter the words. It's why we've worked so well together these past few years. We know what the other is thinking. It's always been beneficial.

Until now.

He sees my weakness. A weakness I shouldn't have.

The ass-ripping Prez gave us has barely faded from my ears, yet here we are, with his princess between the three of us doing exactly what he fears.

Challenge swims in her eyes.

She wants me to own my feelings about her as much as Dane does.

But can I do it?

Can I admit that she's it for me? For me... *and* them?

My eyes flick to Noble, who's now sitting on the shallow rocks, looking a little sheepishly between the three of us, still rocking a semi as he probably remembers what it was like having her lips wrapped around him.

My fists curl beneath the water as jealousy surges through me faster than I can control. Sharing her with Dane is one thing. He's my best friend, my brother in all the ways that matter.

But can I share her with him too?

Dane whispers something in Sadie's ear, but from this distance and with the roar of the water behind me, I don't stand a chance of hearing it.

I do see the actions that follow.

His arms loosen from her waist, his hands pressing against her smooth stomach and climbing until he cups her breasts.

Asshole.

Her head falls back on his shoulder as he plucks her

nipples, but despite the desire filling her eyes, she never once rips them from mine.

"You ready to go again, Sadie, girl?" he asks, loud enough that I can't miss it.

"Yes," she moans as he pinches again and bites her shoulder.

I feel the heat of his stare, but my eyes don't leave my girl.

"Did you want to watch her come, or make her come, brother? She's all yours, if you want her. I bet she's wet for you." A growl rips up my throat. "Want me to find out?"

It's clearly a rhetorical question, because before I even get a chance to answer, his hand descends her stomach. His fingers dip between her thighs just above where the water is lapping at them, and her eyes shutter as he teases her clit.

Out of the corner of my eye, I spot Wes slowly jerking himself off as he watches the pair of them. My cock aches for me to do the same, but I already know it won't be enough. Nothing other than her will ever be.

"Fuck, bro. She's dripping."

My teeth grind, knowing that some of that is from him, that he got inside her first. Again.

"But if you don't want her, then I'm more than happy to go again. Or maybe Pretty Boy wants this round." He shoots a look over at Noble and winks. "So what do you say?" He grabs the back of Sadie's neck as if he's about to move her. "I could bend her over right here and you could watch as she takes my cock like a good little princess, or you could—"

I'm on her before I've even realized I've moved. My

hand wraps around her throat, her dark eyes widening at the roughness of my grip.

"You like this, don't you, princess? All three of us watching you, wanting you? Does it get you horny? Dirty little whore," I mutter, my fingers tightening but not quite enough to cut off her air supply.

I push her back, pinning Stray between the edge of the pool and Sadie—not that I think for a second that he gives a shit. Her ass is pressed up against his cock, after all.

"You want me to fuck you, princess?"

"Rhett," she moans, her hips grinding back against Dane, as if it's going to get her what she needs.

"His turn is over. You're mine now."

Dropping my head to her neck, I bite down on her skin, making her cry out in a mix of pleasure and pain until the taste of copper fills my mouth. "I should have brought my knife with me," I chuckle, darkly. "We both know how much you like that."

"God, yes," she whimpers as I palm her breast, pinching her nipple until she screams in pain. "You're a fucking asshole," she cries.

"And you love it, don't you, princess?"

She stares at me, daring me to take what I want, knowing that no matter what I do to her it'll turn her on more than she's even aware. She wants it all. Everything I've got to give. The pleasure, the pain, the torture, the surprise.

She gasps as I spin her around, pulling her ass against me and grinding my cock against it, my mouth watering as I think about how tight it must be.

My cock aches, thinking about the day we promised her. The day when Dane and I fill her front and back, taking everything from her, owning her completely.

That day is coming.

"Hey, princess." Dane smiles.

"You've had your fun, Stray. Get the fuck over there with Pretty Boy."

I tilt my chin to where he's still sitting, slowly pumping himself at the sight of Sadie's naked body.

I get it; it brings me to my fucking knees as well.

I pull her harder against me to allow Dane to slip from the edge, but the smug fuck doesn't move as fast as I want him to. In fact, he does the exact fucking opposite and presses the length of his body against Sadie, slamming his lips down on hers.

Her moan of pleasure vibrates through me as she returns his kiss.

"Fuck. Off," I grunt at Dane, making him laugh and finally back the fuck up.

"He gets super pissed when he's horny," he mutters to Noble, who's watching the show with a smirk playing on his lips.

"He's always pissed off."

"You've seen our girl, right?"

"Yeah," Noble muses. "I'm always fucking hard too."

Dane sinks down beside him on the rocks—although not too close—his eyes trailing around Sadie's body as my inked hands begin to roam.

"Rhett," she whispers, leaning her head back on my shoulder and kissing the sensitive spot on my neck just beneath my ear. "Fuck me, Savage. Show them who's boss."

A growl rips from my throat as she copies my previous move and bites down on my neck until I swear my skin splits open.

Wrapping my hand around the length of her hair, I push her forward, bending her over and exposing her round ass to me. "So fucking pretty, princess. But it's missing something."

Lifting my hand, I bring my palm down on her soft, flawless skin. The slap echoes around the cave, quickly followed by her cry of pain.

I stare down at my red handprint. "Better. But still not enough."

I do it again, harder this time, making her surge forward from the hit. The only thing that stops her falling face first into the edge of the pool is my fist in her hair.

"Look at them," I muse, taking in both Dane and Wes getting themselves off to the sight of Sadie's pain. "They love watching you."

"So do you," she breathes. "Don't tell me you weren't hard watching them fuck me."

"You get me hard, princess. Not them," I growl.

"You were jealous, weren't you? You wanted in on the action, but they got there first. They had the balls to take what they wanted while you sulked like a pussy. My dad scare you that badly?" she taunts. "And here I was, thinking you were this big, bad, inked-up biker when you're nothing but a— fuck," she cries when I thrust inside her without any warning.

"You were saying?" I twist her head so she has no choice but to look at me.

"Fuck, Rhett," she breathes, her pussy clenching around my length. "Please, you need to move."

"I take what I want, princess. You don't need to worry about that. They've had their fun. Now it's time for mine. And I can already tell you that by the time I'm done, you're not going to be walking out of this river."

"Oh God."

"No, princess. Just a savage."

I pull almost all the way out before pushing back inside her, filling her to the hilt, the tip of my cock hitting her cervix and her screams echoing around the cave.

"Watch her," I demand, looking at the other two—not that they need the order. Their eyes are already locked on her.

I thrust harder, the water splashing around our legs as she mewls and whimpers. "Who owns you, Sadie Ray?"

"Y-you," she whispers.

"Louder," I boom. "Who fucking owns you?"

"You do, you fucking asshole."

"I've got a fucking name."

"Rhett," she cries when I reach around with my other hand and pinch her clit. "You own me, Savage. You. Stray. Noble. All of you... God... *God!*" Her cries echo around us, mixing with her scream of pleasure as she shatters all over my cock.

"Fuck, princess. Your pussy is a greedy little thing." I pound into her, sweat dripping down my back as my balls start to draw up. "Again," I demand, needing to feel her squeezing me tight once more before I fill her.

I pull her hair, arching her back, ensuring I hit that spot inside her which will make her fly as I twist her clit until she's screaming. The second she clamps down on me, I explode, coating her with hot jets of my cum as pleasure engulfs me, making my muscles go limp.

"Oh God. Fuck. Shit," she chants, sagging in my hold.

Pulling out of her the second I stop coming, I twist her around and hold her face in front of my cock. "Lick me clean. Then go and do the same to them. They both just came all over themselves, watching you."

I realize my mistake the second she puts her lips on me, because I'm hard again in a flash. Her wicked eyes flash up to mine; they're full of dirty thoughts, and I fucking love it.

"On second thought, I want to come down your throat too. The boys will have to wait a little longer."

26

SADIE

I'm pretty sure I'm in heaven. Rhett holds my body close as we float in the warm pool, Dane and Wes laughing and joking beside us.

A delicious ache radiates through my body, a reminder of what we did. What we *all* did. God, they drive me wild. The way they take control of my body and give me exactly what I need.

I've spent my whole life fighting for power in a man's world. I rebel and push the boundaries, but with my guys, it's like I can let go and just be Sadie Ray, instead of club princess Sadie Ray Dalton.

Rhett is quiet behind me, but the dark cloud usually circling him has dissipated. I might even say he's... relaxed.

"What?" he asks as a small chuckle leaves my lips.

"Nothing." I glance back at him, inhaling a sharp breath at the remaining intensity in his eyes.

"Careful, princess, or I might think you want to be spanked again." His lip quirks.

"I wouldn't complain." I bat my lashes and Dane lets out a howl.

"She's got you wrapped around her fucking pinky. How does it feel to be pussy-whipped, bro?"

"Dane," I warn. I don't want anything to ruin this rare moment of peace we've found ourselves in.

"He's not wrong, princess." Rhett drags his tongue up my throat, nipping my jaw before smacking my ass. Hard.

I jolt forward in the water, yelping. They all laugh.

Assholes.

Dane prowls forward in the water, holding his arm around my waist and turning me into him so my back is against his chest. "Come sit with me, Sadie, girl." He sinks back against the shallow rocks.

"Hi," Wes says, smiling.

"Hi." I fight a grin. "So what did Ray really say?" I ask the question nobody seems to want to discuss.

"Oh, you know, he threatened to cut off our balls if we so much as hurt a hair on your head."

"That's all?" I lift a brow.

"Don't worry about Prez," Rhett says. "He knows the deal."

"And what is the deal, Savage?"

His eyes flare at the way his name rolls off my tongue. "I think you know, princess."

"I think you should spell it out for me."

He's here, which speaks volumes, but he still hasn't said the words I so desperately need to hear.

I hold his stare, refusing to back down. I need him to be all in on this. More than I ever realized. It's like they each hold a piece of me, completing me somehow. Dane makes me laugh. He shows me how impulsive and wild and reckless life can be. Wes is like my anchor. He's quiet and intense and he makes me feel grounded. Then there's Rhett. He pushes me the way no one else ever has before. He feeds the darker parts of me. The part of me that wants to be dominated.

"Shit, princess," Dane smirks against my neck, "you really shouldn't push him."

"Really? Because I think it's exactly what I should do."

"She's right," Rhett says, and the cave falls so quiet I can hear the steady beat of my heart.

"I am?"

"Don't look so surprised." He glowers. "You forced my hand when you outed us to Daddy Dearest."

"Asshole," I snarl.

"Didn't ever claim to be anything else, princess. But I'm your asshole now, so suck it up."

A triumphant smile tugs at my lips. "Damn right you are."

Dane snorts while Wes laughs quietly beside me. Part of me wonders what he makes of all this. He isn't a Sinner. He isn't in this life.

But he's in my life now.

And I refuse to give him up for anything.

"Do we need to figure out some kind of schedule?" Dane asks with a hint of humor.

"Schedule?" Rhett balks.

"Yeah, like who gets to fuck her and when."

"Hey, asshole." I jam my elbows into his stomach. "We don't need a schedule."

"I don't know, princess," Wes says, finally finding his voice. "It's not a bad idea."

"Seriously, we are not having a schedule."

They're joking.

They have to be joking.

"Sounds reasonable to me," Rhett adds. "So long as you're in my bed the most."

I roll my eyes. "You're going to have to learn to share your toys, Savage."

"The way I see it, princess, there's enough of you to go around. Pussy, mouth... hands."

They're all chuckling again. Feeling indignant, I push out of Dane's arms and swim off toward the mouth of the cave.

"I'm getting wrinkly, and I'm hungry... and before you say anything, I'm hungry for actual food. Not dick." I wink before diving under the water and swimming out of the cave.

Wondering how long it'll take for them to follow.

When we're all dry and dressed, we walk back to the compound together. There are a few guys milling around the shop, but they pay us little attention. But once we enter the clubhouse, the noise quiets down as everyone watches me walk ahead of my guys. Power thrums through my veins, knowing that Rhett, Dane, and even Wes are behind me. *With* me.

"Nice swim?" Pacman hollers from behind the bar. Someone snickers and then a *crack* rings out.

"Enough," Dad booms. "Unless someone wants to get their dick blown off, I suggest everyone keeps their goddamn mouths shut."

Rhett moves ahead of me, making a beeline for the bar, and the noise starts up again. Quinn and River beckon me over and I go to them, dropping down on the leather banquette.

"Where the hell did you go?" Quinn seethes.

"For a swim." I shrug.

"With all three of them."

I don't like the accusation in her eyes. "Quinn, I'm with them. All of them."

"You're fucking crazy," she murmurs.

"How does that work exactly?" River asks, intrigue glittering in her eyes.

"Ew, gross, Riv. That's your brother—"

"Relax, I'm not... forget it." She blushes.

"I agree with Quinn," I say around a smirk. "You probably don't want to hear about how your big brother makes me—"

Quinn claps her hand over my mouth and frowns. "How are you so okay with all of this? We're on lockdown because there's a psycho out there who wants to hurt you, and you're acting like this is one big party."

"What would you rather I do? Sit around terrified, shaking and crying in the corner?"

"No, but this is serious, Sadie."

"I know that. Trust me, I know." My teeth grind together. "But I refuse to be a victim, Quinn."

"Because you'd rather be a dirty whore, right?" Tasha appears out of nowhere, snarling in my direction.

"Seriously, Tash," Dane says, coming over to our table. "You need to take a walk before you say something you'll regret."

"Maybe I'll go keep Rhett company." Her eyes light up.

"Try it, bitch," I hiss, my fist clenched at my side.

"Relax, Sadie, she isn't worth it." Quinn shoots Tasha a cold look.

"Whatever." She flicks her long, dull hair off her shoulder and walks away, swaying slightly.

"Jesus," Dane breathes, dropping down beside me.

"She's either drunk or high," Jax says, shaking his head.

"I don't know why Uncle Ray keeps letting her come around," Quinn adds.

"She's got no one."

"And that makes it okay?" I ask Dane.

He lets out a steady breath. "No, it doesn't. But without the club she has nothing."

I hate the empathy in his eyes, as if he relates to her. Dane is nothing like Tasha. Nothing.

"Maybe she should try to keep her opinions to herself, then," I mutter.

"Hey," Dane squeezes my knee, "don't let her get to you."

My lips purse as I watch her saunter over to Rhett, running her manicured fingers up his inked skin. Red-hot jealousy unfurls in my stomach, and I lurch forward, but Dane holds me back, leaning in to whisper, "Look."

Rhett glares down at her, roughly removing her hand from his arm. Tasha's lips curl in disgust.

"Seriously?" I hear her whine. "You're going to pass up a chance to fuck me for... her?" Her eyes cut to me, and before I know it, I'm up off the bench and storming toward her.

"Oh shit," someone rasps as I grab her by the hair and yank her backward. Her shrieks of pain fill the clubhouse.

"You're done." I drag her toward the doors. "So done."

"Get the hell off me, bitch, you can't—"

"Sadie Ray," Dad bellows across the room. "Put her down, right this instant."

Snickers ring out around me, everyone watching with amusement as I shove Tasha. She staggers backward, hissing at me like a snake.

"You fucking bit—"

"Okay, Tash, let's go take a walk." Rosita and Jada crowd her toward the door, forming a barrier between her and me.

"Get her out of here," I snap, anger zipping through me like wildfire.

"Go cool off." Rosita shoots me a disappointed look, and part of me wants to go at her too. They're defending her... Tasha. After she came at me, spewing her cruel words and blatantly trying to get a rise out of me.

I feel Rhett at my back. He doesn't touch me, but his presence is enough to make me move, and I slink over to the bar, perching on one of the stools.

"You good?" he asks.

"Yeah." I clench my fist again, focusing on the way my muscles expand and contract.

"She's not worth it."

My brow lifts, and he lets out a smooth chuckle.

"You're better than her," he says, as if it's the simplest thing.

I feel eyes on me, and I know if I turn around that half the club is probably watching me, wondering what I'll do next.

"Maybe I slightly overreacted. But she touched you and—"

"You were jealous," he deadpans.

"Apparently my hormones are territorial."

He leans closer. "Just your hormones?"

A small smile tips the corner of my mouth.

"Can I trust you not to attack any more of the women?" Dad asks, coming up to rest his arms on the bar beside me.

"She's a bitch."

"Tash is a little misguided, yes. But she's not a bad girl. She needs the club, Sadie Ray."

"What are you saying?" I balk.

"You need to play nice."

"Seriously? She needs to learn to keep—"

"I'll talk to her. I'll let her know not to come sniffing around Rhett or Stray anymore." He blows out a strained breath, rubbing a hand down his jaw. "No more bitch fights."

"Fine." I flash him a saccharine smile as he pushes off the bar.

"And no more skinny dipping in the river." His jaw tics. "You're going to send me to an early grave if you're not careful."

"Is that all?"

"Oh, I have a growing list of things we need to talk

about, but we've got bigger problems right now." He glances at Rhett. "Keep an eye on her. I'm trusting you to keep her out of trouble."

"Yeah, Prez. You got it."

"Fucking kids," he mutters as he walks away just as a loud *boom* rocks through the place and screams fill the clubhouse, glass shattering everywhere.

"The fuck?" Rhett plasters himself against me, shielding me from the devastation.

Everyone seems to hold their breath as we wait for another explosion, but nothing comes.

"Is everyone okay?" Dad yells, surveying the damage. Aside from the shelves holding all the drinks shattering and a couple of windows blown out, everything seems okay.

But then shouts come from outside and dread races down my spine.

"What now?" Dad mutters as he unsheathes his pistol and storms out of the clubhouse.

27

RHETT

I hold Sadie against me, my arms in a vise-like grip around her body as I shield her from the source of the explosion, keeping my word to Ray.

I will always protect her.

"Fuck. Are you okay?" I breathe, looking down at her and pulling her wild curls away from her face.

She's pale, her eyes wide in fear.

We both know that whatever that was, it was a warning. They can get into our compound if they want.

And they can get to her.

Fear races down my spine, my entire body noticeably shuddering with it.

"Y-yeah, I'm okay. Y-you—where's Dane and Wes?" she asks, stepping up on her toes to look over my shoulder.

"They were right—" I look over at the last place I saw them, but they're no longer there. "Uh..."

"They went outside. They fucking went outside, Rhett," she cries, her body trembling as the realization hits her.

She darts around me, but I catch her waist. "No, princess."

"But they might be hurt. They might need me."

"Or there might be another bomb, and it might hit their intended target," I growl in her ear, fear like I've never known before flooding me.

"Fuck. I hate this."

"The feeling is mutual, princess," I mutter as I stare through the blown-out window in the hope that Dane might just walk past like nothing ever happened and he was taking a piss.

I even look for Noble. Asshole.

"We need to find them, Rhett. Please."

She turns to me, her huge, dark eyes laced with fear and full of tears. "I-if they've been—" A sob swallows her words, and something inside my chest cracks open at the sound.

Sadie doesn't break down. Ever.

She's strong. So fucking strong. So seeing her like this fucking wrecks me.

"Okay," I agree, unable to deny that I also need to see that my best friend is alive and able to continue giving me shit.

We hang back as the rest of the club head outside behind Ray and Micky, and leaving the other old ladies and girlfriends behind, I tuck Sadie into my side and follow, praying to anyone that will listen that both of them are okay.

The scene before us as we step outside is one of pure devastation.

The vehicle that went up is obliterated, parts thrown

across the yard, the main chassis still on fire. There are bodies strewn around the place and my stomach twists. There's no way we haven't lost any brothers in all of this.

I just hope it's not the one I so desperately need to find.

We might be different in so many ways, and I might give him shit like I hate him most days, but Dane's my brother in all the ways that count. I couldn't imagine a life here without him.

I need him. And I know that the trembling girl in my arms needs him too.

Some of the jealousy that was within me abates in that moment, right as I realize just how strong her feelings for him are. She lifts her hand to swipe away a tear that's fallen onto her cheek.

"They'll be okay," I whisper, wishing I knew if my words were true or not.

Guys scream while others shout and run headfirst into the scene to help. As I scan the area, I see brothers at the compound entrance with their guns raised as if they think we're about to get ambushed, but that's not what this is.

This isn't an all-out attack. It's a message. One we've heard loud and fucking clear.

"Call a fucking ambulance," someone barks right as a blond head of hair catches my eye.

"Over there," I say to Sadie, pointing out where I just saw Noble.

She takes off before I have a chance to move and I run to catch up with her, fear still snaking through me that something else is going to happen. We need to get them and get the fuck away from here.

"Wes," she cries as she rounds a smoking part of whatever the fuck was blown up. "Are you—Dane. No. Oh God, no."

She drops to her knees beside Wes and reaches for my best friend. All the while I stand there, frozen by sheer panic.

"Dane. Fuck. Wake up. Please, wake up."

He's got blood and dirt all over his face, but other than that, he looks normal... in one piece.

She cups his dirty cheeks, willing him to come back to her. Noble looks up at me over her head, his own fear clear in his eyes.

"What the fuck happened?" I demand, needing to focus on something other than my best friend out cold on the ground in the middle of what looks like a fucking war zone.

"He followed the bitch out, the one who mouthed off to Sadie. I think he wanted to say his piece about the way she spoke to our princess." My teeth grind at the way he says 'our' but I force myself to put my issues aside for the moment. "He took off ahead of me but never made it, because that truck exploded."

A groan from the ground drags our eyes from the mess in front of us.

"Dane," Sadie breathes as I drop to my knees beside her.

"Stray, you good, bro?" I ask, needing to see some kind of life from him.

His lips part a beat before his eyes do and everything inside me relaxes.

"Y-yeah. Never better," he croaks out, his eyes firmly locked on Sadie. "Princess," he groans. "Gonna be my nurse, yeah?"

"Good to see your outstanding personality is still intact," I deadpan.

"You love it," he teases, finally looking over at me.

I don't respond, but I do hope he can read the truth in my eyes. I might never admit it, but fuck, yeah, I do love him.

"You okay to move?"

"Yeah, I think so," he groans, pushing onto his elbows to sit up with Sadie's help. "Holy shit," he gasps when he gets a look at the scene before him. Clearly the scent of burning, charred flesh, and people's screams wasn't enough to remind him of what just happened. "Is everyone okay?"

"We're only worried about you right now," Sadie says, refusing to let go of him.

"We need to help, we need to—"

"No," I bark. "We need to get you to your room and make sure you're really okay. I'll come back and help out here."

"But—"

"No fucking buts, Stray. Sadie needs you in one piece, so you'll do as you're fucking told."

He looks from me to her, and his body relaxes.

"Okay," he breathes, holding her stare and reaching for her hand. Although if his slight wince is anything to go by, the move hurts like hell.

"Are you hurt?"

"I got thrown against the wall. I'm pretty sure it's just bruising."

"If you're lying, I'll—"

"Sadie, girl, I'm okay. I promise. You won't get rid of me that easily." He winks, and I wait for her to hit him, but this time, she manages to refrain from chastising him.

I look up at Noble, who's watching us all with his brows pulled in concern.

"Ready?" I ask. He nods in agreement despite the fact that I'm sure he has no clue what he's agreeing to. "One arm each."

"Motherfucker," Dane barks the second we lift him from the floor.

"Quit being a pussy, Stray. You only hit a wall," I tease, as if anything about this is okay.

"Fuck you, Rhett. Fuck you. I got blown up."

"Yeah," I mutter as we move toward the clubhouse, Sadie rushing to push the door open for us, "his head is okay."

Only minutes later, Noble and I are lowering him to his bed. Sadie rushes to his side, playing her part as his personal nurse, pulling his shoes off and making sure he's comfortable.

"You okay, man?"

"Yeah, brother. You go help out."

I nod at him before briefly glancing at Noble in thanks and then Sadie.

"We'll look after him. Just be careful," she warns with narrowed eyes. "We don't want to come and have to collect you too."

"They've made their point. There won't be anything else tonight. He'll sit back and wait for us to retaliate."

"You sound a little too sure," Noble says, clearly not believing a word of it.

"Trust me, I'm aware of how a psycho biker's brain works."

Noble scoffs while Sadie and Dane openly laugh. "Yeah, don't we fucking know it," Dane murmurs as if it hurts him to talk.

"I'll check back in later. Be good." I look each of them in the eyes.

"He's hurt. What do you think we're going to do?"

I glance between Sadie and Dane. I'm more than aware of his penchant for watching, especially when Sadie is involved, so I wouldn't put anything past the three of them.

"Behave," I repeat.

"You're just worried you'll miss out on the fun."

My muscles tense at his words. I don't want it to be true, but it is. I want in on anything that has to do with Sadie Ray's pleasure.

"I won't be long."

I slip out of the room before I can come up with any more reasons why I should stay and keep an eye on the three of them.

As I walk back out to the yard, two ambulances come tearing through the gates, followed by two cop cars.

The medics rush toward the worst looking guys and immediately get to work while Micky captures Chief Statham's attention as he climbs out of one of the cars.

"Stray okay?" Ray asks, stepping up beside me.

"Yeah. Sadie and Noble are looking after him in his room. Thought it was the safest place for her."

"I'm not happy about this," he says again. He must have repeated that statement at least five times while Dane and I were in his office earlier. "But I do trust you both to protect her with your lives."

"None of us are going anywhere, Prez. Not today. We'll find this cunt and we'll take him out before he gets near any of us again, let alone Sadie."

"I really hope that's true, Savage. We can't have this happening again. We can't lose our men."

"Fatalities?"

"Two," he admits, pain laced through his voice.

"Fuck," I mutter, rubbing the back of my neck as I once again survey the scene around us.

"Everyone else has flesh wounds." He falls silent for a few moments as a brother is loaded onto a gurney and pushed into the back of an ambulance for treatment.

More sirens approach, and only seconds later a fire truck appears.

"We need to find out where that cunt is and put him down. I'm done being controlled by a fucking feral Reaper."

"You and me both, Prez. You and me both." I never thought I'd say it, but I want life to go back to normal. Which means I actually want to go back to school.

I help the guys tidy up the yard once the fire crew and Chief Statham give us the nod before following my brothers into the clubhouse for a very strong drink.

Something tells me we're going to need plenty of it,

because this is only the beginning. I can feel it, dread twisting up my stomach.

Darren Creed isn't going to give up this fight easily. He clearly wants something from us, and I get the impression it's more than just our blood...

And anything but his own death won't be good enough to put an end to it.

28

SADIE

By the time the cops leave, it's late. The mood in the clubhouse is somber as my dad and his friends—his family—mourn the loss of Cooper and Jango.

Wes rubs soothing circles on my knee as we sit on the banquette, watching my dad, Micky, Rhett, and some of the other guys discuss what to do next. I half expected him to call Church, but things are different now.

Darren has crossed a line. It's a declaration of war, and I know it'll only be a short time before they ride out to seek revenge.

A shiver goes through me, and Wes squeezes my thigh. "You hanging in there?" he asks me.

"Yeah, I'm okay." I force a smile.

"Sadie Ray." Dad calls me over, and I get up and go to him. He pulls me into his arms, dropping a kiss on my head. "I want you to get some rest, okay? The same goes for everyone else." His voice ripples around the room. "There's nothing more we can do tonight. This place is on lockdown;

nothing is coming in or out. Police Chief Statham is leaving some of his guys out front. We're safe, for now."

He tenses beside me, and I peek up at him, laying my head on his arm. Family, this club, is everything to my dad, so I know this is killing him. But he'll do what needs to be done to make sure Darren Creed is wiped off the face of the Earth.

"You're not going to go out there tonight, right?" I ask him quietly.

Rhett catches my eye, something passing between us. He wants to go after Darren, I see it simmering in his murderous gaze. And I don't blame him. Part of me wants to go after him too. But I know my limitations, and what happened tonight proves Darren isn't just out to make a noise.

He's out to destroy the Sinners.

A commotion behind us draws my attention, and I watch as some of our guys file out of the hall, armed to the teeth with an array of firearms. They each nod to my dad and then slip out of the clubhouse, no doubt to take up their posts around the compound for the night.

The cops might be guarding us beyond the gate, but Sinners protect their own. It's how it's always been, how it always will be.

"Didn't think I'd see this again in my lifetime," Dad murmurs, and I hug him tighter.

I know what he's thinking. He's thinking there will be more bloodshed before this is over, and all I can do is pray it isn't anyone I care about. Because if I lost him or Rhett, Dane or Wes, I don't know what I'd do.

"Watch her," Dad says to Rhett, handing me over to him.

Rhett wraps a possessive arm around my waist and guides me back toward our friends. Quinn and River are with the old ladies, huddled around a table, holding each other. Aunt Dee and Rosita will make sure everyone has somewhere to sleep tonight—not that it will come easy for anyone.

"Riv," Rhett calls, and she walks over to us. He reaches for her. "I want you with me tonight, okay?"

She nods.

"You and Pretty Boy can bunk in with Dane." Rhett gazes down at me.

"Yeah, okay." I lean up and graze my mouth against his. He stills but then melts into the kiss, sliding his tongue past my lips to tangle it with mine.

We have an audience, but I don't care. He could have been hurt earlier. Dane *was* hurt.

"Promise me you won't do anything reckless."

"I'll be right here with River, I swear."

With a small nod, I take Wes's hand and lead him to find Dane. He went to get cleaned up, so it's hardly a surprise we find him in his room, just coming out of the shower.

"I... shit, let me get dressed," he blurts out, ducking back into the bathroom.

Wes shoots me a knowing look, and my stomach churns at the image of the scars littering his back. But he doesn't ask, and I don't offer up any details; it's not my story to tell.

"I should probably call my mom," he says. "She's been blowing up my cell."

"What will you tell her?"

"I'll think of something. Don't worry about it." He digs his cell phone out of his pocket before dropping down on the small couch.

I knock on the bathroom door. "Dane, are you okay in there?"

"Yeah."

But he doesn't sound okay.

I try the handle and find it unlocked, so I slip inside. "Hey."

"Hey." He grimaces with pain.

"You're hurt."

"I'll live." His t-shirt is clutched between his fingers as he braces himself over the sink.

"Your back," I say, noticing the fresh grazes.

"Yeah, the blast must have ripped open the new skin."

I move closer, ghosting my fingers over the angry red welts, but I don't mention the old scars. He'll tell me when he's ready.

Pressing my body into Dane's, careful not to touch his injuries, I slide my arms around his waist and rest my cheek on his arm.

"Why is he doing this?" I whisper over the lump in my throat.

"Because he's a fucking psycho hell-bent on revenge." His eyes meet mine in the mirror, swirling with anger.

I still can't shake the feeling that we're missing something. But Dane seems so weary I don't want to bring it up.

"We should get some rest," I suggest.

"What's Pretty Boy doing?"

"Calling his mom."

"Do you think she's okay with his old man? I can't help but think we shouldn't have left her there."

"Wes says she is. It's not really our place to get involved. His dad hates the club; if he finds out Wes is here..." I trail off, hoping that day never comes.

Turning toward me, Dane laces his arm around me and gazes down. "He's going to find out, princess. You need to be ready for that, and so does he." His eyes go to the door.

"Yeah, I know."

But hopefully it will happen after things have calmed down with Darren and the Reapers.

"Come on, let's go to bed."

"What about Wes?" I worry my lip, fighting a smile.

"He can take the couch." His lips come down on mine. "I want to hold you, Sadie, girl. I need to."

"Yeah, okay."

Wes is speaking to his mom in hushed tones when we enter the bedroom again. He looks up, offering me a small smile.

"Yeah, Mom. I know... No, as long as you're okay. Okay, be safe. I love you... Yeah, bye." He hangs up and runs a hand through his hair. "She's okay."

Relief sinks into me. "That's good. Where does she think you are?"

"Staying at a friend's. Dad is away for the night on business." He notices the way Dane is holding me and smirks. "I guess I'm sleeping here then." He points at the couch.

"You don't have—"

"It's cool. After the day we've had, I think I could sleep for a week." He stretches out and shoves a cushion behind his head.

I ease out of Dane's arms and go to him, kneeling down and brushing the strands of hair from his eyes. "Thanks, for today. For being here."

Wes cups my face, brushing his thumb along my cheekbone. "I'm not going anywhere, princess." He captures my mouth in a searing kiss, one that makes my heart flutter wildly. "Get some rest," he breathes. "I'll be right here."

"Night, Pretty Boy," Dane chuckles, but I hear the strain there. Today has taken its toll on everyone.

I hit the light switch, plunging the room into darkness. Dane turns on the bedside lamp and climbs into bed, patting the space beside him. I strip down to my underwear and slide in next to him, curling into his side. His arm wraps around me tightly, tucking me close to his body.

"You think you can sleep?" I ask him.

"Nah, not yet. But you should try." He drops a kiss on my head. "Pretty Boy is right—we're both here, and we're not going anywhere."

They're the last words I hear before sleep claims me.

"No... no, stop. Please..."

I wake confused, my eyes straining against the darkness.

"*It hurts... please, no. No!*" Dane thrashes beside me and I lurch into action, grabbing his arms and trying to gently calm him.

"Dane," I soothe, "you're dreaming. Wake up, I'm here. I'm right here."

His body succumbs to me waking him and his eyes flicker open. "S-Sadie?"

"You were having a nightmare again."

"I... shit." He heaves a ragged breath, dragging a hand down his face. "I didn't hurt you, did I?"

"No. I'm fine."

"And Pretty Boy?" Shame washes over him.

"Out like a light." I glance over at Wes again, smiling at how cute he looks draped over the too-small couch.

"Want to talk about it?" I ask, tracing the planes of his chest with my finger.

"I-I don't remember much."

"Can I ask you something?" He nods. "The scars... do you think—"

"They've always been there," he admits. "Ever since I can remember."

"But you don't know how you got them?"

"No. It's like... it's like there's a wall in my mind. I can clearly recall arriving at the compound. I remember being so scared... Your dad was like this big terrifying monster, but I felt safe with him."

"Who brought you here?"

"That's the thing, I don't know. I see her face, but I don't know her. That's weird, right?"

"You were young." And he had obviously sustained some kind of neglect or abuse.

My heart aches just thinking about it.

"You know you said you recognized Justin..."

"Yeah?"

"Well, I've been thinking, and I can't shake the feeling—"

"Uh, what's happening?" Wes bolts upright, startling me.

"Relax, Pretty Boy," Dane chuckles. "We're all good."

"What the— Dane? Sadie?"

I chuckle this time. "You should go back to sleep. It's the middle of the night."

"Y-yeah," he croaks, barely lucid. Wes shifts and shuffles, getting comfortable, and then his gentle snores fill the room again.

Dane runs his nose along my jaw and steals a kiss. "He'd be useless in a crisis."

"Oh, I don't know. He's handling everything okay so far." I lay my hands on his chest, burrowing closer. "We'll all come out of this alive, right?"

I refuse to allow the fear circling me to strike.

"I don't want to make promises I can't keep, Sadie, girl." Dane's voice wavers. "But know that we'll do everything to catch that son of a bitch and make sure he pays for hurting you."

"It's not just me I'm worried about," I admit. "I can't lose you, Dane." My hand trails up his neck and curves around his shoulder. "Any of you."

"And you won't. But this life, Sadie, girl... it's not always smooth sailing."

"I know." God, I know that.

"Close your eyes. Tomorrow things are gonna get kinda crazy around here. We should sleep while we can."

We hold each other like it might be the last time.

But I refuse to believe that, not when I've only just found them.

29

DANE

The room is still silent when I wake the next morning.

Despite my nightmare, I slept pretty well. Although, I already know that it won't be well enough for what today is going to throw at us.

Reaching over, I grab my cell from my nightstand and look at the time.

Almost midday.

I guess the entire compound had a late one followed by a fitful night's sleep if everyone is still tucked away in their rooms.

Pushing up on my elbow, I stare down at the woman sleeping beside me, my chest aching at the sight of her.

Sadie Ray Dalton.

As kids, she was my best friend. I arrived here at the compound with nothing but the clothes on my back. I had —still have—no clue where I came from or who left me here. I see the face of a woman sometimes, mostly in my dreams, but I can't put a name to her or even a place. Just a soft, kind face of someone who I know looked after me.

She's the only one there was, of that, I'm sure. The other faces I see aren't as clear. They're just dark blurs, hidden in shadows, hiding from me, just like my memories. What I remember all too well, though, is the pain and the smell. I remember there being a knife and a lighter. I remember feeling the slice of the sharp blade down my back, the trickle of blood as it leaked from the wound. I remember the burn of the flame on my ribs, the scorching metal from the lighter pressed into my skin.

Every time I wake from one of those nightmares, my body aches with the pain as if it's just happened. The scars feel raw, the blisters almost unbearable. The second I come around and realize that it's all a dream, that it's all in the past, it doesn't get any better. I feel it for hours after. Even more so if it's dark. That's exactly why I usually sleep with the light on. Even as an eighteen-year-old man, I have to have the light on. Or Sadie beside me, it seems. Because aside from last night, I've never had a nightmare with her here.

She makes everything easier, calmer; she makes me wish like hell that I never left her side when we were kids. But Rhett and I got closer, and as puberty hit, we had more in common than Sadie and me, and the two of us grew apart.

I can't help but wonder how much easier those early teen years would have been if she was still by my side, holding my hand when things got rough. And being a boy with no memory of who he was, where he came from or what his real name even was, there were some hella dark days.

My eyes continue to track over her features as I think about the things she keeps asking me about the past. I know it's my fault because I confessed to Justin affecting me somehow, but she's bringing it all back up. She's only trying to help, trying to get to the bottom of all of this. But I keep thinking that she's putting two and two together and coming out with fifteen.

Why would they want the two of us? It was a coincidence that we were together that day on my bike, but the photo in her locker was of us. The Reapers have no reason to go after me. Hell, I don't even know who I am; I very much doubt they do.

Movement on the other side of the room catches my eye, and when I look up, I find Noble also staring at a sleeping Sadie. "She still out?"

"Yeah," I breathe. "She needs it."

"Yeah, we should probably let her rest..." Something wicked flashes in his eyes, and I can't help but get excited at the sight of it.

"Or we could—"

"Give her a wake up she'll never forget."

"I like your thinking, Pretty Boy." I smirk. "Maybe she's onto something, bringing you into the mix."

He shakes his head as he silently rolls from the couch and pulls his shirt over his head, letting it drop to the floor.

Unlike Rhett and I, his skin is clear of any ink, something I'm sure we'll have to address if he plans on sticking around. But he's also free of any scars. Tan, ripped, and smooth, his body is so perfect that I can't help the wave of jealousy that washes through me.

I hate my scars, and until I find answers for why they're there, I'm not sure I'm ever going to be able to accept them, to own them as part of me.

Stepping up to the bed, he peels back the sheets at her feet, exposing her body. "Damn," he hisses at the sight of her in nothing but her black lace lingerie.

"We're lucky motherfuckers, bro," I mutter, as he kneels on the bed, wrapping his hands around her ankles and parting her legs.

She moans softly in her sleep and falls onto her back.

"Ready?" he whispers.

"Always. Let's make her scream."

I watch for a beat as Noble kisses up her inner thigh before I tuck my finger under the lace of her bra, exposing her already hard nipple to me. I wonder if she's dreaming of us.

Lowering my head, I flick her peak with the tip of my tongue as Wes hits the juncture of her thighs. "No backing out now," I chuckle.

His shoulders shake with a laugh.

No, I wouldn't be going anywhere if I were in his position either.

His finger dips under the lace covering her sweet pussy before he pulls it away, exposing her to him. Our eyes connect and we both move, him licking up her slit and me sucking her nipple deep into my mouth.

Sadie startles not a second later, her body jolting beneath us. "What the— holy shit," she gasps, her eyes wide as she looks down at the pair of us enjoying her body.

None of us move for a few seconds as she comes to her senses. But when she does, she falls back, her body relaxing once more. "Best morning ever," she breathes. "Please, continue."

Deep laughter rumbles in my chest as I take her back in my mouth, my other hand reaching out to expose her other breast and teasing that one too.

"Oh God," she cries. "Fuck." Her body is now fully awake and on board with the situation. "*Yes!*"

Her back arches and her hips roll as her hands find their way into our hair, holding us both tightly against her body.

"I'm not coming without you both," she pants. "You'd better get there too."

Not needing to be told twice, I push my hand into my boxers, pulling out my aching cock, jerking myself off as I tease her.

"Fuck, I'm so close."

"Me too, princess," I groan, kissing up her chest and sucking on her neck.

Her eyes lock with mine before dropping to my hand. "Mouth," she demands. "I want to taste you."

As I scramble to my feet to do as she orders, she glances at Wes. "Pussy. Now."

He moves even quicker than I do, and in seconds she's full of both of us as we all race toward our releases.

My back stings like a bitch where I collided with that wall last night, but fuck if the sight of her lips wrapped around my cock doesn't help.

"Yes, yes. Dane...Wes. Fuck. *Yes*," she cries as her orgasm hits her.

Two seconds later, I come down her throat with her name, a plea on my lips as Wes fills her pussy. Satiated, the three of us collapse on the bed.

"Well, it's safe to say that today is already better than yesterday," Sadie pants, her fingers laced with both of ours.

"I could get used to this whole lockdown thing, you know," Pretty Boy murmurs. "We never even have to leave this room."

The moment dissipates, the reality of what we're about to face descending over us like a dark storm cloud.

"As amazing as that sounds, I'm going to have a job to do very soon in the hope of putting an end to all this bullshit."

"Fuck, yeah. I'm sorry. I didn't mean to—"

"Chill, Pretty Boy. We're all good."

"Okay, well, while you two bicker, I'm going to shower." Sadie smiles, but it doesn't quite reach her eyes. Although we can distract ourselves with each other, it doesn't erase the fact that we're in the middle of a shitstorm that's only set to get worse before it gets better.

"Want company?" I ask, watching as she tucks her tits away and climbs from the bed.

She looks between the two of us. "You two want to shower together?"

Wes and I glance at each other.

"Maybe another time," he says.

I mean, I'm not opposed to the idea. Sadie naked, wet, covered in bubbles between the two of us... sounds like my sort of fun. But Wes is probably right. We've already enjoyed ourselves too much this morning, given the circumstances.

"Okay, well..." She walks to my bathroom, her ass swaying in her tiny thong making my cock harden for her once more.

"Damn, she's hot," Pretty Boy mutters, although I'm sure he didn't actually mean to say it out loud.

"Told you, man. Lucky motherfuckers."

The two of us get up and pull on some clothes while she showers. When Rhett storms in a few minutes later, he finds me resting against my headboard, trying to ignore the pain in my back, while Noble sits on the couch with his cell in his hands.

"Where is she?" he asks in panic, as if we'd ever actually let her out of our sight.

"Shower. She's—"

"Look after River," he demands, dragging his sister into the room and storming toward the bathroom. "Put some music on. My sister doesn't need to hear this."

"How about we go and find some breakfast?" I suggest, also not really wanting to sit here awkwardly while Rhett fucks Sadie in the shower.

"Sounds like a plan, man. I'm starving," Noble says, jumping to his feet.

The scent of smoky bacon hits my nose the second we enter the hallway, and by the time we get down to the clubhouse where Dee and Rosita are serving up, my mouth is watering and my stomach is growling.

"Morning, kids," Dee chimes as she starts loading up plates for us, and my respect ratchets for one of the women who holds this club together in a time of crisis "Sleep well?"

"As well as could be expected."

"You doing okay?" she asks me, her eyes narrowing in concern.

"Yep, just a few scratches. Nothing to worry about. How's everyone else?"

"The clubhouse is a sadder place this morning, Stray..." She trails off, swiping her eyes before pasting on a weak smile. "Jango and Cooper will be hugely missed."

"That they will."

"Stray," a familiar deep voice booms. "Where the fuck is my daughter?" Ray steps up to me, looking between the two of us.

"Uh, she's with Rhett, Prez. No need to get your panties in a twist." I smile. "We've got her under control."

He scoffs. "I very much doubt that. You've met my Sadie, right? Part of me isn't surprised it takes three of you to handle her."

I stare at him, dumbfounded. I guess that's where Sadie gets her attitude from when shit gets hard—just laughs it all off and hopes for the best.

I guess it's not all that different to how I handle stuff either.

"We're all meeting in thirty," he grumbles. "Got some big decisions to make today. Make sure Savage is ready to go. Pretty Boy, can you control Sadie while we meet?"

"Of course. I know how to handle your daughter, sir."

Ray's lips flatten. "I'm not sure if that's a good thing or not, son."

He holds Pretty Boy's eyes for a beat before spinning

on his heels and demanding his main men stop stuffing their faces and follow him to Church.

30

SADIE

My dad and the guys are gone for what feels like forever. My leg jostles up and down as Wes sits with me, Quinn, and River, while the wives and girlfriends prepare yet another buffet table.

If there's anything I've learned growing up in the club, it's that no matter what is going on, bikers need the three F's: food, fast rides, and fucking.

The world could be ending, and there'd still be time to ride hard, stuff your face with Rosita's infamous taco salad, and fuck until you see stars.

It's club life.

But I'm grateful to be here, surrounded by the only people who know what it's like.

Growing up, I never considered becoming an old lady. I always wanted to be the first female member of the club. Princess turned queen. But now, I just want my family, the guys I care about, to make it out of this thing alive and unharmed.

We've already lost two good men; I can't stand the thought that we might lose more before this thing is over.

It's why I didn't protest this morning when Dane and Wes woke me up with their lips and teeth and tongues. Or when Rhett joined me in the shower, making me come on his tongue before fucking me against the tiles. Life is precious. Even more so when you live by a different code to the rest of society.

"They'll be okay," Wes says, gently rubbing my knee. I flick my eyes to his and smile weakly.

"I know."

Because anything else is simply not an option. But Dane has already been hurt twice. And it could have been him or Wes in Cooper and Jango's places yesterday.

It could have been any of us.

A shiver runs through me, but then a commotion sounds down the hall, demanding my attention. Guys start filing into the room. The married ones go to their wives, hugging and kissing them, while the others break out a fresh bottle of whiskey.

I guess whatever was decided wasn't good.

"Daddy!" I leap up when he appears ahead of Rhett and Dane.

"Come here, sweetheart." He pulls me up and into his arms. "We got a lead, Sadie Ray. Ritz reckons he knows where Darren is hiding out. We roll out within the hour."

Fear like I've never known clamps down on my heart like a vise.

"Ritz is going to ride with you?" I ask, because more guys mean better odds of catching Darren and his crew.

"Yeah, we're going to wait for him and his guys to cross into town, and then we end this."

I inhale sharply, my attention going to Rhett and Dane. They both look fierce, bloodlust shining in their eyes. My knees go weak at the knowledge that it's all for me and our club. They'll do whatever they need to do to make sure we're safe.

To make sure *I'm* safe.

"Pitbull and Pacman are going to stay here with a couple of the other guys. Dee and Rosita know the drill. Nobody comes in or out until we're back. River, come here, sweetheart."

I step aside, letting him hug her. She looks terrified, her bottom lip wobbling as he whispers something to her. Nodding, she hugs my dad tight, and this time, I feel none of the jealousy I did before.

This is bigger than me or her or what my dad did with Julia. This is about our family. She and Rhett already lost their dad at the hands of the Reapers. I know she doesn't want to lose him too.

"Come here, Riv," I say to her, offering her my hand. She takes it and I wrap my arm around her. "It'll be okay."

River nods, too choked up to reply. She rejoins Jax, who looks as fierce as Rhett and Dane, and I know he'll protect her with his life.

"Pretty Boy," Dad says, and Wes shoots up. "I need you to do something for me."

"Anything, sir."

"I need you to watch out for my girls while we're gone."

"You have my word."

"You ever handle a gun, kid?"

Wes's brows knit. "My dad and I used to go to the range, but it's been a while. I'm probably rusty."

"Rhett, Stray, find him a piece and take him out back to show him how it works."

"Daddy, is that really necessary?" I balk.

"It's okay," Wes says. "I want to do this. I want to help."

"Right answer." Dad claps him on the shoulder. "I need to go handle some things, but when this is over, you and I need to sit down and talk."

Wes nods, but I don't miss the way his eyes flash with fear.

If we weren't in such dire circumstances, I'd probably laugh at how cute he looks, scared of my big bad biker dad.

"Come on," Rhett says. "Time to see what you're made of, Pretty Boy." He smirks, and it makes my stomach dip.

I wouldn't miss this for the world.

The mood is tense as Rhett and Dane show Wes how to use the gun. After a couple of attempts, he gets the hang of it, but his aim is all off.

"Go again," Rhett demands. "You need to actually hit your target if you're going to be useful."

"Rhett," I warn. "He's trying."

"Yeah, lighten up, Savage. I don't remember you being such a good shot when we first started carrying."

"That was different," he grumbles, correcting Wes's stance for the third time.

Wes shakes him off. "I've got it." He pulls the trigger, and while it's better, it's still not great. "Fuck, I really thought I had it this time."

"Keep trying, Pretty Boy," Dane snickers. "But if anything happens, you just shoot at anyone who comes through those doors that isn't wearing a Sinners cut or a police badge."

Rhett pulls out a pack of smokes and presses one to his lips. I hop down off the stack of tires and saunter over to him. "Didn't anyone ever tell you those things will kill you?"

"There's a lot of things that can send you to an early grave in this life, princess." He lights up the end and inhales a deep hit, holding it in his lungs for a second before grabbing the back of my neck and sealing his mouth over mine as he exhales. The bitter taste hits my lungs and I almost choke, but there's something so erotic about the way he holds me that I don't.

"Now maybe we can go together." He pulls away, sucking his smoke again.

"Rhett, don't say that."

His jaw clenches. "Fuck, I'm sorry... I just..."

"Yeah." I run my hands up his solid chest. "I know. I need you both to come back to me."

He flicks his smoke to the ground and hooks his arm around my waist, pulling me closer. Dropping his head to mine, he inhales deeply. "We don't plan on going anywhere, princess. I promise."

"Look out for him." My eyes go to where Dane is

showing off to Wes with his gun. "I still can't shake the feeling we're missing something, and he's been... distracted."

"What do you mean?" Rhett asks.

"What do you know about Dane's background?" I ask. "I mean, before he came here."

"As much as everyone else. Your dad found him outside the compound. He had no ID, there was no note, nothing."

"I know it sounds crazy, but what if—"

"Rhett, Stray," Dad booms across the compound. "Let's roll."

Rhett grips me tighter, his eyes darker than usual. "Promise me you'll stay here, no matter what happens. Do not leave this compound, Sadie Ray."

I nod, overwhelmed by the intensity in his voice. Tears prick my eyes as I curl my hands into his leather cut. "Be safe." Please God, keep them safe.

A tear slides free, and Rhett catches it with his thumb. "No goodbyes."

"No goodbyes," I say, leaning up to kiss him. It's hard and bruising, and by the time he pulls away, I'm breathless and aching.

"Don't hog our girl," Dane says, joining us. I go to him, wrapping my arms around his waist.

"Look out for each other."

"Relax, Sadie, girl. We'll find Creed, put a bullet through his brain, and end this shit before anything comes of it. You'll see." He drops a kiss on my head. "I love you, Sadie Ray Dalton," he says as if it's the simplest thing in the world. "I think I've loved you ever since we were kids."

"Now?" I shriek, swatting his chest. "You choose *now* to tell me that?"

He chuckles, yanking me back into his arms and burying his face in the crook of my neck. "I love you, princess. Deal with it."

I'm aware of Rhett and Wes watching us, watching Dane act as if he didn't just change our dynamic... again.

I care about him. I care about all of them... but love?

That's something I haven't allowed myself to think about, not yet. Not so soon after convincing them all that this—the three of us—is what I want.

I peek over at Rhett, but his expression is a stone mask. "We should go," he says, barely looking at me.

My stomach sinks.

"I want you naked and waiting for us when we get back," Dane whispers. "There's something about blood and violence that gets me horny as fuck."

Swatting Dane's chest again, I gawk at him, but he only smirks.

"Pretty Boy, take care of our girl while we're gone."

"You know it." Wesley steps up to me, wrapping his arm around me and pulling me into his side as I stand there and fight the building tears.

Rhett and Dane don't look back, focused solely on the task at hand. But as I watch my guys leave, I can't shake the feeling that this isn't the end.

It's just the beginning.

31

DANE

Rhett's glare burns into the side of my face as we walk toward where the rest of our brothers are waiting to head out to find this motherfucker. Sadie watches our every step, her attention making my already aching body tingle with awareness.

I hadn't intended on saying what I did to her. It was a spur of the moment thing fueled by the unease I'm feeling about what's going to go down today.

I'm not usually one to give a shit, mostly happy to run into any kind of fucked-up situation without giving it a second thought. But recently, since Sadie, everything is different.

For the first time, I'm starting to feel like I know who the real Dane Stray is.

He's not just some abandoned kid no one wanted. I'm Sadie's, and she's mine, and fuck if that doesn't mean everything to me right now.

My life has always been built on the knowledge that I'm only here because the club felt sorry for me, because they didn't know what else to do with me. I know they love me, that I belong here. But Sadie has chosen me for me, because of who I am. And that—

I bite down on my knuckles, a wave of emotion racing through me and begging me to turn around to be with her.

I trust Pretty Boy to look after her. He might be a shit shot, but I know he won't go down without a fight. She's as important to him as she is to me, and he gets that. I just... I don't want to leave her. Even if I'm protecting her by leaving. By finally putting a bullet through this cunt's head.

"What?" I finally bark when I can't cope with Rhett's interest any longer.

"You fucking love her?" he asks. I knew it's what was bothering him. I saw it in the way his body jolted when he heard me say the words.

"Yeah," I say simply. Because it is simple. I fucking love her, and what I said to her was true. I think I always have. "Don't worry, brother. She's not expecting a confession out of you anytime soon."

His eyes widen in shock, telling me what I already know. Rhett has barely acknowledged his feelings about her; he's far from confessing his love yet. But that's okay, these things can take time. Despite what he's fighting, I already know he loves her. I see it in the way he stares at her when he thinks no one is looking. His jealousy, his possessiveness. He's totally fucking gone for her. He just needs to wait for his brain to catch up with his heart and to listen to the damn thing for once.

"Or ever," he scoffs, making me laugh. "What?"

"Nothing, man. Nothing at all. Let's just focus on the task ahead, huh?"

"This cunt is dying today."

"Agreed, brother. Agreed."

Ray nods at us as we approach. "You boys ready?"

"Always, Prez," I say.

"More than ready." Rhett nods as he tugs on his helmet and throws his leg over his bike.

We already know the plan; we went over it in Church. The Reapers are due over the border any minute. We'll join them and then we'll go hunt this motherfucker down until he's no longer breathing the same air as us. Until he's no longer a threat to the club...

Or our princess.

After a few words from Ray, the rumble of our engines fills the compound and we set off across town. My body aches from the blow yesterday. I might not have been badly injured, but I collided pretty hard with the wall when the explosion happened. Holding my bike steady is harder than usual as my muscles burn, begging to be relaxed.

Just as they agreed, we meet with the Reapers.

It's the first time in my lifetime that I've known the two MCs working together like this. We might have had a truce since the war a few years back, and things have been amicable, but not to this level. It just shows how big a threat Darren is to both our princess and the Reapers' future.

I can't deny it's nice, being surrounded by brothers from both clubs, fighting for the same cause.

We park down the street from the address Ritz gave us before heading toward the old rundown house we believe Creed is hiding inside. Our guys surround the place as Rhett and I move around the back with a couple of Reapers. We all share a silent look, and, after a countdown of three, Rhett blows the door handle off and storms inside.

Screams pierce the air as the people who were inside jump to their feet, taking cover. I notice a woman grab a child and duck behind the couch.

This ain't right, a little voice inside tells me.

Ritz has been fed bogus intel.

I cover the door with a Reaper Prospect and watch the chaos as both Ray and Ritz try to calm the situation down with the residents of the house losing their shit.

This was not how today was meant to go. But I guess it explains why that dread was sitting heavy in my stomach earlier.

This is a setup.

It has to be. And we've left Sadie behind with little protection.

Glancing across the room, my eyes lock with Rhett's, and I see the same concern in his blue depths.

This isn't good.

Once we've got the situation inside the house under control, we all head outside.

"I don't like this, Prez," Rhett says to Ray the second we reach him. "What if it's a diversion... what if that fuck plans to attack—"

"The intel was solid," Ritz says, cutting him off. "I don't know what to say."

"You sure about that?" Rhett gets all up in his face. "Because if you played—"

"Whoa, easy there, son." Ray wedges himself between Rhett and the Reaper VP. "Ritz came to us with this. We gotta trust that."

"And you're willing to put Sadie's life on it?"

Ray scrubs his jaw, indecision flickering in his eyes. "Pike," he barks, "call Pacman and get an update on the compound."

"Consider it done, Prez."

"I swear to God, Ray, if Darren's sending us on a wild goose chase, I had no fucking idea."

Rhett bristles and I move closer, ready to intervene. The last thing we need is him and Ritz going head to head while Darren runs circles around us.

"No sign of trouble at the compound." Pike strolls toward us. "The place is locked down tight."

Relief slams into me and Rhett visibly relaxes.

"Okay, let's just take a second." Ray slaps Ritz on the shoulder. "We need to find this motherfucker before he does any more damage. Let's head to those other locations your guys have come up with, and if there's no sign, we'll just have to keep searching."

The group splits into two, Rhett going with Ray and me going with Ritz so we can check both places faster. After this bust, I don't think any of us are expecting him to be at either location, but hopefully we'll get a clue as to where the prick is actually hiding.

In minutes we're taking off again, Prez and Rhett's crew heading back toward our side of town while I follow Ritz toward the Red Ridge border.

I ride at the back of the group all the way to a warehouse that doesn't settle anything inside me. My eyes scan the surrounding woodland, aware that anyone could be hiding in the shadows waiting for us.

We pull to a stop, and as the others climb from their bikes, they also look around nervously.

"I don't like this, VP," one of the Reapers says, clearly feeling the same unease I am.

"We'll check it out then move on if it's a bust. We're sitting ducks right now," Ritz says, agreeing with his brother.

Ritz nods at us and we climb from our bikes, pulling out our guns and heading toward the warehouse. I follow instructions and head inside while a few others remain outside.

The place is deserted. I have no idea if it's a Reapers warehouse or what, but it's clear he's not here.

"This is bullshit," Ritz spits. "He's fucking playing us. We're smarter than that psycho. Why can't we get ahead of him?"

I stare at the Reapers VP. He looks exhausted with swollen, dark circles under his eyes. The stress with his father plus Darren going rogue is clearly getting to him.

"We'll get him, Ritz. He'll fuck up at some point and we'll take him and his guys down. They're not going to take this club. Not over my dead body," Crank, his Sergeant-at-Arms, growls, his own anger and frustration over this cat and mouse chase obvious in his tight expression.

"Let's get out of here, head back. Regroup."

Ritz turns to me and my brothers beside me. "We're

gonna find him. And when we do, we're going to kill him."

"Damn fucking right," I state, holding his eyes so he can see how serious we are.

Ritz takes off toward the door, more than happy to leave the damp and dusty warehouse, and we all take off after him.

"This place gives me the creeps," Munster says beside me. "I feel like I'm being watched." He visibly shudders.

"He's playing us," I say, confident that we're currently just pawns in the sick bastard's game. But until he plays his hand, we're unable to take control.

"I hope Prez has had more luck."

"Yeah," I mutter, although I don't have a lot of hope. They're going to have been led on a wild goose chase as well. I'd put money on it.

"Few more days in lockdown it is, then. At least we've got a few club whores to keep us company. We can't all be banging the—"

I'm on him before he's even realized he's said the words out loud. His back collides with the wall as I fist his shirt, my nose only a breath away from him. "What the fuck were you about to say?" I seethe in his face.

"I—"

My arm trembles with the strength I need to keep my hold on him. "Keep your fucking thoughts to yourself. And if I ever hear you say anything like that about my girl again, I'll fucking kill you. You got that?"

He nods once and I release him, shaking my arm out at my side.

"You okay, bro?" he asks, immediately putting our little moment behind him.

"Yeah, I'm good. Let's get out of this shithole."

Turning around, I find that everyone has already left, leaving the space even more ominous than before. "Fucking hell," I mutter, heading for the door with my gun hanging from my fingers.

Right when I hit the entrance, someone yells, and all hell breaks loose.

Dark bodies jump from the undergrowth with guns as Sinners and Reapers alike begin shooting in retaliation. The sound of the gunfire pierces through me, my body jolting with each one as I watch bodies fall and blood begin to soak into the gravel beneath them.

"Holy shit," Munster shouts, but before either of us can pull up our weapons, gunshots land in the building beside us.

More guys emerge from the shadows. They easily outnumbered us even before they took half of us down. We don't stand a fucking chance.

I fucking knew this was wrong. I knew today was going to go to shit.

Raising my arm, I fire off rounds to my left as I try to duck around the side of the building to find some cover, but there's nowhere to hide. We're completely out in the open, exposed. Exactly like I feared. Sitting ducks ready to be taken down one by one.

I look over just as Munster hits the ground, clutching his shoulder in agony as blood oozes from it. My heart thunders in my chest, sweat coating my body. I've been in some seriously fucked-up situations over the years.

Ambushes. Fights I wasn't sure I'd get out of. But none of them were like this.

This is a fucking massacre.

Just as I think the word, a bike explodes to my right, sending bodies flying, some screaming in pain. One of the guys in all black turns on me and I get one second to look him dead in the eyes.

I gasp as a memory hits me.

I know him.

But how? And who is he?

He takes a step closer and raises his gun.

Fuck. This is it.

This is where I die.

32

SADIE

"Fold," Quinn says, chucking in her cards.

"I'm out too." I do the same, checking my cell phone for the hundredth time.

"Relax, sweetie," Aunt Dee says, eyeing me from her position perched at the bar. "It's only been a couple of hours."

"Yeah, I know." But it doesn't stop me from worrying my lip.

"They'll be okay," Wes says quietly, running his hand up my thigh. My eyes shutter as I succumb to his touch. He's been right here beside me since the guys left.

"River takes the pot, again," Jax mumbles, shoving the pile of poker chips toward her.

"You sure you've never played this before?" Quinn asks.

"I promise. It must be beginners' luck."

"Somethin' like that," Jax shoots her a grin but doesn't let it linger. He's cooled off with her a lot recently, but I see the way she watches him with longing in her eyes.

If we all make it out of this okay, I'm going to talk to Rhett about letting her and Jax explore whatever's going on between them. Life's too short to waste by not going after what you want.

Jax is a good guy. Sure, he might be a prospect, but so is Dane. That's how the club works. But it won't be like that forever. One day, they'll both patch in.

My cell phone vibrates and relief splashes inside me, but when I check the message, it's Kel asking if we're going to be at the Arches this weekend.

I don't text him back. It's not like I can broadcast our current situation. Of course, when shit goes down, it'll probably be plastered in the local news by Monday, but it's always a bunch of hearsay and conjecture.

"I need to get a drink," I say, nudging Wes to let me out.

"I can go," he offers.

"No, I need a second."

He gives me a nod, moving aside to let me out. I go to the bar and Aunt Dee frowns. "If you think I'm going to serve you—"

"Soda is fine." It isn't, not really, but getting ass over elbow drunk right now isn't going to do anyone any favors. So I accept a soda and crack it open.

"I hate this."

"Don't we all," she says.

"How do you do it?"

"I knew what I was signing up for when I got with Micky." Her lips curve with nostalgia. "Your dad would have let me walk away from the life. He wanted more for me. Your granddaddy too. But I knew what I wanted, and Micky was it."

She wipes down the counter. "Once you're in the life, you have to take the rough with the smooth. And I only had one guy to deal with." She pins me with a knowing look. "You know, Sadie Ray, I've watched you grow into a determined, strong young woman. But I hope to God you know what you're doing with the three of them."

"I can handle it."

Soft laughter bubbles in her chest. "I don't doubt it. If anything, I think it's them who need to be worried about handling you. But Rhett alone is—"

"He would never hurt me." Not unless I wanted him to, or unless it was going to guarantee me a mind-blowing orgasm.

"Anyone can see he's fiercely protective of you. But he's an alpha. They tend not to share their toys very well."

"Good thing I'm not his toy then, isn't it?" I smirk.

"Shit, sweetie, listen to your—"

"Look, Aunt Dee, I know it isn't conventional, and I know most of you won't agree or understand, but I care about them. All of them. I didn't plan on this, but I'm not going to deny myself either."

Something like admiration shimmers in her eyes. "You grew up good, sweetie. And your momma, God bless her soul, would be real proud of the woman you've become."

There goes my good mood. I don't need validation from a woman who didn't care enough to stick around.

"Shit, Sadie, I'm—"

"It's all good." I stand and drain my can of soda. "I just want today to be over with."

"Don't we all, sweetie." She stares at the door. "Don't we all."

"I can't do another round," I grumble, folding my arms over my chest. It's been hours.

Hours of waiting, wondering what's happening.

I feel like I'm going out of my damn mind. I've texted Rhett and Dane at least a couple of times despite knowing it's unlikely they're in a position to reply. But the not knowing is killing me.

"Come on," Wes says, standing.

"But—"

"You need to relax," he lowers his voice so only our table can hear, "and I can help with that."

Quinn snorts, throwing me an amused look.

"Wes, I don't think now is a good time to fool around."

He snags my arm and gently tugs me to my feet. "There's nothing we can do to help them, but I can't sit here for a second longer, watching you drive yourself crazy and staring at your cell phone."

"I just..."

"I know, I'm worried too. It's been a long day. Let's go somewhere quiet and... relax."

"Fine." I concede. "We can go to Dane's room." I take his hand and don't even look back as I lead him down the hall.

We enter Dane's room and I instantly wrap my arms around myself, suppressing a shiver.

"Hey, he's going to be okay." He steps up to me and runs his hands over my arms.

"You don't know that," I say, leaning back against him. Wes nuzzles my neck, kissing me there.

"Let me distract you, princess." He traces his lips up to my jaw, nipping. His hands slide to my cheek, moving me where he wants me, and then he's kissing me—hot, wet kisses that make my knees buckle.

I manage to turn in his arms, clutching his t-shirt and anchoring us closer. But Wes steps away, smirking.

"What the hell, Wes—" I start, but his eyes darken with intent.

"I want you naked and on the bed." He starts scanning the room—for what, I don't know. But desire ripples through me, making my pussy throb with anticipation. It feels wrong to be so turned on when Rhett and Dane and our family are out there, in danger. But Wes is right. I need a distraction before I do something reckless like go after them.

"I'm not—"

"On. The. Bed." He growls the words, moving to Dane's small dresser to place his cell phone there. When he turns around, he pins me with a dark look that sends shivers racing down my spine. "You're still clothed."

"Maybe I want you to undress me."

His brow lifts. "I'm going to fucking devour you." Wes stalks toward me and begins tearing at my clothes. My t-shirt goes first, his hands tracing my stomach, gliding up between my breasts and hooking into my bra. I moan when he lowers his head and teases each nipple with his tongue, licking and sucking in a way that has me trembling.

"Wes," I cry, sliding my fingers into his hair.

He chuckles against my damp skin and rasps. "Get on the bed, Sadie."

I step backward, sitting on the edge of the bed, gazing up at him. He drops to his knees, carefully removing my sneakers before running his hands up my calves, going higher and higher until his fingers disappear underneath my skirt. He cups my pussy in a total Rhett and Dane move, and I snort.

"Careful, Pretty Boy, or I might start to think you want to be just like them."

Something simmers in his eyes, but all thoughts melt away as he yanks down my skirt and buries his face between my thighs, licking me over my underwear. It's so dirty but so fucking good, I fall back onto the mattress and fist the sheets.

Wes practically tears my panties off my body so he can get to my pussy, spearing his tongue deep inside me.

"Jesus," I breathe, consumed by how good it feels. He laps at me like a man starved.

"I want you to come on my tongue and then my cock," he demands, replacing his mouth with two thick fingers that rub my walls until I'm clenching around him.

"More," I cry... "God, more..." I'm almost there, flying toward that magical place where nothing else matters.

Working me with his fingers, Wes greedily circles my clit with his tongue, sucking it and licking it. Another curve of his fingers and I shatter, crying his name and locking my thighs around his head.

With one final kiss to my inner thigh, Wes rises to his feet, yanks off his t-shirt, snaps his belt, and pushes his jeans down slightly to fist himself. "Hands and knees, princess. I want to fuck you from behind."

I gush at his words, desire already building inside me again as I roll onto my stomach and lift my ass in the air.

His hands trail down my spine and around my hips, yanking me backwards. He runs a finger through the crease of my ass, dipping it inside my pussy and back up. "Maybe I should get this first." Slowly, he works a finger inside me, just the tip. I rock back, desperate for more.

"Such a greedy girl," he chuckles, withdrawing his digit. "I think Stray will have something to say if I take your ass first. He seems pretty fascinated with the idea."

God, why does the idea of it get me so hot?

"Guess I'll just have to make do with this." Wes drives into me without warning, so hard I have to fight to keep myself steady.

"Fuck, Sadie," he grits out, pounding into me without mercy, grazing my cervix with every thrust. It's fast and hard and everything I need to get out of my own head, until I can think of nothing but the way Wes feels using my body.

"More..." I cry. "I need more."

He works a finger into my ass again, deeper this time. "I won't fuck you here," he groans, "but I'll get you nice and ready for Stray." He stretches me, and I feel so full, I can't imagine what it'll feel like the first time I take two of them together.

"You're thinking about it, aren't you?" He works his finger inside me to the rhythm of his thrusts. "Thinking about having two of us, aren't you?"

"Yes... *yes*," I choke out. My hands claw at the sheets as Wes rides my body into complete oblivion. "I'm coming.... fuck, I'm..." Words escape me, turning to mewls of pleasure as another orgasm rocks through me.

"Fuck, Sadie, fuuuuck." Wes jerks inside of me and collapses onto me.

He presses little kisses to my spine as we both come down from blissful highs.

But as the silence envelops us, the worry creeps back in. Wes must sense it because he rolls to the side and pulls me into his arms.

"It's going to be okay," he says, holding me tight.

"Yeah." I whisper, wanting so badly to believe it.

33

RHETT

My body trembles with anger as the others peel out of the parking lot behind Micky.

"Ready?" Ray asks, shooting me a look over his shoulder.

"Cunt needs to die."

"Couldn't agree more. Let's just hope we're about to find him then, yeah?"

My teeth grind, my grip tightening on my handlebars until it hurts.

"Let's ride," Ray barks, kickstarting his bike and taking off in the opposite direction, the Reapers Road Captain following his tail.

The rumble of the rest of the bikes flows through me, calming me slightly but nowhere near enough.

Creed is playing us, that much is obvious. This intel from Ritz is bullshit. And something tells me that the location we're heading to is going to be equally as pointless.

Knowing that we have no choice but to check it out, I

follow my brothers, and thirty minutes later, we're pulling up to what looks like an abandoned apartment building just over the Red Ridge border at the other side of town to the first location.

The parking lot is deserted, all the windows on the bottom two floors are smashed, and the building is covered in graffiti.

"This is bullshit," one of the Reapers barks when we all come to a stop, staring up at the building.

"We've got to check it out," Ray instructs. "One floor at a time, let's go."

A rumble of agreement flows around me as I climb off my bike and pull my gun from my waistband.

"If you do find him, don't kill him. I want that pleasure," Ray adds before a few of the Reapers go ahead. "Savage, with me."

"You got it, Prez."

"You think we're gonna find him?" he asks as we follow the rest of the group into the building.

"Nah, he's playing us like fucking puppets."

"Yeah."

"We've got to get ahead of him," I say. "We're playing right into his hands. This building is probably laced with explosives and is gonna go up any second."

Ray looks around, taking my words seriously. "We'd better fucking hope that ain't true."

"All clear," someone shouts from down the hall. "Let's go up."

The heavy fall of boots on the stairs makes the floor vibrate beneath me, but just as Ray and I are about to follow, his cell starts ringing. He pulls it from his pants and stares down at the screen, his brows pinching as he looks at whoever is calling.

"What is it?"

He turns the screen to me. "Unknown. You think it's him?"

"Only one way to find out."

He nods, swiping the screen and putting it to this ear. "Dalton," he barks in his scariest voice. As a young kid, it used to fucking terrify me. But I know Ray better than to be scared of him now. Even after he's discovered me, Stray, and Pretty Boy are sleeping with his daughter. I respect him too much to be scared. If he wants me dead for touching Sadie, then he'd have pulled the trigger before now.

Someone speaks on the other end, but I can't hear any of it.

"Yes." Silence. "Fuck. Okay, we're coming now."

My heart hammers in my chest as I watch his expression fall, the color draining from his face before he hangs up and pockets his cell once more.

"What's wrong?"

"We need to go," he grunts.

"I'll call the others."

"No," he says quickly before I'm able to call up the stairs. "Let them search. This is just me and you."

"Okay. Where are we going?" I ask, taking off behind him when he suddenly bolts for the door.

"Nolan's place."

"Nolan's?"

"Yeah. Shit's gone south. Come on."

He doesn't hang around long enough for me to ask

any questions. I jog behind him as he runs ahead of me and climbs on his bike, the engine immediately coming to life.

I'm barely on mine when he's speeding out of the parking lot. Gunning my engine to catch up with him as he takes a left, we head deeper into Red Ridge.

I've been here a few times over the years, but I've never been to Nolan Creed's home. I follow Ray all the way to a huge ranch that's surrounded by rolling hills in the distance.

The second we pull to a stop beside Nolan's bike, the front door opens, and his old lady appears.

"Come on," she says, sparing no airs or graces. "He's inside." She gestures for us both to enter her home.

Dread sits heavy in my stomach as Vivienne leads us to the back of the building. We find Nolan in a hospital bed in the middle of the room, overlooking the view of the countryside in the distance.

He looks nothing like the man I've met in the past. His face is slim, his cheeks hollow and his skin pallid. If we needed evidence that what we've been told about his health was true, then it's right here.

"I'll leave you to it. Call if you need anything," Vivienne says, quickly ducking out of the room.

"Nolan, it's good to see you," Ray says, lowering himself into the chair beside the Reapers Prez and taking his hand when he just about manages to lift it from the bed. "You remember Rhett?" he asks, glancing at me.

"Of course," Nolan rasps. "Welcome."

"What do you know?" Ray gets straight down to

business. "Your old lady said that something happened and you needed to discuss some things with us before—" He cuts himself off when he registers what the end of that sentence is.

"Our brothers got ambushed earlier."

My heart jumps into my throat. "Micky? Dane?"

"Ritz is dead," Nolan says, sadness bleeding into his expression.

Holy shit. All the air rushes from my lungs as I think of my brothers. Of Dane.

We lost two men yesterday because of that car bomb. Now this?

"Fuck. I'm sorry, Nolan," Ray says softly, once again taking his hand in support.

"Darren, he's... he's going to destroy my club." His voice is broken. "I can't let that happen. With Ritz gone, I—"

"What can we do? How can we help?"

Nolan stares at Ray before his eyes flick to mine briefly, although I'm barely registering the conversation because my head is spinning with the fact that we've lost more brothers.

I think of Sadie, emotion clogging my throat. I can't go back to the compound and tell her that Dane is gone. I just can't.

Lifting my hand, I scrub it down my face, trying to gather myself together enough to focus on the here and now.

For all I know, Dane is fine. He could have gotten away. He could have—

I shut down my own thoughts, knowing it's useless

hoping. Ritz is dead. I have no reason to believe anyone walked away.

"I can't have Darren take leadership, Ray. It isn't an option."

"Agreed." Ray nods. "We're trying to find him. We want him gone as much as you do."

"No," Nolan says, his voice suddenly harder, more serious than only seconds ago, and it catches my attention. "There's something you don't understand."

"Okay."

"You have the answer."

"The answer? What do you mean?" Ray asks, frowning, as we both sit forward in our chairs.

"Your boy. Dane."

"What about him?" A protective edge I usually only hear when he's talking about Sadie enters his voice.

"You really don't know where he came from, do you?"

"N-no, I—"

"He's a Reaper," I blurt out, the pieces of the puzzle finally falling into place.

Nolan nods, confirming what I only just realized. "He's my brother's kid. It's a long story, one I don't have time for right now. But if we can get rid of Darren," he says, "Dane is next in line to take the gavel."

"A Reaper... I don't understand..." Ray stutters, completely blindsided.

"Your prospect isn't a stray, Ray. He's a Creed. And it's time he took his place within my family."

Despite seeing it coming, my chin still drops in shock.

Dane is a Creed.

He's a fucking Reaper.

"But he was with the group who were ambushed," Ray says grimly, causing what little color that was left in Nolan's face to drain away as realization hits him.

He didn't only lose his son today.

He might have lost his only shot at saving his club.

And we might have lost our shot at avoiding all-out war between the Sinners and Reapers.

Sadie, Rhett, Dane, and Wes's story continues in Sacred,

DOWNLOAD NOW

Two angsty romance lovers writing dark heroes and the feisty girls who bring them to their knees.

SIGN UP NOW
To receive news of our releases straight to your inbox.

Want to hang out with us?
Come and join CAITLYN'S DAREDEVILS group on Facebook.

TAUNT HER

SNEAK PEEK

Ace

I look around at the only home I've ever known and feel conflicted. It's a shithole, but it's our shithole—the only place I and my brothers have ever called home. And if I wasn't convinced that this move would benefit them, it wouldn't be happening.

They throw their bags into the trunk of their heap-of-shit car without a word. Dread sits heavy in my stomach as I move on autopilot, as if we aren't about to leave our home. The feeling isn't an unusual one, nor is the fury that fills my veins on a daily basis.

Our uncle should have been here ten minutes ago to take us away to start our new life in Sterling Bay. Maybe he's decided we're not worth it after all. Chance would be a fine fucking thing.

I'm just about to tell them to give up and go back

inside when the crunching of gravel by the trailer park entrance hits my ears.

Fucking great.

A black town car with equally blacked-out windows comes to stop in front of the three of us.

"I hope he's not planning on staying long, that thing'll be on bricks in minutes," Conner mutters, his eyes locked on the driver's door.

We haven't seen our uncle in years, not since he left us with our shit show of a mother. It seems family only matters when his hand has been forced by the state.

I'd have quite happily been my brothers' guardian for a year, but apparently an eighteen-year-old with a rap sheet like mine isn't a responsible enough adult to look after others.

The door opens and I lean to the side to get my first look at the man who abandoned us to this life instead of fighting for his family, but the guy who stands isn't one I recognize.

"Who the fuck are you?" I bark, much to the guy's irritation if the widening of his eyes is anything to go by.

"I'm your uncle's driver. He sent me to pick you up."

"Fucking brilliant." The laugh that accompanies my words is anything but amused.

"If you'd like to put your bags in the trunk, I'll take you home."

Home. *This* is my home.

My body tenses, my fists curling at my sides, as I step up to the man. He already looks totally intimidated by his surroundings, and I delight in him taking one step back as

I approach. Slamming the door as I go, I stop him from an easy escape should he feel he needs it.

No motherfucker, you've probably not dealt with anyone like me before.

The scent of his expensive aftershave fills my nose, and it only makes me want to hurt the privileged asshole that much more.

"Let's get a few things straight." I don't stop until I'm right in his face, so close I see the fear in his eyes. Now *that's* something I can work with, something I can feed off like a fucking leech. "Firstly, that place you're meant to be taking us to is not our home. It'll never be our home. And second, we're not getting in this fancy-ass fucking car. Where the hell is James? I thought he was coming to collect us."

"He's been called out on business."

This is a fucking joke. First he demands we move into his pretentious mansion—blackmails me into it when he knows it's the last place in the world I want to live—and then the motherfucker can't even be bothered to turn up himself. He's probably too good for this place. No wonder he looked down his nose at us all those years ago and turned his back as fast as he could.

"He will be home later to greet you."

I stare at him, no emotion on my face and a storm brewing in my eyes.

"If you could just get in and—"

"Un-fucking-likely. We can make our own way."

I told James as much when he instigated this whole thing in the first place, but he insisted. Probably because he doesn't want my brothers' rust bucket sitting in his fancy driveway and bringing the tone of the area down.

"I really don't think—"

"I don't give a fuck what you think, *Jeeves*."

All the blood that was left in his face from when he first stepped out of the car drains away, and he swallows nervously.

"D-do you want to f-follow me then?"

"Marvelous, Jeeves. What a fantastic plan," I mock, mimicking his posh British accent.

The second I take a step back, he scrambles into the car as quick as he can. Fucking pussy.

"I can't believe he sent a car," Conner mumbles as my brothers join me, and together we watch the town car roll slowly down the dirt track.

"Really?" I balk. "James isn't our savior, Con. You think he'd even be taking us in if it weren't for the court deciding I'm no good..." I swallow the rest of the words. Of course, no one would trust me with my brothers. Apparently, the fact that I've raised both of them since we were just kids doesn't matter.

My chest tightens.

"It'll be okay, Ace." My brother squeezes my shoulder. "A fresh start could be just what we need."

"Yeah, whatever." I shrug him off. "We should probably get going." There's nothing left for us here.

Conner gives me a weak smile before following Cole to their car. It's an ancient Ford they somehow manage to keep running despite the fact that it should have been scrapped at least ten years ago. Cole doesn't even spare our trailer a backward glance as he climbs inside and guns the engine. I'll need to keep my eye on him; he's always been a quiet kid, but lately he's been even more brooding.

They follow Jeeves' lead before I throw my leg over my bike and rev the engine. The vibrations instantly help to cool me off. The anticipation that I'll soon be flying down the coastal road helps to push my ever building anger over this fucked-up situation down a little more.

I gun the engine once both the town car and my brothers have disappeared from sight and take one last look at this place. It's dark and dingy, like Hell on Earth. But it's our home... *was* our home. We're moving. Heading over the border to the rich side of town. Like we're ever going to fucking fit in there.

Dust and gravel fly up behind me as I speed off to find my brothers' taillights somewhere up ahead. We know roughly where James lives, but I've no idea which of the insanely pretentious houses actually belongs to him. Probably the biggest one, knowing that pretentious stuck-up prick.

I catch them just before the road opens up and the bright blue sea appears in the distance. I guess that's one good thing about where we're going: the girls on the beach. It's just a shame they're all going to talk like Jeeves, as if they've got a spoon permanently stuck in their pouty mouths.

"Fucking hell," I mutter to myself as I follow the two cars up a long ass driveway. It's not until the very last moment that the actual house appears. It's a huge place on a hill overlooking the ocean. The kind of house I've only ever seen images of in magazines, or on the TV when the piece of shit worked.

Images of the parties we can have here start to fill my mind. Maybe this place won't be so bad after all. I can get off my face and attempt to fuck some rich chick looking to take a walk on the wild side... in every room of the house.

Parking between my brothers' car and a flashy Mercedes, I throw my leg over my bike and head in the direction I just watched Jeeves walk into the house. He obviously thought against helping with our belongings. Wise man. He's learning quickly.

With our bags in hand, we climb the stairs to the double front door. It's a damn sight different to the one on our trailer that swelled up so bad in the summer we had to crawl out through a window, and that allowed the wind and rain to come inside during any storms.

"Holy crap," Conner gasps as we walk into the entrance hall of all entrance halls. I swear to fucking god that the only house I've seen quite this lavish is the Playboy mansion. I'm half expecting scantily-clad women to pour through the doors for a welcome party at any moment.

Sadly, the only person who emerges from one of the many doorways is Jeeves.

"Would you like a tour?"

"Or a fucking map," Conner mutters. Cole, however, stands totally mute and looking bored out of his skull. I know he's taking everything in, though. It's how his brain works.

"Just point us in the direction of our rooms. I'm sure we can figure the rest out ourselves. We might be from a trailer park, but we're far from stupid."

"I'm well aware of that. I'm William, by the way."

"I would say it was nice to meet you, Jeeves," I spit, curling my lip in disgust, "but in all honesty, it wasn't."

"Right, well. You can get to your rooms via this staircase, but you do have your own at the other end of the house. If you'd like to follow me."

For once, the three of us do as we're told and trail behind him until he comes to a stop at a slightly less audacious staircase, although it's still much grander than any I've seen before.

"At the top you'll find four rooms. Each has a fully stocked en suite, but if you need anything extra please speak to Ellen. You can usually find her in the kitchen, which is directly behind the main staircase, and she'll see you have everything you need."

"How about an ounce of weed and a few bottles of vodka?"

He stares at me as if I'm going to laugh at my own joke. It's not a fucking joke. I'm going to need that and then some if I'm meant to live here.

It's only a year. You can do this for a year for your brothers.

"If that's all, I'll leave you to find your feet." He spins on his heels and fucks off as fast as his legs will carry him.

"Shall we do this shit then?" Conner asks as we all stand like statues at the bottom of the stairs.

"Fuck it." I move first, but they're not far behind me.

I take the furthest door from the stairs, and the one I'm fairly sure will have the best view. I might be here for them, but they can fuck off if they think they're getting it.

"Fucking hell," I mutter, walking onto the insanely

spongy cream carpet and looking around at my new digs. This one room alone is about double the size of our trailer.

I dump my bag on the window seat and look out at the ocean beyond, exactly as I'd hoped. Staring out at the perfect postcard view, I hope its calmness will somehow transfer into me. No such luck, because when I turn and take in the room around me, the need to smash it up is all-consuming.

I don't want to fucking be here.

I want my old life. My shitty trailer. My state school and dead-end opportunities.

Pulling my cell from my pocket, I sync it with the speakers I find on the sideboard and turn it up as loud as it'll go. This house might be a mansion, but I'll make sure Uncle fucking James knows we've arrived.

Retrieving the packet of smokes from my bag, I pull one out and place it between my lips before falling down onto my bed. I can only assume there's a no smoking rule in a place like this. I smile as I light up and blow smoke right into the center of the room.

I didn't follow any rules before, so like fuck am I about to start.

I can't hear anything over the sound of my music, so it's not until the door opens that I realize someone wants me. Looking up, I expect to find my brothers, but instead Uncle James stands before me in his sharp three-piece suit, slicked-back hair and clean-shaven face.

"What do you want?" I bark, turning away from him and lighting up once again.

"I was coming to see how you were settling in, but I see you've already made yourself at home."

"What the fuck?" I seethe when the cigarette is plucked from my lips, seconds before it's flicked out the window.

He pulls up the front of his perfectly pressed pants before sitting down on the edge of my bed. If he's trying to look authoritative, then he needs to try fucking harder.

"A few house rules are in order, I think."

I scoff but allow him to continue so he can list his challenges, because you can bet your sweet ass I'm going to breaking each and every one just to piss him off.

"No smoking in the house. You want to kill yourself with those death sticks, then you do so outside. You will not bring any drugs or drink into this house. If you want friends here, you can use the pool house. I've set it up as a den of sorts for the three of you. That's your domain."

"So we can smoke, drink, and do drugs in there?"

"No. There will be no parties, no girls, nothing that will cause any trouble of any kind."

"If you're not looking for trouble, then you invited the wrong guys to come and live with you."

"You are no longer in Sterling Heights." He frowns. "Things are different around here. I think it might be important for you to remember that."

"Whatever."

"School starts in two weeks. Your uniforms are already in your closets. I suggest you familiarize yourself with the place before the hard work starts, because there is no way you're not graduating this year," he jibes, knowing full well that I fucked up what should have been my senior year last year. Not my fault that someone had to earn some goddamn money to support my brothers.

I look to the other side of the room as if his mere presence is boring me.

"Dinner will be served in an hour. I expect you all to be cleaned and dressed appropriately." I see his gaze from out of the corner of my eye drop to my ripped jeans and oil-stained shirt. "My girlfriend and her daughter are coming to welcome you to town, and I shouldn't need to tell you that you will be nice to both of them."

Well, doesn't that sound like a fucking fun way to spend our first night in Sterling Bay? A nice, cozy family meal with the man who only wanted us when we had no parents left in this world.

He makes out like he wasn't aware of what our lives were like.

He's a fucking liar.

"An hour. I've already warned your brothers. We'll be waiting."

I do shower and change—not because he told me to, but because I fucking stink, and to be honest, I can't deny that the rainfall shower in my en suite wasn't appealing. It was a shit load better than the open pipe we had in the trailer.

Wearing a different pair of ripped jeans and a slightly cleaner shirt, I step out into the hall at exactly the same time both Cole and Conner do. They're dressed similarly to me; it seems they took Uncle's warning about as seriously as I did.

The sounds of voices direct the three of us toward the dining room. My curiosity as to what hides behind each door we pass is high, but I don't look. I don't want to seem like I care, because I really fucking don't, I'm just intrigued as to why a man who's always lived alone needs so many fucking rooms.

As we join them, all conversation stops and three heads turn our way. I know our uncle is here but don't pay him any mind. The brunette, however, captures my imagination quite nicely.

He might have warned me about no girls already, but he didn't mention one who clearly already spends time here.

He walks over and wraps his arm around both the brunette and her mother. "Ace, Cole, Conner..." He grins like the cat who got the cream, and I fucking hate it. "This is Sarah, my girlfriend, and Remi, her daughter."

DOWNLOAD TAUNT HER to continue reading Remi and Ace's story now.

Printed in Great Britain
by Amazon

38062133R00175